*No one ever told me that grief felt so like fear.*
—C.S. Lewis, *A Grief Observed*

# FRIDAY

# 1

Someone was watching me. I could feel it. That tingle you get at the back of your neck, between the shoulder blades. I scanned the dim, misty forest behind me: the skunk cabbage along Hunter's Creek; the western hemlock strewn with witch's hair; the moss-covered and impossibly large trunks of the towering red cedars; the ferns sheltering the mossy forest floor at their roots. I saw no one, though the unsettling feeling persisted. Someone *was* watching me.

But then, there was always someone watching within this temperate rainforest, a chickadee, a crow, a cougar, a black bear—or a grizzly. I put a hand to the bear spray in the belt holster at my hip. A huge cinnamon-coloured grizzly, a sow, had stalked my husband, Ben, through this forest earlier in the fall, though on the far shore of the lake, likely the same bear that had mauled a young woman to death there the previous summer. Ben and Jackson had never been able to catch the animal. The cinnamon grizzly, with a taste for hunting humans, was still out there. I shook off the thought as I turned back to the giant stump I'd just discovered and snapped a few photos of it with my phone, to share on social media when I caught some bars. There was no cell reception out here.

This stump of an old-growth red cedar was inflicted with heart rot as so many of the elderly trees were. Aside from the mound of waste branches left behind, most of the wood of the felled tree had been bucked into rounds and split into blocks small enough to be hauled away. The tree had survived hundreds of years, storms and fires, and then a century more of logging within this rare inland rainforest. It had been a giant, an ancient, an old soul, alive in a way my puny human mind would never fully comprehend. And now, senselessly, it was dead, only so some homeowner could slap cedar shakes on their house or keep the weeds at bay in their garden with cedar mulch.

*Shit.*

I knelt in front of the stump and wrapped my arms around it as far as they would go. Which wasn't far. The stump was massive. To anyone watching, I would have seemed like a child in comparison. The cut wood pressed against my cheek felt like the bristle of Ben's freshly trimmed beard as I lay in his arms, prickly, comforting, familiar. *Home.*

But then I again felt eyes on me, as I had so many times in these woods. It might have been a deer or even that grizzly, but no, I knew it wasn't. It was the bushman. I stood, scanning the shadows in the thick, lush understory beneath the hemlock and cedars. "Who's there?" I yelled. "I know you're there. I know you've been watching me." Not just this day, but at other times too. "Show yourself!"

And then, only metres from me, a thread of mist swirled away, revealing a dark-green shadow of a man, before he backed up silently on the mossy forest floor, disappearing into the gloom. But I knew he was still watching me.

"What do you want?" I shouted after him. In response, there was only another stirring in the mist, the shift of branches and leaves, as the wind, rippling through the forest, brought with it the chill of snow, heralding the turn of the season into winter.

# 2

There was a *crack*, like a twig broken underfoot, and I turned to squint down the overgrown tree poacher's trail that I had followed to find this stump. Overhead, clouds skittered too fast, nervously jittering around the mountain peaks that loomed over the valley. Someone, or something, was out there, blocking the way to the logging road, even as a man lurked in the forest behind me. I looked back and forth in each direction of the trail as I pulled the bear spray from my holster, removed the safety clip and took a step toward the road, my truck, safety, holding the canister in front of me, my gloved hand out to guard my face against the broad-leafed, spiny and aptly named devil's club that stood on guard throughout the forest. Another, louder *crack*, and I stopped, held my breath.

And then Ben appeared, striding around the corner of the roughed-in trail. I let out my breath as I slid the safety clip back on the bear spray and tucked the canister back in the holster. My husband wore his uniform, black pants and jacket, projecting an official persona so different from the easy, relaxed man he was at home. Even so, his bearded face was, as always, kind and welcoming, an advantage in his role as public educator, as he informed the people he met in the bush about the many laws and regulations governing the wilderness and its resources. But that friendly face was also a disadvantage, I imagined, when trying to enforce the same laws on those determined to break them.

"Oh my god, Ben," I said as he reached me. "You scared me. How long have you been here?" Did he see me hugging the stump?

"I only just arrived." Seeing the fear on my face, I imagine, he squeezed my hand. "Hey, what's going on?"

I lifted my chin in the opposite direction, to where I had seen the figure in the mist. "The Green Man was here."

The Green Man. The bushman who had haunted this forest over the past year, stealing from summer cabins and homes around the lake. Ben's buddy Jackson, who was a wilderness guide and had seen the bushman on occasion, had given him the name because he wore green camouflage and the green face paint soldiers use, to blend into the forest foliage, to hide.

The Green Man was a squatter and a thief, and very likely suffering from some kind of psychiatric disorder. He had escaped RCMP searches over the last year since cabin owners started reporting his thefts and, on rare occasions, saw him fleeing from their properties. Ben had seen him a couple of times through the screen on his smart controller while flying his drone on patrol. In the images the drone captured, the Green Man was bearded and shaggy-haired, and seen from above and at a distance, resembled a sasquatch, a Bigfoot, loping through the bush.

"Are you sure it was the bushman and not one of the tree poachers?" Ben asked.

"I'm sure."

I tucked my gloves in my pocket and nodded sideways at the giant stump. The rusty red of the cedar was that much more vibrant in the rain. "But you see what Owen's done now?"

I felt the sting of tears and turned to the steep hills shrouded in cloud, trying to hide my emotions, embarrassed at how keenly I felt the loss of this old-growth tree, even if Ben would never judge me for it. My father certainly would have, and though he'd died when

I was in my teens, his voice still echoed in my head. *Don't be a flake.*

Ben wrapped his arms around me from behind and kissed the top of my head in that way that always made me feel safe. He was so tall. Six foot four, broad-shouldered and barrel-chested. He smelled of fresh air, this forest. "I'm so sorry, Piper, about the tree," he said.

Rain fell harder still, thumping against our waterproof jackets, making a sound like drumming fingers. Rain was a frequent companion here, and when winter hit suddenly, as it almost always did, the clouds dumped piles and piles of wet snow. The snowline was already low on the steep mountain slopes, and we were due for that first winter snowfall in the valley. Overdue. It seemed winter arrived later and later every year. I felt a chill run through me and pulled away from Ben to zip up my jacket, adjusting the orange safety vest I wore to avoid being shot, by mistake, by those out here for the November deer hunt.

"You followed me again?" I asked.

"I found your note on the fridge."

Always leave a travel plan, Ben had taught me. So that morning before I left the house, I had hastily scrawled my plans, to spend the day up here at Hunter's Creek, on an oversized sticky note. The area was part of the swath around this end of the lake that we hoped to turn into a park, for recreation use and to preserve the giant trees.

"We discussed this," Ben said. "It's hunting season. You shouldn't be out here alone. You shouldn't be out here *period*. And you know hunters and poachers aren't the only danger you're facing in this forest."

"I know, I know." I shook both hands by my ears in mock fear. "Coyotes and cougars and bears, oh my!" Something I said when he warned me of the many hazards I could encounter in this wilderness. But he was right. There was no end to the dangers I might face out here. Bears had become more aggressive in recent years as humans encroached on their territory. The cinnamon grizzly had mauled and killed that young woman, Andrea Peterson, and had taken several swipes at her husband, Elijah, when they were honeymooning on the far shore, searching, Ben had told me, for Valentine's legendary lost cave. (Valentine was a prospector who stumbled across a cave in the area that he described as "glorious," but died of a heart attack before telling anyone where it was, spawning searches that continued to this day.)

"I carry bear spray and a bear banger," I said. To scare bears away should they get too close.

"And then there's the Green Man," Ben added, his eyes scanning the dark maw of the forest where I had seen the ghostly figure.

*Yeah, there's that*, I thought. The bushman had scared the crap out of me not just today, but a few other times. Still. "He's been out here for more than a year now," I said. "If he wanted to hurt me, he would have."

"But now we know he's armed."

The Green Man had recently stolen a rifle from a truck belonging to one of the local loggers when the guy was out cutting up firewood, with a permit, on Crown land. Or at least the logger assumed it was the bushman. The lock on the guy's truck box had been busted, and the rifle had disappeared, along with an emergency kit, a chainsaw and the guy's lunch. Salami on rye, Ben had said.

I shook my head to dismiss my own fears as much as Ben's. "The bushman likely took the gun to poach deer, to feed himself, to protect himself. I'm sure he has no intention of using it on me, or anyone else."

"We don't know that. We don't know anything about him."

"I'm sure he's harmless," I said. "Sometimes I even get the feeling he's watching over me." In a creepy sort of way.

Ben put his hands on his hips. "Yes, exactly. He *watches*. Ask

6

yourself why he's taking such an interest in you. A woman out here alone." He pushed my wet bangs out of my eyes. "A beautiful woman."

I felt my cheeks heat up. *Hardly*, I thought. Carrot top, Ben called me, both for the colour of my hair and how my cropped cut often stood straight up, as I'm sure it did now.

"I'm not going to hide in our house," I said. "I moved here for this wilderness."

Ben dropped his hand and grinned. "Thanks a lot."

I smiled in return. "You know what I mean." We both lived for the outdoors. When we weren't working in it, we were in our kayaks, or bouldering—rock climbing—on the far shore, or hiking the wildlife trails, or, in winter, backcountry skiing with Jackson and others. This landscape, and all it offered, was one of the things that had brought Ben and me together, after Jackson introduced us.

I stood a little straighter. "I can handle myself out here. Besides, if I hadn't searched this part of the forest for poaching today, I wouldn't have found this tree."

My husband pressed his lips together. Finally, he spit it out. "I don't want you facing these tree poachers alone, should you come across them. When it comes to defending the environment, you sometimes get—"

I finished the sentence for him. "Confrontational. I know." I pushed a hand through my damp hair, feeling the sting of the remark. It was something he had complained about before. But I never meant to raise a stink. Quite the opposite. I *hated* conflict. Still, I also felt *compelled* to speak out against an injustice. It wasn't out of some moral or religious code, to do the honourable or decent thing. The drive was hard-wired into me, a compulsion. I couldn't stop myself from protesting. Even my father's fist hadn't stopped me.

"Hey, hey," Ben said, seeing the hurt in my face. "You know that's one of the many things I love about you, right?"

"That I'm pissy?"

"That you're passionate. You dare to stand up for what's right when others don't." He took my hand. "At least promise me you won't venture this far into the bush alone until hunting season is over, and not until the bushman has been caught, and emotions over this park proposal cool. Maybe limit your longer hikes to weekends when Noah or I can go with you."

I let go of his hand. "I'm a grown woman, Ben. You know I love Noah. I'll spend all the time I can with him. But he's seventeen. Are you really saying you expect him to protect *me*?"

"He's already six foot two. Whoever is making those threats toward you over the park proposal will think twice about approaching him."

"But not me?" I grinned. We both knew I was anything but intimidating. I'm petite, only five foot two, and wiry from a lifetime of active living. With my pixie cut, I know I look boyish.

"My concern is not a reflection on you," Ben said. He put a hand to his black vest. "When I come out here, I wear body armour, for good reason. I'm vulnerable, and I know it." His official uniform included this soft body armour, but no gun, and not even a baton. "I start to sweat when I'm about to ticket somebody for fishing without a licence. Many of the guys I run into are carrying guns and knives, and a few of them are either drunk or battling demons." Dealing with mental illness, he meant. "Piss off the wrong one and—" He had only his defensive and conflict-avoidance training to fall back on.

I laughed a little, to get him to stop. He was freaking me out. I already entertained these thoughts when he was on patrol. "Okay, okay. I'll be more careful." I took his big hand again, almost twice the size of my own. "I worry too, when you go out alone."

He squeezed my hand in response. "I know."

I didn't just worry. Each time he went into the wilderness alone, the same thought entered my mind: *This could be it. This might be the last time I see him alive.* Such bleak, dark thoughts. The kind of anxieties that I had struggled to contain for most of my life. But then, if I had these fears about Ben as he went into the wild alone, could I really fault him for worrying about me too?

I directed his attention back to the giant stump, to change the subject. "What are we going to do about this?"

"I'm not sure there is anything I can do. The tree was cut down and bucked some time ago, maybe in the summer. The wood is long gone. And I have no witnesses. The poachers are likely felling, bucking and trucking the wood out at night. In any case, who is going to see them on these back roads even during the day?" He walked a circle around the stump, kicking the wet grass and ferns in search of broken saw blades or tools the poachers might have left behind. "It appears they were careful not to leave anything that might identify them. But I will do a thorough search."

"So unless you literally catch the poacher in the act—"

"Then it's very hard to identify the thief or make charges stick, yes." He ran a hand over his mouth. "I know it's frustrating, especially after all the work you and Jackson have done to make the park a reality, but tracking down tree poachers takes time and—"

"And in the meantime, we lose more of these old-growth trees. Ben, there are so few of them left." I sank to the stump. "Dammit."

Ben let his arms drop to his sides as if he too felt helpless. "I'm so sorry, Piper."

I lay a hand on the fragrant wood beside me. So many rings, hundreds of them. The tree could be six hundred, seven hundred years old, maybe more, but, although ancient to humans, it was cut down in middle age. It might have lived to be two thousand years old, like some of the trees found in what was left of this once vast inland rainforest. The strong, spicy scent of cedar rose up from the stump, bringing to mind the aftershave my father used to wear in an attempt to cover the stink of whiskey.

"You know it was Owen," I said.

"There are plenty of men and women in the region with the skills to do this. Everyone in town, in fact." Most of them hard-drinking, hard-smoking, hard-working sorts—that is, until the small independent mill had closed, putting not just the mill workers but many of the local loggers out of work, Owen among them. "Two men with chainsaws and pickup trucks could have hauled this cedar away in no time."

"Owen has the equipment and the crew," I said. He would have roped his buddy Nelson into tree poaching, and likely his son, Tucker, too. Though I wouldn't fault Tucker for going along with him. Owen bullied the kid, kept him pressed under his heavy thumb. Tucker would have little choice.

"I know you and Owen have had your differences over the park proposal," Ben said. He tapped the base of the stump with his boot. "But a crew from outside the valley could just as easily have done this. Tree poaching is big money now. Organized crime is getting in on the action globally. Yank an old tree out of the wilderness, disappear down an abandoned logging road, sell the wood at a mill where no one is asking questions. Easy, low-risk money—"

I nodded wearily. I'd written on the subject for online magazines and news sites. "You *know* it was Owen," I said again. "He fits the profile. He's got the skills, and the criminal record." He'd been caught stealing from a mill he'd worked at before moving to Moston, and he'd been charged with assault after a drunken bar fight. Rumour had it his wife had left him because he was abusive when drunk. I knew the type all too well, having grown up with an overbearing father, a cop, who drank too much. "And Owen hasn't been struggling for money like the other loggers or mill workers since the mill closed. He paid cash for that truck." His Ford F-350 wasn't brand new, but still. It was a newer model, a private sale.

"He paid cash?" Ben asked. "Who told you that?"

"Noah." Who got it from Tucker. They went to school together, hung out at our place together. "Of the few locals opposing the park proposal, Owen has been the most vocal, with me, at least. The things he's said to me . . ." *Fucking tree hugger.* "I'm convinced he's the one who broke my truck window." On the passenger side. I'd had to make the hour-long drive into Clifton to get it repaired. "You *know* he keyed the tailgate." *Go home bitch.* As if Moston, where I had lived for nearly three years now, wasn't my home.

Ben scratched the hair on his chin. "Yeah, about that." He glanced up the poacher's trail and grimaced. "Did you see the new graffiti on your truck?" he asked. "The door?"

"*What?*" I headed down the trail toward the logging road where I had parked my Chevy Silverado. Ben followed me. "What now?" I asked. "What did Owen do now?"

"You'll see."

"He must have been up here today, then," I said. "What if he cut down another one of the big trees?" I picked up my pace.

We reached the overgrown logging road and then followed my own muddy footprints back to where both our vehicles were parked, and there it was, the fresh graffiti spray-painted on the driver's side of my truck: *I'm watching you.* A track, other than Ben's and mine, led back down the logging road. Owen was long gone, of course, likely back in town.

"He can't get away with this," I said. I waved a hand in a circle. "Not the truck. I don't care about the truck. But the trees, the threats." I unlocked the door. "I'm going to talk to him."

"Please, just stay away from Owen."

I threw my pack onto the passenger seat and turned to my husband. "I've got to stand up to him, or he'll just keep threatening me." Like any bully would. Like my father had. "Maybe I can reason with him. Make him understand how important this park is to the town."

Ben snorted. We both knew how unlikely that was. But I had to try.

I gave Ben a peck on the cheek and climbed into the truck. "I'll see you at home," I said. "I may be a little late starting supper."

When I closed the truck door, he knocked on the window. "Piper, wait."

*Piper.* As I started up the truck, it struck me as an odd name. Why had my parents chosen *Piper*? Ben once joked that he felt the name suited me as I had a determined, no-nonsense way of walking and talking that made him think of a Scottish piper, brave and stubborn, marching noisily down the street, leading the way for the parade. Or the army.

"Piper, don't—"

But I was determined to face Owen, to end his intimidation, and, hopefully, his poaching of our precious old-growth trees. I turned the truck around, then put it into gear to make the trek down the mountain road.

"Don't do anything stupid," Ben shouted after me.

# 3

The rain had stopped by the time I drove my pickup down the last leg of a neglected, pitted road into town, or what was left of the town. Moston. Everyone called it Moss Town, for the moss that choked out the grass of the unkempt lawns, clung to the trees, grew on roofs and nearly anything that was stationary in this rain-drenched region. Once, silver and gold had brought prospectors and then miners here, but the precious ores ran out and the mine closed even before the Second World War began. After that it was logging, a mill, that kept men employed and their families in this valley. Their log cabins and clapboard houses were clustered on the east side of Black Lake—a long, deep and, yes, inky-black lake—as the steep slopes dropping almost directly into the lake made it difficult to access the west side. Not long ago there was a school in Moss Town, and shops, a movie theatre, an ice rink and a library.

But then the mill closed and most of the residents left to find work elsewhere. Now there was only a tiny post office inside a grocery that I would have called a convenience store back in the city; a Legion inside a community hall where coffee houses and dances were held; a museum and visitor centre combo in what was once the library, a grand brick building covered in ivy and, of course, moss. The only restaurant was Maggie's, a diner with a logging theme, attached to the one gas station.

After that, the rutted road continued through ravaged timberland, the mountains above patchy in replanted clear-cut, for more than an hour before hitting the next town, Clifton, where Ben's office was based. Ben had chosen to live in Moston because it was smack in the middle of the vast wilderness he monitored on his own. As he said, it was useful to know the locals, to be a member of the community here, as his friends and neighbours alerted him to those misusing or abusing the Crown land that surrounded the town. And there were few places, he said, more beautiful.

Moston was a village now, with a tiny population of dogged souls who refused to leave, or, unable to sell their houses, couldn't leave. The village would die completely in the near future if it didn't reinvent itself, and soon. Jackson, Ben's best friend and the self-appointed "mayor" of Moston, had set up a website trying to promote the village to outdoors enthusiasts, hipsters searching for a simpler, rural way of living, and healthy retirees who didn't need a hospital close by. Anyone selling property in an urban area could find a real estate bargain here and live on the difference. But even though houses were dirt cheap in Moston, there were still many homes sitting empty because there was so little work to be had, and so few amenities.

When Jackson first contracted me to write material for the town website, for his wilderness guiding business and to help promote the park proposal, he joked that I was just the kind of person he was trying to attract to Moston. I do communications and copywriting work for industry, non-profit environmental groups, online magazines, and news sites—anyone promoting environmental issues who would pay me to write a story or clean up copy. I had taken English and environmental studies at university, come out with a BA as an environmental writer. So yes, I was that thirty-something with a portable job that Jackson was hoping to bring to Moston, a freelancer and environment nut who would put up with the area's isolation and work from home, so I could live a low-cost lifestyle in this astonishingly beautiful landscape. While Jackson hadn't yet had much success luring telecommuters like me to Moston, he *had* started to bring in ecotourists for wildlife tours, sport fishing, kayaking, hiking and bouldering in the summer, and backcountry skiing in the winter. With Jackson's help, former residents who couldn't sell their homes by the lake started renting them out to tourists over the summer, and to skiers in the winter.

Jackson's bigger project, though, and one I had passionately embraced, was working to safeguard what was left of the old-growth forest from Hunter's Creek on over to the far side of the lake as a park, which would ultimately bring tourists to worship in that majestic outdoor cathedral. But we would have little to protect if poachers kept cherry-picking the old-growth trees.

I *knew* Owen was responsible. And I knew where I would find him, at Maggie's diner, the last business on the Moston strip. Owen met his son, Tucker, there for an early supper most days after the kid got off the bus.

Sure enough, Owen's truck was in front of the diner, its sides and back end mud-splattered as if he'd taken it off-road. After parking next to his pickup, I snapped a photo of the latest threatening graffiti on my truck—*I'm watching you*—before swinging open the door to the diner, the handle greasy under the palm of my hand. There were *No Smoking* signs everywhere, yet the place reeked not only of french fries, but cigarette smoke. Owen's buddy Nelson, facing in my direction, sucked his cigarette and, as he blew out a stream of smoke, nodded at me to get Owen's attention. "Here's trouble," he said.

Owen chewed as he spun lazily in the booth to face me. His face was heavily lined from a decades-old smoking habit and working under the sun, but his expression remained as inscrutable as a professional poker player's. "Well," he said flatly, "look who the cat dragged in." Owen had already finished off one can of Budweiser. He slurped from his second can and placed it on the table beside him, chewed another fry.

*Breathe*, I told myself, *breathe*.

Owen raised his eyebrow to me. "*Yes?*" he said, drawing out the *s*.

I cleared my throat and tried for a cordial tone. "I see your truck is muddy. Just back from a drive up to Hunter's Creek?"

Owen exchanged a glance with Nelson. "No, we were on Jill Mathewson's property, bucked some firewood for her. Nelson will tell you." He popped another fry into his mouth. I could see it moving around as he spoke. "You need a few loads for the winter? How many cords you want?"

The few loggers who remained in Moston had resorted to selling firewood to homeowners in Clifton to make ends meet. When Ben questioned them about where they got the wood, most claimed it was from private land, just as Owen had, and there wasn't much Ben could do to prove otherwise. If they took trees from Crown land to sell as firewood, they were supposed to arrange for a forestry licence to cut. Instead, most just got a free permit to cut firewood for personal use. Either way, they could only take already dead or downed trees. The scent of freshly cut cedar on Owen and Nelson made me doubt it was firewood they had been cutting.

I turned to Nelson. "You were at Jill Mathewson's all day?"

To avoid answering, Nelson bit into his burger, cigarette still in hand, and kept his eyes on his plate. Mayo slid down his little finger. He still wore his corks, even though a sign on the door read *No Cork Boots Allowed*, as the spikes on the bottoms punctured the floor. He wasn't the only one. The floor was chewed to shit.

I tilted my head at Owen. "So, you weren't near Hunter's Creek today."

"I told you. We were at Jill's. Why do you keep asking?"

Maggie, on her way out of the kitchen carrying a coffee pot, stopped to watch us, and I realized others in the café were watching too. The unemployed loggers and mill workers who ate together, clustered in the red booths. Old Hen and Archie at the window table. Friends on the park committee seated along the wall. Maggie nodded at me and wiped a hand down her full-length barbecue apron that read *Keep Calm and Grill On.*

"I was up there today," I said. "At Hunter's Creek."

Owen smirked. "You don't say?"

My phone vibrated several times, finally picking up texts now that it was within cell tower range, and I quickly checked it. A text from Libby, my mother, wondering why I hadn't called. Another from Noah, who was still on the bus, asking if I had plans for supper. A call from Ben that had gone to voice mail. I slid to photos on my phone, the new graffiti on my truck door, and held it up for Owen to see. "Somebody spray-painted this on my truck while it was parked on the logging road."

There were rumblings around us. From the corner of my eye, I saw Hen touch a translucent hand to her mouth.

Owen squinted at the photo, then put on a pair of black-rimmed glasses to take a better look. The glasses transformed him. He now seemed less the logger and more the astute businessman. He made a show of taking off the glasses and tucking them back in his pocket. "What exactly are you suggesting?" he asked.

I turned to Hen for support. She and Archie had arrived in Moston fifty years before as back-to-the-landers and had lived here ever since. Together they had initiated the effort to create the park years before, though Jackson now headed the committee. Hen nodded slowly, grey pigtails bouncing. She wasn't one to step back from a fight. In the early nineties, she had joined the War in the Woods on the coast, chaining herself to an old-growth tree to stop loggers from cutting it down.

I turned back to Owen. "*Did* you—" I started. *Breathe.* "Did you spray-paint my truck?"

Owen's voice bristled with offence, real or manufactured I wasn't sure. "Piper, I'm astonished you would ask." His mouth remained a straight, unreadable line, but the spark of a smile flickered into his eyes. I wasn't sure whether he was playing me or not. Certainly, he was playing to the supper crowd. He spoke just a bit too loudly, theatrically. "I would never threaten a woman like that."

"That's not what I heard," Maggie said under her breath.

Nelson cleared his throat, a warning to her, and I heard murmurings from the booths closest to us.

Owen ran a nicotine-yellowed finger under his nose and sniffed as he stared Maggie down. "Lady, you need to be a lot more careful about what you say." His gaze slid sideways, at our neighbours. "Especially in public."

Maggie harrumphed and went on her way, carrying the coffee pot to a nearby table to refill cups.

The door opened, ringing a bell, and Owen's son, Tucker, pulled his hoodie back as he entered, revealing a mess of straw-coloured hair he must have inherited from his mother. Outside, the bus that ferried the few students to school in Clifton and back lumbered away as the kids that had just disembarked scattered in all directions. My stepson was among them, though Noah evidently didn't notice my truck parked at Maggie's, or he would have ducked in with Tucker to catch a ride. Instead, he crossed the road to walk the kilometre home to our cottage on the lake.

Tucker slid into the booth next to Nelson, dropping his backpack on the floor as he took in the tension at the table, the locals watching us. "What's going on?"

"Piper here was just leaving," Owen said, pointedly, to me. "So we can finish our supper *in peace.*"

"You ordered for me?" Tucker asked.

"The usual."

When I didn't immediately leave, Owen glared up at me. "Was there anything else?" he asked, but in that way that said *Fuck off.*

Something clawed against my throat, trying to escape from the cage of my chest, but I spoke anyway. "I know you don't want me here in Moston," I said quietly, keeping my head down, only flicking him glances. "You might even be trying to scare me into leaving."

Owen shifted uncomfortably in his seat.

I lifted my head a little. "And I know you don't like the attention I've been bringing to the park proposal." In blogs, on social media, stories in online magazines and on news sites, the work Jackson was paying me for. "I know you'd rather I disappeared." I caught Maggie's eye and she nodded, encouraging me on. "But Moston is my home now," I said, with more confidence. "And the park proposal is important for this town. In fact, it's the one thing that may save it, bring in tourists, new blood, young people, jobs."

Old Archie croaked, "Hear, hear!" from his window seat opposite Hen. There were a few scattered claps from others on the park proposal committee. But there were grumblings too, from Nelson and other loggers, former mill workers. Hen offered me a tired smile as she held her husband's veined hand. They had been fighting this same fight for decades, trying to protect the old-growth forest within this area, and others, from logging interests. Now that thin strip of old-growth forest from Hunter's Creek around to the far shore, the area we hoped to turn into a park, was all that was left untouched. Almost everything else was clear-cut or second-growth.

Owen ran a finger under his nose again, craving a smoke, I thought. "You came here from the city, Vancouver, what, two years ago?"

"Three."

"I've been here nearly twenty-five." He slapped his chest. "I've made a life for myself and raised my son here, stayed when others didn't. So many people have left, and they'll keep on leaving unless we give them work. Logging, jobs at the mill, that's what's going to save this town. Not some goddamned park. If you really care about this community, how about you bring in some investors to get that mill up and running again?" He turned to his son. "I'd like to see Tucker stay, raise his own family here. That's what you want too, isn't it, son?"

Tucker's eyes shifted from his father to the table. He shrugged in a quick, jerking movement. "I don't know."

Owen's voice deepened to a growl. "You don't *know*?"

Tucker squirmed in the booth. "I guess," he said quietly. As Owen continued to eye him, Tucker sank both hands between his thighs, hunkered down in the booth. The boy needed to get away from his father.

"The park *will* bring jobs to the town," I said quickly, to divert Owen's attention from his son. "Jackson, me"—I waved a hand around the room, at Hen and Archie and the others on the park committee—"all of us involved in the park proposal, we're trying to bring people back into this community, not just tourists but people who want to live here. And they *will* come, because of the beauty of this landscape and—"

Owen cut me off. "There's nothing in that park proposal for us. Not the loggers or mill workers. You're just locking up more big trees."

"Yeah, plenty of trees on the other side of the lake," Nelson said. He stubbed out his cigarette. "Plenty of big trees, if we could just get at them. That game trail over there is a muddy mess. Can't barely get a four-wheeler down—" He stopped when Owen glowered at him, shutting him up.

I exchanged a knowing look with Hen. Nelson had all but admitted they had been poaching those trees. I flipped back through my photos and held my phone out to show Owen the image of the giant stump. "Someone cut down this old-growth cedar near Hunter's Creek. It was maybe seven, eight hundred years old."

"Well, that is a crime," Owen said.

"Yes, it is, actually," I said. "Anyone taking down those old-growth trees illegally could face fines as high as a million dollars, and years of jail time."

Across from Owen, Tucker was wide-eyed. "A million bucks?" he asked. "*Years* of jail time?" He turned to his father. "Is that true?"

"Shut it," Owen told him.

Hen piped up then, her fragile elderly voice lilting across the room. "When somebody takes one of those ancient trees down, they take something from all of us, not just from this town, but this country, the world. That's how rare those trees and that ecosystem is now."

A few others clapped in support, even a couple of the younger loggers, I noted.

"Dad never touched any of those big trees at Hunter's Creek," Tucker told me, and then the room. "Or anywhere that park's going to be. We, we—none of us did."

If I hadn't been before, I was certain now that Owen had dragged his son into the sorry business of poaching old-growth trees.

Owen skidded a fork angrily across the table at his son. "I said, shut it!"

Tucker withered in the booth under his father's glare. When

Owen was satisfied his son *would* keep his mouth shut, he turned slowly back to me. "As my son said, we've left those big trees alone. The only thing we harvest on Crown land is salvage on the clear-cuts and roadside, for firewood. We've got a permit for that." But as he spoke, his eyes flickered past Maggie to the framed black-and-white photo on the wall of old-time loggers felling a gigantic cedar with a misery whip saw, an oversized two-man crosscut. He was lying.

The words tumbled out of my mouth before I'd thought them through. "You *did* take down that tree at Hunter's Creek, didn't you?" I asked Owen.

Owen took his time wiping his mouth with his paper napkin, then stood, forcing me to step back. He wasn't as tall as Ben, but he was big, heavier. His skin was pockmarked with old acne scars, and he'd gained a paunch in his middle years, but he had been handsome once. Even now he held himself with the confidence of a man used to getting, or taking, what he wanted. Under his plaid wool jacket, he wore a blue T-shirt that read *Forget the trees, hug a logger.* Had he worn it for my benefit, to taunt me? He must have known I would track him down after he spray-painted my truck.

Maggie, holding that coffee pot off to the side as if she feared it would get broken, put out a hand. "Now, Owen, we don't want any trouble."

But Owen pushed a finger into my upper arm, throwing me off balance. "You come in here, interrupting my supper, accusing me of theft in front of my friends, my neighbours, my *son*." His eyes watered with rage as he roared. "What gives you the goddamned right?"

I took a step back. "I'm sorry—" I started, my voice rising in panic.

But Owen had already taken hold of my safety vest, yanking it up so his fist, twisted within it, knocked against my chin. His hazel eyes staring into mine were yellowed, bloodshot, and broken capillaries lined his nose. The telltale signs of an alcoholic that I was all too familiar with. For a split second I had the uncanny, dizzying sensation that I had slipped back in time and was standing in close quarters with my father.

When Tucker jumped up to yank at his father's arm, to stop him, I cried out, "Tucker, stay back!" But it was too late. Owen jerked his arm out of Tucker's grip, elbowing his son square in the face, by accident or on purpose, I wasn't sure. Either way, he let me go.

As Tucker held his bloody nose, Owen pushed his son roughly. "Don't you ever—"

Maggie danced out of the way with the coffee pot as Owen pushed his son again.

"Stop!" I cried. "Owen, stop it!"

Owen swung back to me, both fists pumped, his face red with rage, but then the bell over the door rang as someone opened it. Owen dropped his fists, took a step back. I turned to find Ben marching toward us in his uniform and body armour. The expression on his bearded face was determined, pissed, as he eyed Owen. But he didn't confront the man. Instead, he took me by the elbow. "Let's go," he said quietly.

As Ben led me through the door, Owen snorted at me, like a bear does before a charge.

# 4

Still holding my elbow, Ben walked me out of the diner and into the lot, where he had hurriedly parked his truck, with its official government logo, at an angle, blocking the gas pumps to customers on the one side. He stopped and flicked back his jacket to put his hands on his hips. "You want to tell me what just went down in there?"

I crossed my arms and glanced through the café window. The overcast late-afternoon sky was dark enough that I could see clearly into the well-lit diner. Both Owen and Tucker were back in their booth. As the boy dabbed his bloody nose with a napkin, his head was bowed, like Owen was giving him hell. "I tried to make Owen understand how important that park, that forest, is to the town," I said.

"You confronted him about the stump."

I nodded. "And then Owen flipped out. He grabbed me and hit Tucker. I mean, he elbowed him. It may have been an accident, but—"

"He *grabbed* you?" Ben asked.

"He grabbed my vest."

My husband took a step toward the diner, and for an instant I thought he might rush in and tackle Owen. But he stopped himself and turned back. "Did he hurt you?"

"I'm okay."

"You're shaking."

"I'm a little rattled, I guess." Triggered, actually. I felt the same jittery wash of fear and adrenalin coursing through me as I had as a child after one of my father's rampages. I felt foolish about it and tried to hide it, but my husband knew me too well.

Ben pulled me into a bear hug. "Hey, hey. Hug me," he said. "Breathe deep to calm yourself." Something he always said when I was upset. Enfolded in his arms, my face against his chest, breathing in the fresh, forest scent on him, I did start to relax.

After a few minutes he asked, "Better?"

I nodded into his chest, and he let go.

"Do you want to press charges?"

I hesitated. "No. It was nothing." In any case, I knew from experience that pressing charges would only make things so much worse for Tucker. Owen would take out his frustrations and anger on his son, as my father had on me.

"I should have spoken with Owen alone, privately," I said.

"And if you had, you would have put yourself at more risk." Ben turned back to the diner. "*I'll* have a chat with Owen."

"Don't do anything stupid," I said, smiling a little, echoing his earlier advice, which I obviously hadn't taken.

Through the window, I could see Maggie carrying a plate over to Owen's table, for Tucker. She came back with an empty container and a brown bag, for takeout, I guessed. I turned back to my husband. "Listen, Nelson all but admitted he and Owen are poaching on the far side of the lake," I said. "He talked about how their ATVs got stuck in the mud over there, on their way to the really ancient trees."

Ben rubbed his beard as if he were thinking something through. "I was going to hold off telling you this until I had a chance to get over there, but Jackson called, said he was across the lake this afternoon with his GPS unit, mapping out where the future trails should go."

"Yeah, he told me he was heading out there today."

"He knows I'm investigating the tree poaching, of course. I asked him to alert me to any activity he comes across in the forest. New trails, equipment left out there, felled trees. Today he found a newly felled cedar. The log is still in place." He hesitated. "It's one of the ancients, Piper."

I put a hand to my mouth. "Where?" I asked.

"Within the Boulders."

The Boulders was an area named after the huge, cracked, moss-and-fern-covered boulders that littered the foot of the slope on the far side of the lake, boulders the size of cars or in some cases a house, chunks of the mountain that had once fallen from the cliff above. It was a magical landscape that made me think of the floating rocks in the movie *Avatar*. The rocky terrain had deterred logging, and most of the remaining old-growth trees of the valley were found there. Owen would have had to drive that overgrown, long-abandoned logging road past Hunter's Creek down the other side of the mountain, and then follow a game trail around to the far side of the lake. He would have had to use four-wheelers, quads, to ferry the wood back and forth to his truck, because he couldn't have gotten a full-sized vehicle through there. When I hiked the Boulders, I took Ben's aluminum boat or my kayak across the lake. One of the plans within the park proposal, pending funding, was to develop a road and trail system to make the Boulders more access-ible to tourists, largely for bouldering, rock climbing.

Ben looked across the lake to the area now. "Sounds like they started to buck the tree, so I figure they'll be back for the rest of the wood soon enough. I'll go over there tomorrow."

"It's Saturday." His day off.

"I'll make up for it with a day off next week."

The diner door opened. Tucker. Ben lowered his voice as Tucker approached. "I'll head out first thing in the morning, check it out. Hopefully, I can scrape together enough evidence to figure out exactly who's responsible." Then his voice rose, a bit too loud. "But I hear we're in for snow tomorrow night."

Tucker's backpack was slung over his shoulder, and he carried a bag with grease stains on it, his supper, a burger and fries, I was sure. He sidled up to us, a shy grin on his face, like he wasn't sure he was invited to the party. While he'd wiped his nose with a napkin, there was still blood in his nostrils from his father's blow.

"You okay?" I asked him.

He ran a finger under his nose in a gesture so like his father's. "Yeah, I'm okay." He glanced back at the diner. "Hey, I'm sorry about Dad," he said. "The way he acted."

"Tucker, you don't have to apologize for your father." I offered him the sad smile of someone who had gone through a shared trauma: a drunken father's cuff to the head, a slap, a shove against the wall, maybe worse. Tucker hadn't told me anything about it, but he'd come over to our place with bruises, and I could see it in him, the nervous, hangdog stance when he was around his father, the defensiveness and defiance when he wasn't.

The boy kicked gravel. "Yeah, well." He glanced nervously back at the diner, then stood a little straighter as he spoke to Ben. "I told Noah I'd hang out with him tonight. Can I catch a ride to your place now?"

"No problem."

"Are you sure your father's okay with that?" I asked. "I mean after . . ." After I'd taken a stick to the hornet's nest.

Tucker nodded awkwardly, like a bobble-head, then squinted up at Ben as if he expected the answer to his next question would be no. "Noah said he'd let me try out his drone. I thought maybe you could teach me how to fly it?"

Noah had just got his drone pilot licence, after Ben had bought him a drone for his seventeenth birthday. Tucker was fascinated with the machines, coming over to watch Ben and Noah fly them any chance he got. He clearly wanted a drone of his own.

Ben scratched his neck. "I don't know, Tucker. It's been a long day and we haven't had supper yet."

I put a hand to Ben's arm, asking him to reconsider. "We're always happy to have you," I said to Tucker. The boy needed all the kindness we could offer, and I didn't want him near his father right now.

"Yeah, I guess, sure," Ben said. "But only if the rain doesn't start up again. And it will be a short flight, since it's getting dark. But I can offer some tips."

Tucker rocked on his heels, obviously delighted. "Cool."

Ben nodded sideways at the diner, Owen paying for supper at the till. "I think it's time to go." He gave me *the look*, and I nodded, rushing back to my truck before Owen came out.

Tucker jumped in the government truck with Ben, and I quickly slid into the driver's seat of my own pickup, backing out and swinging to the road just as Owen walked out. As I waited for a car to pass before crossing over to Lakeshore, I glanced in the rear-view mirror. Owen stood by his muddy truck, staring after me. He pointed at his own eyes with two fingers, then pointed them at me. *I'm watching you.*

# 5

I drove home along Lakeshore, a road that wound along the beach where most of the houses were situated. The small, squat cabins built by early pioneers were nestled next to the Edwardian and Craftsman homes that followed during the heyday of gold and silver mining, and beside them, the clapboard houses built still later by loggers and mill workers. Many of these homes, rich or poor, were constructed by Scottish immigrants who planted rowan trees, mountain ash, near them for good luck, and their bright-orange berries now bobbed in the wind.

Ben and I lived with Noah in one of those white clapboard houses, a cottage literally at the end of the road, tucked into the cliff base. Its door was long ago painted red by a former Scots owner to indicate it was finally mortgage-free. When I parked my truck next to it and got out, I could hear that Ben and the boys were already flying the drones on the beach in front of the deck. Those irritating mosquito whines. Once, while visiting my grandparents at their prairie farm, I had heard a similar ominous buzz and had stepped outside to see a huge black cloud of mosquitoes directly over the tin roof of their hundred-year-old farmhouse. As I walked down the slope of pebbled beach now, Ben and Noah's drones felt no less menacing, hovering there, watching.

Nevertheless, the drone was a powerful tool, revolutionary in the way GPS technologies had been for natural resource management.

Ben saw just how useful a drone would be for his work, and when he couldn't get funding, he bought one of his own, professional-grade but small enough that he could tuck it in his backpack. Ben now flew his drone on patrol as he kept an eye on the trails and roads, Crown forest and logged timberlands, hunting for evidence of "non-compliance," as he put it, or even photographing offenders in the act. In the past, a costly helicopter or plane flight was the only way to patrol the forests from the air.

Ben flew his drone next to Noah's now, as Tucker watched from the side. Noah's height, and those skinny jeans, made him seem that much thinner. I imagined it would be some time before he filled out, but he already had Ben's build, the rounder chest, the wide shoulders, exaggerated now in his black puffer jacket. I could see his mother in him too, of course, her dark hair and eyes, and warmer skin tone, her Italian roots, so different from Ben's ruddy Scottish complexion, which was more like my own. The blend made Noah a handsome kid, though he refused to believe it when compli-mented, and hated having his picture taken. Whenever I pulled out my phone to snap a shot, almost without fail he twisted away. I trashed photo after photo of his blurred image. But then, weren't all teens like that? Doubting their beauty and power. I had doubted my own. My father had made sure of it.

I stood close to Ben. "Hey," I said gently.

He clicked the home button on his smart controller to bring his drone down to land on the beach near his feet, in the position it had taken off from. "Hey."

I searched his face. "Am I forgiven?" I asked. For confronting Owen, and so publicly? He gave me a quick kiss and I took that as a yes.

"How was school?" I asked Noah.

"Okay, I guess," he said. His thumbs worked the sticks of the drone controller. Noah had grown so fast in the last year that he wasn't yet comfortable with his new height. Even standing out here on the beach, he ducked his head as if afraid he might hit the top of a doorway.

"You got your calculus exam grade back today, right?" I asked him.

"Yeah."

"How'd it go?"

"I did all right."

"Should we be celebrating tonight, with pizza?"

He grinned, glancing sideways at me. "Maybe."

I bumped shoulders with him. "You aced it, didn't you?" As he almost always did.

"Ninety-two percent." Noah shrugged. "I could have done better."

I shared a knowing glance with Ben. Noah was such a perfectionist. We had been trying to get him to chill a little, fret less about his grades. But he was aiming for a career in tech, a computer engineering degree, and was worried about getting accepted into his universities of choice. I put an arm around him. "Ninety-two is amazing," I said.

Tucker sunk his hands into his pockets. "I'd be happy with seventy-five percent."

"You just need to study," Noah told him. "I could help you, if you want."

"Nah, too much work."

"You may need calculus," I said to Tucker. "You might want to go back to school. Maybe in the trades?"

Tucker shook his head. Sadly, he had made no plans for post-secondary education. Owen was determined to have Tucker join his family business, whether the logging was legal or not, it seemed.

Tucker was one of the few friends Noah brought home, though my stepson talked often of other friends at the high school in Clifton. Then again, Tucker was one of the few teens who lived in Moston. The population had aged to the point that Jackson wondered if the village would die off as the residents did, of old age. Even Noah would be gone in a year, off to university the next fall. I was excited for him, but the thought of his leaving punched a hole in my stomach. Ben and I talked a lot about how we might entice him back for visits once he left for school. But when compared to city life, what did Moss Town have to offer?

Owen was right about this, at least: we *had* to bring young blood into the community, give them something to come here for, a reason to stay. But I didn't believe that meant logging and mill work, as Owen did, because the surrounding forest was already depleted and the replanted trees would take decades to grow into a mature second-growth stand, generations more to develop into an old-growth forest. And faced with global warming and logging pressure, it was unlikely that would ever happen. Once these old-growth forests were gone, they were gone forever. Tourism was the answer, recreation. We needed a destination to draw young people here: the park and within it bouldering, kayaking, hiking and back-country skiing. But even I wondered if that would be enough to convince people to move here, to rebuild the town, or even to keep what was left going. We were so far off the beaten track.

Ben turned to the boys. "So, Tucker, you've come for a lesson." *Let's get this show on the road.* He must be hungry for supper, I thought.

Tucker, with his hood up, bobbed his head. "If you want," he said. He was a kid who, when offered a choice between root beer and Coke, would say, "It doesn't matter to me," and when pressed, "You choose." As if he was afraid that if he made the wrong choice, he would be punished for it. Which I imagine he often was, at home. Moody and distant, sometimes rude, he wasn't an easy kid to love. But he stirred my maternal instincts because I knew, or at least I thought I knew, what he was going through with Owen. He had no one but his father. He was trapped.

"Want to let Tucker try?" Ben asked Noah. "Let's start with the drone on the ground."

"Sure." Noah landed the drone and handed his controller over to Tucker. "Careful. They bust easy."

"I know," Tucker said, a little defensively.

"Okay, the basics," Ben said. "First, you always want to check your battery level. Remember, you need enough power not only to send your drone where you want it to go, but to get it back home too. If you don't . . ." He made a gesture like an aircraft nosediving to the ground. When Tucker appeared alarmed, Ben added, "But don't worry. By default, the drone records the location it took off from and sets it as the return-to-home location."

"So, it automatically comes right back to the place it took off from," I clarified.

"When it has used up half its battery power," Ben added.

"Got it," Tucker said.

"Okay, take it up. Pull both sticks in and down to get the motors spinning." The drone started whirring. "That's right. Now move the left stick forward to lift the drone."

Tucker, with his eyes on the controller screen, which showed the view from the drone camera, pushed the stick up too far and sent it skyrocketing upward until I all but lost sight of it.

"Whoa, bring it back down," Ben said. "Remember, you want to keep your eye on the drone as you're flying it. Only check the screen when you need to, for battery or radio signal strength, or, if you're taking a video or still, to see what the camera is seeing."

He pointed at the controller. "The sticks are spring-loaded. If you panic, just let go and the drone will hover in place."

"Right." Tucker wiped a sweaty hand on his jeans.

"You're doing fine," I said. I put a hand on his shoulder, to reassure him that no one would criticize him here, as Owen so often did. He craned his neck back to stare up at the drone as he brought it down.

Ben nodded. "Good. The main thing you've got to learn is how to put yourself in the pilot's seat. You want to imagine you're right in the drone, viewing things from the drone's perspective as you're flying it. It can be a little counterintuitive to operate when it's flying toward you." Ben glanced at the joysticks as Tucker thumbed them, then up at the drone. "That's it. Keep it away from the house. Now bring it closer to us."

Tucker brought the drone down until it hovered, nearly stationary, at eye level in front of us.

"Closer."

Alarmed at the buzz and whir of the blades, Tucker stepped to the side, into me. "Sorry," he said quickly.

"It's okay," I said. "You don't need to worry about it flying into you. It's programmed to back off if you get too close."

"Seriously?"

"Walk toward it and you'll see."

With a grin on his face, Tucker stepped up to the drone and, sensing him, the drone automatically moved backward, keeping a safe distance from anyone, anything around. It was easy to project intelligence on the thing, a consciousness. It appeared to be a large, alien insect, studying us warily, watching with that one black eye.

Ben pointed at the screen. "Now hit the home button, to bring it down."

The drone gracefully, and automatically, buzzed down to the ground, landing on the spot Tucker had taken off from.

"There you go!" I said. "Your first flight."

Tucker grinned at me, his face lit up in joy. He seemed like another kid entirely. But then his face fell as Noah held out his hand and Tucker gave him the controller. "Thanks, man," he said. Then he was back to his sullen self.

"No problem."

"I'll do better next time," Tucker said to Ben. His expression made me ache for him; he was desperate for Ben's approval, for a father's approval, I thought. But Ben missed it, his eyes on his controller.

"You did good this time," I told Tucker. "Way better than I did on my first flight." I only played with the thing. I hadn't bothered to get my drone pilot's licence. If I needed images, a video for the website, say, Ben or Noah did the flying.

"What's the range on your drone?" Tucker asked Ben. "I mean, how far can it fly away from the controller?"

"About fifteen kilometres. That's a huge range, if you think about it." Ben ran a hand across the expanse of the far shore. "That's all that wilderness above the beach. But the law requires a drone pilot to have his eyes on the drone at all times. I've applied for an exemption to that regulation, given the vast territory and isolation of my patrol area, as I want to do bigger grid searches, but I haven't been approved yet."

Ben lifted his drone into the air again, and as he tipped his head back to watch it fly above the water, I hung at his side to view the video the drone sent back, our figures on the pebbled beach, the red tin roof of the house tucked into a rocky outcrop at the end of Lakeshore Road. In summer, tourists often turned in our yard before going the other way. Our house was surrounded on one side by cedar and hemlock that clung to a steep, rocky slope that rose almost directly from the lake, making it nearly impossible to build a road beyond it, though we had plans in the works to create a trail system on this side of the lake as well. I imagined that would mean more traffic to the rough turnabout behind our home. I would have to talk to Jackson about that, see if we could drum up funding for a parking lot that would keep tourists out of our yard.

Ben handed me the drone headset, like a VR headset. "Have a go?" he asked me.

I slid the headset over my face and, instantly, I was flying over the house, Ben, myself, and the boys below. I felt a little dizzy, disoriented, quite literally out of body, as I always did when using the thing.

"Easy there, girl," Ben said as I bumped into him.

"Can I try?" Tucker asked.

"Sure," I said.

"In a minute," Ben said. "First, I need to sweep my wife off her feet."

I grinned at his cheesy comment as he manoeuvred the drone so that, hitching a ride through the VR glasses, I flew over the red roof of our cabin, over the cedar deck, the pebbled beach and then, circling back, out over the dark, misty lake. "It's beautiful," I said, my arms out.

Ben lifted the drone, and me, to the tip of a cedar clinging off the rock face of the slope next to our house. I felt I could reach out, touch the top of the tree as the drone circled it. Ben rotated the drone so that it faced back to the house far below and hovered there. I could be an eagle sitting on that tree, observing myself and my family in the failing light.

"Can I try?" Tucker asked again, and I took off the VR headset and handed it to him.

Ben gave him the same quick overhead tour of the beach, the lake, the treetop, then clicked on the home button. Tucker groaned as the drone headed back. "Can't we take one more pass?"

"It's getting too dark," Ben said.

"Can we fly again tomorrow morning?" Tucker asked. "I could stay overnight."

Recently, he often stayed over, sleeping in our spare room in the basement.

"Of course," I said. "You're always welcome here."

But Ben took my arm. "Just not tonight," he said.

"Why not?" Noah asked.

"Yeah," I said. "Why not?"

Ben didn't answer at first. He only said, "Some other time."

Tucker hung his head. There wasn't just disappointment there; he had hoped to avoid his father's bad mood.

"Ben," I said, "having Tucker stay over is really no problem. I have the spare bed already made."

"We have plans," he said.

"Plans?" Noah asked.

That was the first I'd heard of it. "What—"

But before I said "plans?" Ben shook his head ever so slightly at me, asking me to drop it.

I threw Noah the keys to my pickup. "Give Tucker a ride home?" I asked. "And pick up a pizza from Maggie's to celebrate that excellent mark on the exam."

He handed me his controller to take back to the house. "Sure. The usual?" The pizza, he meant.

"I'll pay you back later."

Tucker shuffled up the beach, hands in his jeans pockets, without saying goodbye. Noah followed.

"Come over Sunday," I called after Tucker.

"Yeah, Sunday," Ben said. "We'll get in another flight."

Tucker kept walking, as if he was sure that would never happen. I expected his life was full of disappointments. I just hoped Tucker would escape this town and his father after graduation in the new year. In the meantime, I had to do a much better job of keeping an eye out for him. Maybe I could arrange for him to get a place in Clifton, or he could crash in our basement during his final year in high school. Noah would like that, and Tucker too, I was sure. I would have jumped at the chance to escape home, and my father, at his age. I'd have to talk to Ben about it, ease him into the idea, but now wasn't the time.

As the boys drove away, Ben and I retrieved the drones and carried them up the beach toward the deck stairs. We had a good-sized deck that ran along the front of the house and down one side, high enough that the patio door of the basement walkout was just below it. Another patio door off our bedroom opened to the side deck, affording us a spectacular view of the lake that was better, even, than the view from the open kitchen and living room.

"We have plans tonight?" I asked, giving Ben a sly smile.

But he chose not to run with the innuendo. "I'm heading across the lake in the morning to investigate that downed cedar Jackson told me about," he reminded me. "I don't want Tucker to know, because he might pass on that information to his father. I'm hoping Owen left some equipment behind, to pick up later. If we find something, we can identify him as the poacher that way." He started for the house. "Or who knows? I might get lucky and capture a video with the drone of Owen and Nelson bucking the wood."

"You won't involve Tucker, though, right?" I asked as I followed. "He can't face charges. He's just a kid." When Ben didn't answer, I pressed the point. "Owen would have forced Tucker to help him. The boy would have no say. Or face a beating if he refused."

Ben hesitated on the deck stairs, then spoke as he climbed them. "I think you may be projecting too much of your own experience onto Tucker."

I joined him on the deck. "You've seen the bruises on the boy, how he acts around his father." Like a kicked dog.

My husband put his hand on the base of my back. The weight, the security of it there. "But, Piper, Tucker isn't you," he said. "And Owen is not your father."

"He's a bully," I said, stepping past him to enter the house. "Bullies are all the same."

# SATURDAY

# 6

I startled awake. Though I couldn't remember the nightmare, I had the dim sense that I had called out, that throaty, otherworldly cry of the dreamer. I rolled over, arms and legs splayed as if I were making a snow angel, to look around the room: Ben's stocky forties bureau, the tall eighties dresser where I kept my jewellery box and wedding photo, the matching mid-century night tables I'd found at a yard sale, where I housed our hand towels and personal lubricant on my side, and Ben kept the thriller he read before bed on his. The house was filled with a hodgepodge of used furniture from different decades. But it was the best I could do with the resources in the area and, really, I couldn't care less. Ben and I both spent our days on the lake or in the forest. The wilderness was where we truly lived.

I sat up to find Ben's large form silhouetted against the glass of the patio door, his hair wet from his shower, a towel around his waist, the ugly green sweater I had knitted him draped around his shoulders, his favourite mug in his hand (a Father's Day gift from Noah that read *World's Greatest Farter*). We didn't have window coverings, even here in our bedroom. There was usually no need, as there was rarely anyone out on the lake to see us. Behind Ben, the morning light was hazy, the sun not yet up. The days were shorter here, on the valley floor. The sun rose later and set sooner behind that mountain range. Through it wasn't raining, for once, the forecast called for heavy snow starting that evening. Our first snow of the season. Even now, the tips of trees poked through the low cloud cover across the lake, and fog had rolled in over the water.

"Good morning," I said, my voice hoarse, my tongue dry.

"Nightmare?" he asked.

"I guess." Recently Ben had stopped asking me what my nightmares were about, because they were so frequent, though he had pressed me for details early in our relationship, hoping, I think, for clues to my psyche, what he was getting himself into. But I could never remember much about these unsettling dreams, only flashes of dark and ramshackle houses, often blackened as if burnt, and a feeling of dread, the fear that something large and dark, like a bear, was chasing me; or, at other times, that I was responsible for something, no, for *someone*, an animal, or a child, and had to get them to safety, through a burning landscape, a war zone. In my twenties I had written the dreams down, and remembered more, before realizing I didn't want to remember.

I shifted as Ben sat on the bed next to me. He put his mug on his night table, next to his book, and took my hand in both of his, holding it to his chest.

"What?" I asked, laughing a little.

"It's silly. I'll worry you."

I squeezed his hand. "Tell me."

"I woke from my own nightmare this morning."

"What about?"

He gave me an earnest look. "If something happened to me out there, you would take care of Noah, right? You'd make sure he was okay?"

"Of course." I sat up farther, covering my small breasts with the sheet. "Why? What did you dream?"

"I don't know. I just woke thinking, feeling . . ." He paused. "And then your nightmare just now. Things happen, don't they, to people out of the blue? No one goes to work thinking, *Gee, I'm about to have an accident.* It just happens. But if something *did* happen to me, Noah has no other family. I'm it." He rethought that one. "You and me. *We're* it. I just need to know he would be safe, secure, with you."

"You know he would. I love Noah. And he loves me." Why would Ben think otherwise? Or was something else going on here? "What do you know that you aren't telling me? Is Owen more of a threat than you're letting on?" Had he got himself involved in organized crime? As Ben had said, poaching trees was easy, low-risk money. More and more criminal organizations around the world were adding the trade in trees to their ugly but more established business rosters of drugs and human trafficking. "What exactly are you expecting to find out there?" I asked.

He paused. "Nothing out of the ordinary." He grinned. "Just coyotes and cougars and bears . . ."

I hesitated a beat too long before responding, "Oh my!"

We held each other's gaze and then he kissed me, the sweetest kiss, like our first kiss across the lake at the Boulders at the start of our relationship, when everything, even the forest, seemed charged with sex. I saw phallic shapes everywhere then, in the mushrooms at the base of the cedars, in the towering boulders. I saw the shape of a woman's vulva in the mossy crotches of trees. My mind unabashedly, rudely hungry for Ben in that first flush of passion, as we fell headlong into love.

"You should go," I said, "so you can get home before the snow hits. It's supposed to be heavy. I don't want you on the lake during the storm."

"I suppose." He kissed me again. "Or I could leave it for tomorrow. Or Monday. It is the weekend, after all."

I patted his chest. "No, we have to stop Owen from taking

those big trees. There are so few left. There's too much at stake, not just for the forest, but for the town. You need to see what evidence you can find before the snow covers it."

He laughed. "Okay, okay. I'm going."

He let his towel fall away, and I watched his smooth butt as he padded to the dresser by the window. As he pulled on underwear, I sat, naked, on the edge of the bed. My feet didn't touch the floor. "You'll be careful, won't you?"

"I always am."

"I know. But the way Owen reacted to me yesterday, like he might hit me . . . I worry that if he feels threatened by your investigation, he might—"

Ben shrugged on his shirt. "Any man with something to protect, or prove, is dangerous."

I slid out of bed and threw on my fluffy mustard bathrobe. "Is it true of *any* man, even you?" I smiled coyly, opening my robe to him.

Ben grabbed me, tickled me. "Even me."

I ran back to the bed squealing and Ben ran after me, lying on me in his underwear and shirt.

"I love you, you know," he said. "I love you so very much."

I held his bearded face with both hands. "I love you so much it *hurts*."

He kissed me again, then got up to put on his official self—the pants, body armour and jacket of his uniform. When he turned around, he was now the officer.

"I imagine you'll be out of cell range," I said.

"I've never had much luck catching bars on the other side of the lake. You?"

"No." Or even at home. Cell reception was sketchy here. When trying to phone Ben or Jackson, I walked the house waving my cell around, visualizing floating bubbles of reception that, with any luck, I might walk into. Standing out on the deck often seemed to work best.

"I'll have my radio," he said. "I'll call if I'm going to be late."

"You'll keep an eye out for that grizzly, right?" The cinnamon bear that had stalked Ben earlier in the fall and had killed that woman.

"She's in hibernation by now, in her den." Ben bent to give me a last kiss. "I'll try to get home before dark, before the snow hits. Give Noah a hug for me when he wakes." He left the door half-open behind him. I could hear his footsteps through the house as he grabbed his gear from his office in the addition, then carried the bag through the kitchen patio door to the deck and the beach below. He had programmed a flight path into the drone the night before, a search grid of the general area around the Boulders where Jackson said he'd seen the felled old-growth cedar. Once Ben boated across the lake, he intended to launch the drone from the beach on the far shore, then hike into the forest of old-growth giants while the drone surveyed the area from overhead. He could keep an eye on what the drone saw through the screen on his controller.

I threw on jeans and a sweater and went into the kitchen to pour myself a cup of coffee, then carried my mug out onto the deck as I watched Ben load his gear into his aluminum boat moored at the dock. He put on his yellow life jacket and started the engine. As he roared off, he lifted his hand to wave goodbye. A raven clucked from a nearby cedar, the sound like thick wooden dowels struck together, then took off over the water toward the far shore, flying over Ben as if guiding the way. The putter of the boat engine echoed over the lake. His boat entered the bank of fog, and he appeared to fade in colour and then disappear, leaving a V behind him in the still black water.

# 7

I stood at the patio door in our bedroom, tugging the silver necklace Ben had given me on my birthday, scanning the dark water. Ben had told me he'd be home for supper, before the storm hit. Now it was well after eight and the heavy snowfall had begun. At any other time, I would have stepped outside to watch the snowflakes drift down, magically, through the giant cedars, or lifted my face to the sky to feel them melt on my tongue. But tonight, the first snowfall of the season seemed dreary, foreboding. The clouds hung low over the lake and the heavy, wet snow, with its large, clumping flakes, fell like a shower of ammunition, puckering the black water as it hit.

Noah appeared at the bedroom door in jeans and a grey sweatshirt, barefoot. "Any sign of Dad?"

"Not yet." I kept my eyes on the black stretch of lake between us and the far shore, hoping to see the lights on his boat. Shortly before my father died, I dreamed of him standing on a pebbled beach like ours. One of his eyes seemed dead, clouded, but was still seeing somehow, staring across a dark lake at the far shore, at his own death. It wasn't a premonition. I knew he was dying. He was on life support at the time, following the accident. The dream was really about me. I was the one searching the far shore, coming to terms with the inevitability of my father's death. I had woken from the dream feeling both terrified and relieved.

"He should be home by now," Noah said.

I turned to my stepson. "I'm sure he's on his way back now." But the anxiety in my voice betrayed me. He came into the bedroom, something he rarely did, and stood beside me to stare out over the lake. Wanting reassurance, I thought. I offered him a smile. "He's fine," I said. "There's nothing to worry about."

Noah's look said, *Don't bullshit me. You're worried too.* "Have you phoned?" he asked.

I nodded. I'd called repeatedly over the last couple of hours. "He must still be out of cell range."

"I'll try." Noah dialled and the call went straight to voice mail, as mine had.

"Why don't you call Tucker?" I asked. "See if he wants to come over, watch a movie. Tell him I made apple crumble. He likes crumble, right?" I didn't need to ask. Tucker quickly gulped down anything put in front of him, as if he were afraid someone would snatch it away before he was done.

Noah made a face. "You're just trying to distract me."

"Call him," I said.

As soon as Noah left my bedroom, staring down at his phone, I slipped the second handset of Ben's two-way radio out of my hoodie pocket and pressed the push-to-talk button, trying to keep my voice low so Noah wouldn't hear my desperate attempts to reach his father, but the static of the radio crackled loudly. "Ben, can you hear me? Over."

I released the button and listened, but he still wasn't calling back. He carried his radio on his vest or, when he wasn't wearing the body armour, on his belt. "Ben, you there? Please respond. Over." We were well within range if Ben had searched the area around the Boulders as he'd said he would, and he had promised to call if he was going to be late. "Ben, *please.* Are you there? Over."

At the sound of Noah's feet padding down the hall, I tucked the handset back in my hoodie pocket. But of course, Noah had heard me.

"Did you reach him?" he asked, entering the bedroom again.

"Trees or rocks can interfere with the signal." I gave Noah another thin smile. "He must have found something interesting in the Boulders."

Noah grunted as he tried phoning his dad again.

"He's been this late before," I added.

"Yeah, I know." He clicked out of the call as it once again went to voice mail. "This time feels . . ."

*Different.* I'd been carrying around that same heavy feeling— that something was wrong, very wrong—for most of the day.

"Is Tucker coming over?" I asked, trying to redirect the conversation, to keep Noah from fretting.

"He's not picking up."

"Well, keep trying. I felt bad that we had to send him home last night."

"Why couldn't he stay? Dad said we had plans, but then we didn't do anything. Were you just trying to ditch Tucker?"

"No, no. He's always welcome here." I scratched my temple with one finger. "Listen, Noah, please don't let Tucker know your dad went across the lake today."

"Why not?"

"Just—please keep it to yourself, okay?"

"Dad thinks Owen has been cutting down the big trees, doesn't he?"

"How did you—"

"Everyone's talking about how Owen went after you in the diner yesterday."

Of course they were. "It was nothing," I said. "A misunderstanding."

Noah lifted his eyebrows as if to say, *Yeah, right.* "Anyway, Tucker already knows Dad was checking out the tree poaching across the lake today." Noah held up his phone to indicate he and Tucker had been texting. "He told me he overheard you and Dad talking outside the diner yesterday and pieced it together."

Which meant Owen likely knew. "Dammit." I turned back to the lake. Owen could have gone over to the far shore overnight and got rid of whatever evidence he might have left behind.

Noah pressed his phone to his ear.

"Trying Tucker again?"

"Dad." He clicked out of the call. "He's still not picking up." His expression was beyond worried; now he was scared. "We should phone Jackson."

Under normal circumstances, if a person was missing, their family or friends would phone 911 and the RCMP would initiate the search with a service request to the search and rescue manager, in this case Jackson, but we were well over an hour from the nearest police detachment, and Jackson was a friend, and the locals of Moston were in the habit of taking care of their own. If Ben really was missing, I knew Jackson would have the entire SAR crew muster at our place in no time.

But that was a significant undertaking and a waste of everyone's energy if Ben was, in fact, simply late and I was only calling the team out here because of my own anxiety. Which I had done once in the past, when Ben was three hours late coming back from patrol. I had phoned Jackson, asking him to find Ben after he had been called to check out smoke high in the mountain range, a campfire someone left burning deep in the bush. I couldn't reach him because he had been out of radio range, and busy handling the situation before it grew into a wildfire. Jackson and members of his SAR crew tracked him down as he hiked back to his truck, and Ben came home pissed about it. "What if some tourist had flipped his boat and needed rescue?" he asked me. "Or a hiker had fallen and gotten injured out there? Someone could have died because you sent Jackson after me and they weren't here to respond. I can handle myself, Piper." His face had been red as he chewed me out. I had, I realized, shamed him in front of Jackson.

"Just give Ben another hour or so," I told Noah now.

"I had this feeling the day Mom died," he said. He thumped his belly with his fist. But then, his mother had been dying for some time, of stomach cancer, before she finally passed. I wrapped an arm around him, and we stood there together until he headed for the door, dialling Ben's number again. "I'm going to keep trying."

Once he left the room, I pulled out the two-way radio and, over the next hour, repeatedly tried calling Ben myself as I sat on the bed, watching for his boat lights through the large patio windows. The dark water, the grey clouds hanging low over the mountain ridge across the lake—all of it was barely discernible now in the black, as the snow continued to fall heavily. Temperatures would have fallen quickly after sundown.

"Ben, you there? Over." I released the push-to-talk button as I listened, then tried again. And again. "Ben, you there? Over."

And then, suddenly, Ben *was* there. Dressed in his uniform, reflected in the patio window as if he were in the room with me.

I stood. "Ben?"

But as soon as I spoke his name, his image in the window was gone. Just *gone*. I heard his voice whisper my name, *Piper*, but right into my ear, as if he were standing directly behind me. I swung around, but there was no one there. "Ben?" I cried. Then, louder, "Ben!"

Noah thundered out of his room and into mine. "Is Dad here? Did you see him?"

I shook my head a little, uncertain, not understanding what had just happened. "I thought I saw . . ."

*Oh god. Oh god. Oh god.*

I had just seen Ben's *ghost*.

# 8

I slid open the patio door and cupped my hands to my face to call out into the snowy night. "Ben? *Ben!*" But my voice was dampened by the heavily falling snow. When Ben first brought me to the house, he called my name to demonstrate the echo that reverberated across the lake like a skipping stone, bouncing back from the stony cliff on the far shore. On a still, quiet day, when the lake reflected the trees on the steep slopes, I could hear him, he said, if I were to stand on that beach on the other side of the lake. I didn't believe him, until one day I was hiking alone at the Boulders, finding inspiration for a piece for the town's website, and heard Ben's voice calling my name all the way across the lake from our deck. *Piper. Piper. Piper. I love you. I love you. I love you. Marry me? Marry me? Marry me?* I shouted back, *Yes!* And my voice, my answer, bounced back to him from the far shore.

Noah cupped his hands to call alongside me now. "Dad!" But the sound was muted by the snow and low cloud that hid the far shore from us.

I tried calling Ben on the radio again. "Ben, are you there? Over?" We waited, listened, as the snowflakes accumulated in our hair and slid down our necks. "Ben. Ben, do you hear me? Over." When there was still no reply, I went back into the house, hastily slipped on my jacket and boots, and rushed out to jog down the stairs of the deck.

"What are you doing?" Noah called after me.

"I'm going to find him." I pulled my kayak out from under the deck and dragged it down the shore over the snow.

"In a kayak? In this snow? In the dark? That's dangerous." When I slid the kayak into the water, he thundered down the stairs to stop me. "Piper? Piper!"

I turned to him.

"If something *has* happened to Dad, you can't help him by yourself." He paused as his face twisted in panic. "And what if something happens to *you* out there?"

He feared he might lose me too, as he had his mother. I thought, then, of what Ben had said that morning before he left. *If something happened to me out there, you would take care of Noah, right?*

I pulled the kayak back onshore. "I'm sorry, Noah," I said. "I didn't mean to scare you." Trying to head out on the lake alone in this snowstorm to search for Ben *was* dangerous. Panic had taken hold of me, made me stupid. I was too easily triggered. I thought of what Ben always said, as he hugged me—*Breathe deep to calm your-self*—and I did just that. Then I pulled out my phone and held it up in the snowy air until I found a signal, and clicked on Jackson's number. He picked up right away.

"Jackson—" My voice caught, and I covered my mouth.

"Piper? What's going on?"

I gulped back the tears. "Jackson, we need your help."

"Anything."

I took Noah's hand and gripped tightly. His slim fingers were cold in mine. "Jackson, I think something has happened to Ben."

• • •

Noah and I stood on the dock as Jackson backed the trailer holding the SAR Zodiac, a rigid-hull inflatable, down the ramp and into the water. It was a good-sized rescue boat, with seats for four and enough room on the solid deck for an injured person on a litter.

As we waited the few minutes for Jackson to arrive, we had continued to call Ben over and over by radio and cell. He was either out of range or . . . I didn't want to think about it. The image of Ben's doppelgänger that I had seen in the patio window intruded on my thoughts. His ghostly whisper in my ear. *Piper.* But even though I had seen his ghost, I couldn't believe he was dead. I *wouldn't.*

I had made a Thermos of hot chocolate, not for us but for Ben when we found him. No matter what, he would be cold in this heavy, wet snowfall. I also had a blanket ready in a plastic bag, though I was sure Jackson had a full emergency kit packed.

Once the boat was floating, Jackson pulled the trailer back up from the water, parked and got out to coil the dock line as he drew the boat toward us with the rope. Like us, he was geared up in his winter parka and insulated pants. He was in his early fifties, with longish salt-and-pepper hair, and sported a walrus moustache that made him look somewhat like Sam Elliott; the kind of man who would have seemed at home in a cowboy hat and boots. But he would have found that insulting, to be thought of as a cowboy. He was something of an artist, a photographer, carrying an expensive digital camera with him when he took clients on ecotours, kayaking, bouldering or skiing. I'd used many of his images of the region alongside my stories. Like me, he had come to the interior, to Moston, from Vancouver, though many years earlier, attracted by the cheap housing, the stunning landscape, the outdoor lifestyle and the chance of forging a new life here, after losing his wife to breast cancer. He had never remarried. It was a loss that continued to haunt him, one that had cemented his friendship with my husband. Jackson and Ben had known each other for years but had become close after Ben lost Shannon to cancer, as the two of them shared this common grief. Now I got the sense Jackson and Ben would do nearly anything for each other. There were times when I had felt a little jealous of their bromance.

Jackson handed us each a life jacket. "We're not waiting for the rest of the search and rescue team?" I asked him as I put mine on.

"They're on standby," he said, clicking his in place. "I'll call them if we need them."

He held the boat steady to the dock as Noah and I got in, carrying our supplies. I sat on the seat behind Noah. "Am I over-reacting?" I asked Jackson. As I had the one time before when I'd called Jackson and his crew out to find Ben in the bush.

Jackson tossed the coiled dock line to the bow and got in. "No, you were right to call. Too many people have died because their loved ones hesitated to phone for help. But Ben is only a couple of hours late, right?"

"Going on four hours now," Noah said, peering down at his phone.

Jackson started the boat engine. "He's been this late before while out on patrol."

But not in winter, or in a storm. "He isn't answering his radio," I said.

"The snow is likely interfering with the signal." Jackson offered me a smile. "And things come up. It takes longer to get back home than we think, especially in weather like this."

"I know, I know." I had told Noah as much. I hoped to god I *was* overreacting. Ben was okay, I told myself. He had found something interesting out there or had to drag a piece of equipment out of the bush. Proof of Owen's tree poaching. At worst, maybe he'd fallen, dropping his radio, and sprained an ankle. He knew we'd come looking for him. My vision of Ben standing at the patio window was only my own anxious mind playing tricks on me. I was forever imagining the worst, and then believing it to be true. But still. "He said he was only going to check out that tree. He hadn't planned to go past the Boulders. He shouldn't have taken this long."

Jackson manoeuvred the boat away from the dock, raising his voice over the rumble of the engine. "Ben is well trained, he knows this forest and what to do if he gets into a situation. If he's hurt, he'll build a shelter and stay warm until we find him. But I'm sure we'll meet him on the lake."

"And if we don't?" Noah asked.

Jackson revved the engine, nosing the boat to the far shore. "Then we'll pull up on the beach and holler for him," he shouted over the engine noise. "Chances are he'll just holler right back."

Noah put up his jacket hood and kept his eyes on the lake ahead, blinking into the wind and snow. I reached over and squeezed his arm. "We *will* find him," I said, though my voice was drowned by the engine's roar.

We sped across the water, the hull slapping against the waves. The musty orange life jacket was damp under my chin. Even in my parka, I felt chilled, as the air was always so moist here. In front of me Noah sat with his hands on his knees, leaning forward, tense. My knuckles were white as I gripped the seat behind him. Halfway across, I took out my gloves and put them on. Snowflakes collected on the hoods of our jackets, on our backs. Great, wet, heavy snowflakes. In the dark and snow, we could see only metres ahead even with the boat's searchlight on, and yet Jackson pushed forward, bumping, bumping over the choppy water. Normally I would have been frightened by the speed we were going, but now I felt a desperate need to get there, to find Ben.

As the shore came into view, Noah stood up next to Jackson, hanging on to the console of the boat. Jackson tugged at his sleeve to get him to sit, but he remained standing. "We should have seen the lights on his boat by now," Noah shouted into the wind, "if he was on his way back."

Jackson pulled on Noah's arm again. "Sit."

I pressed the push-to-talk button on the two-way radio. Perhaps he would hear us now that we were closer. "Ben, you there? Over." I listened, the radio pressed to my ear, and called again, and again.

As we drew close to shore, Jackson slowed and scanned the beach with the boat's searchlight. He reached into his bag and handed me a pair of binoculars. "See if you can spot him, or his boat."

He pulled out his own set of binoculars, and together we took in the length of beach, but the lenses were quickly dotted with snowflakes. In any case, the falling snow created a swirling transparent curtain between us and the shore.

"Do you see his boat?" Noah asked.

"No. It's not tied up onshore."

Then Noah asked Jackson the question I didn't want to say out loud. "You think something happened to Dad on the water?"

I dropped my binoculars to my lap.

Jackson tugged on his moustache, as he almost always did when nervous. It was his tell during our Wednesday night poker games. "Let's not get ahead of ourselves."

He didn't say what we were all thinking: that several boaters and fishermen had drowned here over the years. The narrow valley often shunted winds down the long lake, working up waves that could toss a small boat.

"We may be looking for him in the wrong place," I said. "If he spotted something through the drone camera, he may have taken the boat up the lake, into the bay under Hunter's Creek. It's quicker than trying to hike these trails."

"But if Dad *did* go out on the lake, then he's . . ."

I imagined his body, weighed down by his boots and gear, sinking into these deep black waters. I choked up a little as I tried calling Ben on the radio again. "Ben, you there? Over?" I listened, then, still getting no response, wiped off the lenses of the binoculars and scanned the shore again. Nothing.

And then, *something*.

I swept the binoculars back, trying to capture the fleeting image I'd seen in the dark. There were boulders and small trees clinging to the rocky shore, a span of pebbled beach covered, now, in snow. And then, there it was again: a dark human figure standing on the beach.

"Look," I cried, pointing. "He's there!"

"Where?" Jackson asked.

Noah took the binoculars from me. "I don't see him."

"There, there!" I stood, gripping the back of Noah's seat to point at the dark span of beach where I'd seen him. But when Jackson swung the searchlight in that direction, the figure had disappeared.

# 9

As our boat covered the last stretch of water before shore, I took the binoculars back from Noah and tried to find the figure, to find Ben. The dark shoreline was rocky, littered with water-rounded stones of various sizes and dotted with large, angular boulders. Farther in, piled up the base of the steep mountain slope and under the canopy of majestic old-growth cedar, there were even larger boulders, some the size of vans, others as big as a house, covered in moss and ferns and small trees. This was the area we called the Boulders, where the few in the know went bouldering, rock climbing. A maze of game trails ran among the many boulders and up the slope. A person could disappear into that area easily, and a body might never be found.

"I don't see him," I said. "He's gone."

Noah grabbed the binoculars and combed the snowy beach, the tree line, the cloud-covered slopes and even the cliff above. His voice took on an angry, childlike whine. "Why would he leave? He must have seen us." Or at least heard the roar of the boat's engine. Even now, the sound bounced back to us off the cliff face above, dampened by the snow.

"Are you certain it was Ben?" Jackson asked as he steered us into shore.

I gripped the back of Noah's seat. "I thought it was." But now I wasn't so sure. At that distance and through the snow, I hadn't seen him clearly. A figure had been there, and now it was gone.

Just like Ben's doppelgänger back home.

Was I only seeing things? Ghosts? It wasn't the first time.

Jackson cut the engine to coast into shore and, still in the boat, Noah and I called out in unison.

"Ben!"

"Dad!"

We listened, squinting through the falling snow, as the boat slid into the shallows.

"Where was he, exactly?" Jackson asked.

"Right there." I pointed at the spot. "He was standing right there."

"Could you have mistaken that tree for a person?" A pine, clinging to the rocky shore, bent like a gnarled, arthritic hand by the prevailing winds.

"No. It wasn't the tree." But was it my imagination?

Jackson sidled the boat up to the rocks. "Noah is right. Ben would know to stay put, to wait for help."

"I know."

"Maybe it was the Green Man," Noah said.

When Jackson had come up with that name for our local bushman, I doubt he'd made the connection to the Green Man of ancient mythic lore who was carved into the stonework of churches and had a face fashioned from leaves and branches. Still, that's how I envisioned him now, as I often did when I was out here, as a supernatural being made of twigs, bark and leaves, his mouth open, a dark cave, as it was so often depicted in the sacred stonework, with roots snaking out of it. A frightening creature not only camouflaged by the wildwood, but spawned from it; the forest taking human form to protect itself.

Jackson jumped out, calf high in the water in his rubberized boots, and pulled the boat onto the beach. "It could have been one of the poachers," he said.

"Owen." Though I had been so certain it was Ben. I *wanted* it to be Ben.

Jackson secured the dock line around a boulder, then held out a hand to help me as Noah hopped down on his own. Jackson pulled out a flashlight as I rushed to the spot where I thought I'd seen Ben. There were no fresh footprints in the snow, but then the snow was falling hard enough that it would have already obscured the tracks.

Jackson swept the area with his flashlight. "You say you saw him here?"

"I saw *someone* here."

He pocketed the flashlight and cupped his hands to his mouth. "Is there anyone there?" He listened, called again. "Anyone?"

"The Green Man's not going to answer," Noah said.

I nodded. "Neither is Owen."

Impossibly large snowflakes fell through the darkened stand of giant cedar just up from the shore. I had always felt small, magically small, within this landscape. The first time Ben took me into the Boulders under this canopy of giant trees, I felt I had entered a sacred space, and came out feeling changed, renewed. I had made my decision to give up my old life in Vancouver and live in Moston on the spot, in that grove. I had said yes to Ben's marriage proposal on the edge of that forest as he called to me across the lake. But now it seemed this gloomy landscape had swallowed my husband. In the dark, it felt frightening, cursed.

"Ben!" I cried again. All three of us yelled, standing back to back to back, each of us facing a different part of the landscape, our calls and echoes threading together into a desperate, mournful dirge.

After a time, we all just stopped, listened. Jackson threw the beam of his flashlight toward the trees, the Boulders, then down the beach. "Piper, I—" Jackson began.

Noah interrupted him. "What's that?" he asked, pointing, and Jackson trained the light back.

I squinted through the falling snow. "What?"

But Noah was already running down the shore. Jackson and I jogged after him, over wet, snow-covered stones, both of us losing traction and nearly slipping to our knees. As we reached him, Noah brushed away snow from something silvery perched on a large, flat-topped boulder.

Ben's drone.

Noah took off his jacket and flung it over the machine to protect the electronics within its housing before picking it up.

Jackson spoke quietly. "Ben must have been flying the drone from the water." As he often had when patrolling these mountains. The terrain was so rocky and steep; it was much easier to take the boat down the shore and fly the drone from it, viewing images of the dense forest from there.

Noah shook his head. "Dad must have launched it from here," he said. "The drone would have flown right back to its launch point when it was close to running out of power."

"Or if it had lost connection with the controller," Jackson said. If the controller had ended up in the water, he meant, along with Ben. "He may have launched the drone from the beach, but then went out in the boat to fly it once the drone picked up something to investigate. He may have intended to fly the drone back to the boat manually, but before he could—"

"No. No." I refused to believe it. If Ben had been out on the water, if he hadn't come home, then— "He must be here. I saw him."

"You saw *someone*," Jackson said.

"Ben!" I yelled into the forest, more desperately now. "Ben! Can you hear me?" I tried calling Ben on the radio yet again. But there was no response.

Jackson reached into his pocket and pulled out an orange pen-shaped device. "I'll try a bear banger," he said.

I habitually carried one of those, just as Jackson did, along with the can of bear spray, to scare off bears that I might come across in the woods. Jackson twisted the cap in place and pulled the spring-loaded firing pin on the banger to set it off. The contraption banged once as it shot off, and then a second time as it exploded. *Bang. Bang.* As loud as a rifle blast. The sound continued to echo off the cliff face above for several seconds. We listened, hoping for Ben's response, as the echo faded.

"Anything?" Noah asked.

Jackson scanned the hills above us. "If he was anywhere on this mountain, he would have heard that," he said. "He would know to call back or hit a tree." With a stick, knocking wood on wood, so the noise would reach us.

"If he was conscious," Noah said, his young face crumpling.

I hugged him and thought, *If he was alive*, remembering Ben's ghost in our bedroom.

Jackson pulled back his hood, ran a hand through his damp hair. "Okay," he said, as if he'd decided something. He marched back to the boat, waving for us to follow. "Come on. We need to hurry."

"What are we doing?" I called as Noah and I raced after him.

"We've got to go." He untied the rope, coiled it and tossed it back on the boat's bow. "Get in. I need to get the team out here, *now*." The search and rescue team. "The temperature keeps falling. If Ben is injured, or his clothes are wet . . ." He didn't need to finish. We all knew Ben could easily die of hypothermia if he couldn't get to shelter. "Once we're out on the water, I'll radio my team to muster at your house."

"I'll stay here and keep looking," I said. "If he's hurt . . ." My voice rose as my emotions spiralled. I started to march away, determined to search the forest for Ben, but Jackson ran after me and gripped my arm to stop me. I half expected him to hug me fiercely, as Ben so often had when I started to lose control, to whisper into my ear, *Breathe deep to calm yourself.* But Jackson let go, stepped back, as if he'd suddenly realized an impropriety on his part.

"Piper, I can't let you search alone. That only puts Ben in more danger. If my team is stretched thin, trying to find you too . . ." Jackson paused and nodded sideways at Noah as if to say, *Pull it together for the kid.*

Noah slouched by the boat, hugging the drone beneath his jacket.

"Ben knows how to take care of himself until we get to him," Jackson said. "Please, we're wasting precious time."

I nodded. "Of course."

We got back in the boat and Jackson pushed off, started the engine. Once we were out on the water, he raised his voice over the roar of the engine as we sped through the dark, the falling snow. "We *will* find him," he shouted, glancing back and forth between me and the rough water ahead. "Piper, you hear me?"

I heard. But my eyes were on the shore behind us, the dark outlines of cedars through the veil of snow, the boulders on the beach, searching for the figure that had appeared and disappeared as if it were a ghost.

# SUNDAY

# 10

Shortly after midnight, I stood on the deck hugging myself, the chill of our first search for Ben creeping down my back. While on the water, and as soon as we got cell reception, we had called the RCMP in Clifton, who officially initiated the SAR search, though it was Jackson who would manage it. He would continue to work in close liaison with the police throughout the search. Then Jackson, one hand guiding the boat and the other holding his phone to his ear, had immediately started rounding up his team to muster at our house. Most of them lived close by and were there within minutes of our arrival, quickly launching their own small boats into the water. Now they were gathered around Jackson on the beach as he offered instruction, all of them dressed in their orange-red SAR jackets, and many of them holding trekking or hiking poles.

"Piper?" A woman's voice called from the side of the house. Maggie.

"Up here!"

"I knocked, but I guess you didn't hear me," she said as she joined me on the deck, carrying two boxes, one stacked on the other. As she set them down on the round patio table, several Thermoses rattled together within the bigger of the two. The smaller box was filled with plastic-wrapped muffins and squares. Someone must have woken her with the news that Ben was missing. She seemed so different without her makeup, younger for it. I could see the teenaged girl she had once been. The freckles on her nose. Instead of the stained checkered blouse and barbecue apron she habitually wore at the diner, she had thrown on a clean button-up blouse and puffer jacket over slacks. Still, her greying hair smelled of the fryer.

"Maggie?" I gave her a brief hug. "What are you doing here?"

"I stopped by the diner and stocked up as soon as I heard about Ben," she said. She nodded at Jackson and the search and rescue team below us. "Got to keep the troops fed and warm."

It was something Maggie *would* do, as her kitchen was the centre of this small community, but I knew there was another reason she was here. "Jackson called you, didn't he?" I asked, smiling a little. "I mean, for me."

"You're a smart one, aren't yah?" A half grin slid up Maggie's face. "Jackson thought you could use a friend about now." A woman friend. She picked up a Thermos and sat it on the railing in front of me. "This one's for you," she said.

In that instant, her care seemed like an overwhelming kindness. "Thank you."

"Ain't nothing." She squeezed my wrist. "How are you doing, love?"

I thought of what I'd seen in the bedroom, Ben's reflection in the window, his ghost. I couldn't get the image out of my mind. "What if they don't find him?" I whispered, my eyes stinging.

Maggie rubbed my back. "Jackson and his crew *will* find Ben," she said. "You can count on it."

But what if they didn't find him *alive*?

I turned to my friend. "Maggie, I saw Ben's ghost."

She hesitated before speaking. "That doesn't mean anything," she said. "A worried mind, is all. People who lose a loved one see them all the time."

"People see the ghosts of their loved ones *after they're dead*."

"Does it *feel* like he's gone?"

I shook my head. "No." I felt like he could walk in that door any minute. "But I saw his *ghost*."

Maggie leaned into the railing next to me. "Let me tell you a story. One day I'm chopping onions in the back, at the diner. Going to make chili out of leftover hamburger patties for the supper menu. You've had my chili, right? Everybody loves my chili. Anyway, there I am chopping onions. Chop, chop, chop with my big knife. In my head pops this godawful image of a hand, a man's hand, all mangled, tore to shreds. I didn't just see it. I *felt* it. I was *there*. Like a vision. Clear as day. Felt the searing pain, the heat, like my hand was on fire. Then, poof. The vision was gone. But I *knew*, see, I *knew* my Ted was hurt, hurt bad. I put down my knife and phoned his cell. When it went to voice mail, I phoned the mill. At exactly the same time I saw his hand all cut up, felt that terrible pain, Ted had caught his hand in a slash-saw, mangled it." She tapped the railing with her finger. "At that exact moment, I *knew*."

Ted often helped Maggie at the diner now, sometimes dropping dishes on the way to a customer as he'd never quite got the hang of his prosthesis, an artificial hand he named Willy.

"I'm not sure what you're saying," I said. "Do you think Ben's alive, or dead?"

"It's what *you* think that's important. Love connects us in ways we'll never understand. Maybe that sounds corny, but I know it's true. If you believe Ben's still alive, then hang on to that. Have faith. It will keep you going."

"I'm scared, Maggie."

She put an arm around me. "You got somebody I can phone for you? You want family around at a time like this. Your mother is still alive, right? But I understand you aren't that friendly with her."

A jolt of adrenalin shot through me. "Ben told you about Libby?" I had stopped calling her "Mom" in my late teens.

"Not much, only at your wedding, when I said I was surprised you didn't have family there." When practically the whole town of Moston had come out to celebrate with us. "Should I call her?"

I shook my head. My mother was the last person I wanted around right now.

"How about for Ben? I know his parents have passed. Anyone I should phone, for him? His office, maybe?"

I wiped the tears from the corners of my eyes. "We'll find him before his workday tomorrow," I said.

"Yes, yes, of course we will."

But the expression on her face—it immediately brought to mind that cop, that female officer who had come to our house after my mother phoned the police on Dad. The cop had looked at me that same way, with crushing pity.

"Let me know if you change your mind," she said.

"I'm so glad you're here, Maggie." I leaned my head on her shoulder and we stood there together watching the SAR team put on their life jackets and helmets, switch on their headlamps. Noah joined us outside, locking the door behind him. He was dressed in his insulated ski pants and jacket, as I was, to keep dry during the search. "You going to be warm enough?" I asked him.

He blinked rapidly, as if to keep his emotions at bay. He was the size of a man, but his face was still that of a boy. A scared boy.

I hugged him. "As Maggie says, Jackson *will* find your dad," I said.

"Jackson's team is the best," Maggie added. She nodded toward the far shore. "They know that area inside out."

Noah allowed me to hug him for a moment longer, then

stepped back, embarrassed, wiping the tears from his eyes. "Yeah, sure."

"Your dad's a smart guy," Maggie said. "Whatever happened, he can take care of himself."

Tucker emerged from the darkness at the side of the house, carrying one end of an inflatable boat. Nelson carried the other. "What are they doing here?" I asked Noah. My heart skipped a beat. "They didn't come with Owen, did they?"

Noah jogged down the stairs to meet his friend, presumably to find out.

"Hey," I called after him. "Grab our hiking poles and throw them in Jackson's boat, okay?"

Noah nodded and disappeared under the deck, where we kept a lot of our outdoor gear, then reappeared carrying the poles.

As Tucker greeted him within the yard light, I saw his face. His left eye was swollen shut, and the area around it red, beginning to bruise. From the way he favoured his ribs as he moved, I was sure he had bruises there too.

I put my hand to my mouth. Was that my fault? If I hadn't wound up Owen like some mad mechanical chimp, if I had insisted Tucker stay with us overnight, perhaps he wouldn't have suffered that beating.

Maggie, following my gaze as Tucker and Nelson set the boat in the water, spit out Owen's name like an expletive. "Somebody's got to stop that bastard," she said.

"We will," I said. "But right now we've got to find Ben."

"Yes, of course."

I added my Thermos to those for the SAR crew and picked up the box, and Maggie stacked the second one, filled with baked goods, on top.

"Thanks again, Maggie."

"Call me as soon as you find Ben, okay?" she said as I carried the boxes down the stairs.

I kept my eyes on the icy steps. "I will."

"And if you need anything—"

"I'll call," I said. I smiled back up at Maggie as I reached the base of the stairs, but she was watching Tucker with a pained expression on her face.

I waited until Nelson joined the members of the SAR crew before approaching the boys. And then I handed my stepson the two boxes of snacks and Thermoses. "Noah, can you put these in Jackson's boat?" To give me a moment with Tucker.

"Sure."

As Noah walked away, I reached out to Tucker's bruised face, lowering my voice so the others, Nelson in particular, wouldn't hear me. "Oh, Tucker, what did he *do*?"

But the boy turned his face away to avoid my touch. "I fell," he mumbled.

"I know you didn't fall."

"It's nothing."

I studied his bruised face. "We can help you."

"I told you, I *fell*."

Tucker's gaze slid past me, and I turned to see a large, dark figure rounding the corner of the house. Owen. As he ambled toward us through the yard light, unlit cigarette in hand, he cast a large shadow that slid over the stones on the beach and up the dock. His stroll was lackadaisical as he rummaged in his pocket and pulled out a pack of matches that read *Maggie's Diner*. As he reached me, and in a gesture so like my father's, he struck a match, and that old burning ember inside me flared. I clenched a fist.

But Tucker gave me a pleading look. *Please don't say anything.*

And this really wasn't the time. We needed to stay focused on finding Ben.

Owen sucked on his cigarette and blew the smoke upward into the falling snow. "Sorry about Ben," he said. "We'll do everything we can to bring him home tonight."

"I appreciate your help."

"Ben's a good guy. I mean that."

I nodded.

"Well." Owen scratched his chin, then pointed his cigarette at Nelson's boat. "I guess it's time to load up. Tucker, let's go."

Noah lifted his hand to his friend as he returned. "See you on the far shore."

Tucker glanced back, first at Noah and then at me, with that black eye.

Jackson joined Noah and me as I watched Tucker slump behind his father to Nelson's inflatable. "Tucker's got some shiner," he said.

"He says he fell."

"I take it you don't believe him."

"He 'falls' a lot," Noah said.

"Owen isn't on your crew now, is he?" I asked Jackson.

He shook his head. "When he heard from Nelson that Ben was missing, he texted right away, volunteered to join the search."

"He *volunteered*?" I lowered my voice. "But he knows Ben is building a case against him."

"Piper, this isn't going to be an issue, is it? Owen knows that forest as well as anyone on my team, maybe better. We need his help."

I nodded. "Okay. I'm not happy about it, but I understand."

Jackson checked his phone for the time and falling temperature. "Let's head out. It's only going to get colder, and this snow is only going to get heavier."

As Jackson held the rescue boat in place against the dock, Noah and I climbed in. Jackson was right. The forecast was for dropping temperatures and a huge dump of snow tonight and in the coming days, and Ben was out there, somewhere, alone and likely injured, in this storm.

# 11

The lights on the boats lit up the dark waves ahead of us, and the snow we plowed through felt like needles on my face. I lifted the hood of my jacket over my head as our boat pushed through the water alongside the others. As we neared the far shore, Jackson opened the throttle and took the lead to direct his team to our starting point on the beach, close to where Noah had found Ben's drone. He cut the engine and we drifted in, then, hitting shore, he jumped out and pulled the inflatable onto the rocks. Noah and I climbed out as the others brought their boats into shore. I was both buzzed on adrenalin and already exhausted, even before the search had really begun. I could only imagine what Ben was feeling, wherever he was.

Noah scanned the beach, the dark forest beyond, the mountain above, this vast wilderness that surrounded us. "So, what do we do?" he asked.

"What *is* the plan?" I asked Jackson.

"I've instructed Chase and Trevor to search the shoreline for any sign of Ben's boat, in case he went to shore higher or lower on the lake, or—" Or his boat capsized. Chase's and Trevor's aluminum boats were still on the water, one following the shore down the long lake, the other heading up into the bay below Hunter's Creek, their searchlights dancing across the snowy shore and waves. "Ben was going to check out that old-growth cedar I stumbled across, that the poachers felled." He glanced Owen's way as he and Tucker jumped out of Nelson's boat. "We'll head there first, and then spread out, in case Ben followed one of the trails for some reason." The game trails, trod by deer, coyotes, black bears and grizzlies. On this side of the lake, there were few man-made paths, only those around the Boulders created by the locals, Ben, Jackson and me, and the ecotourists Jackson boated out here for bouldering. Most of those trails followed the shoreline at first, then split off into a maze of established game trails among the huge boulders and trees that cluttered this steep, rocky slope. "But the snow is going to complicate things," Jackson added, holding out his glove to the falling snow. "We're unlikely to find footprints in this." And the snowline had already been low before this storm. The snow would only get deeper the higher we climbed.

When Noah's brow puckered in worry, I looped my arm through his. "We've got this," I said. "Your father's got this. He knows exactly what to do." If lost or injured in this wilderness, in summer or winter. When Ben took Noah and me out here for hiking or backcountry skiing, he offered us both tips on wilderness survival, on what to do should we become separated or hurt.

"Piper is right," Jackson said. "Ben would find shelter."

"But what if he's unconscious," Noah said. "What if—"

"We've got this," I repeated, though I harboured the same fears.

Once the others had secured their boats, we all headed up the slope toward the felled cedar, each of the searchers following one of the many trails that led from the beach up to the Boulders, calling out for Ben, listening, calling again. Jackson and most of the searchers used hiking or trekking poles, as Noah and I did, to navigate the rocky slope through snow that was already ankle deep. The searchers' headlamps and flashlights bobbed against the trunks of the giant trees and boulders.

"Dad!" Noah called. "Dad!"

"Ben!" Our voices were muted by the heavily falling snow. At times I thought I heard Ben's voice whispering in return. *Piper.* But when I stopped to listen, I heard only Jackson and the others, the hush of falling snow, the rumble of Chase's and Trevor's boat engines on the water. I often heard voices or even music when the heater or air conditioner fan was blowing in our cottage. I imagined I was now experiencing a similar auditory hallucination, brought on by stress and hope. I was *desperate* to hear my husband's voice. "*Ben!*"

As we reached one of the larger stands of old-growth trees within the Boulders, I saw Owen wave at Tucker and Nelson to hurry up, and they plowed ahead up a trail parallel to ours, shouldering their way through the snow-heavy devil's club.

"What's he up to?" I asked.

Jackson turned to Owen and his crew, the light from their headlamps bouncing off the trail and each other. "He's just checking out the trail. It also leads to that downed cedar."

"How much farther?" Noah asked.

"Not far," Jackson said. "A few metres above the Hourglass." The Hourglass was the largest boulder on this slope, a favourite among those who came bouldering here. Just as its name suggested, it was shaped like an hourglass and towered over our heads. At some point, I imagined, it had been part of the cliff above, and, along with the other massive boulders that had collected here, had split off and fallen sometime in the deep past. The boulders were moss-covered and alive with trees and plants that grew like hair from their massive heads. As these boulders in turn split through erosion, a jumble of smaller rocks had broken off at their feet, making the climb between them a scramble. Even in summer we had to use our hands to climb some parts of this area. Now Noah and I used our hiking poles to pull ourselves up and forward in the snow.

As soon as we reached the Hourglass, Jackson started a systematic search of the area with the others on his team, disappearing around the corner of the giant rock to check out the cedar. I could smell the downed tree before I saw it, even in this snowstorm. The strong, spicy-sweet scent of cut cedar. And then, as I climbed above the Hourglass, there it was, the gigantic body of the felled old-growth tree, lit up by the headlamps and flashlights of the searchers, its stump much larger than the one I'd found the day before near Hunter's Creek. It was one of the oldest in the grove. Ben had posted a seizure notice on the end of the log. I put a gloved hand to it. Whatever had happened to him the day before had occurred after he had found this downed cedar.

The massive log and stump were covered in snow, but I could see mounds where the poachers had begun to cut the wood into rounds and triangular-shaped blocks to haul it away. I'd known the tree had been felled, but it was only on seeing its giant corpse lying there on this hill, in the dark forest, that the impact, the loss, fully hit me, and it only served to magnify my fear and worry over Ben. I bent over, hands on my ski pants, feeling like I would be sick.

"Are you okay?" Noah asked.

I held up a gloved hand. "Just give me a minute."

"Oh, here we go with the theatrics," Owen said to Nelson in a lowered voice, but I heard him. Behind him, Tucker shifted from foot to foot, as he so often did around his father, his bruised and swollen face tortured with embarrassment.

I held out a hand against the glaring light of Owen's headlamp as I approached him. "You did this," I said quietly, nodding at the felled cedar.

"You're so sure of everything, aren't yah?" Owen asked. He leaned into me, his breath rank with beer and cigarettes. "Don't believe everything you think." I recognized the phrase as a bumper sticker I'd seen, and then I remembered where: on Jackson's truck. Owen didn't, I noted, deny taking down the tree.

Jackson gripped Owen's jacket, pulled him back. "Ben is our priority, right?" Jackson asked him. "How about we all just get back to the search?"

Owen swung his head back and forth like a caged bear, the light from his headlamp sweeping an arc over the snow and bark of the giant cedar beside us. "Yeah, yeah," he said.

"Okay, people," Jackson called out. "Ben clearly isn't here." He clapped his gloved hands. "All of you, pick a trail and fan out. Let's find Ben." He pointed at Noah and me. "You two stay with me." Then he led us around the stump and headed up one of the trails. "If you don't think you can keep up, go back to the boat and wait there. The temperature is continuing to fall. If we can't find Ben soon . . ." He paused. "We need to get a move on."

But before we got too much farther up the slope, Jackson stopped, held up his hand and signalled us to be quiet. When I raised my eyebrows at him, he pointed his flashlight to the side of the trail, to a gaping hole within the root wad of one of the old-growth trees, a hole that had been purposefully dug into the slope. There were claw marks in the packed earth just inside, and bits of hair clung to the surrounding root system. Piles of leaves were visible at the entrance. A grizzly den.

"I think it's new," Jackson whispered. "At least, I hadn't noticed it before. She must have just dug it this fall."

Noah's voice rose. "There's a grizzly in there?"

Jackson and I both shushed him.

"Maybe. But if not, Ben might have used it as shelter." He waved us off. "Get back."

As we retreated, Jackson crouched down, inched forward in the snow and shone his light into the cavern. Then he stood up. "The den is abandoned," he said.

"But you said it was new."

"If the grizzly was in there, something must have disturbed her." He glanced back down the hill at the felled log. "That old tree would have made a hell of a noise when it fell."

"So, when the poachers felled that tree—"

"They likely woke the bear, yes." A grizzly's hibernation wasn't like that of other animals. They were light sleepers, easily woken. If disturbed, or feeling threatened, the creature would find or dig out another den. And in the meantime, there would be one grumpy beast roaming the forest.

"That cinnamon grizzly?" Noah asked.

"Likely," Jackson said. "I doubt she would allow another bear in her territory."

"So she's out here with us now?" Noah asked.

"Probably."

If that was the case, the bear may well have stalked Ben as she had earlier in the fall, just as she had hunted down that poor young woman the year before.

I put an arm around Noah. "Ben carried his bear spray, always, even in winter," I said. "In any case, I'm sure the bear found another den, right, Jackson? She's likely fast asleep right now."

But Jackson didn't answer me. He clicked the push-to-talk button on his radio and alerted the others to the disturbed den. "It appears we could have a grizzly out here with us, folks. Stay alert." And then to Noah and me he said, "Stay close."

The headlamps of the others danced over the snow and tree trunks as they hiked adjacent game trails. Ferns sprang up as our passage released the fronds from the heavy snow. We were still in the lower-elevation forest of cedar and hemlock. Above us the growth would transition to fir and spruce.

I leaned on my poles to catch my breath on the steep trail, and Noah, just above me, directed my attention to the dark scene below. At first, I wasn't sure what he wanted me to see. The lights on Chase's and Trevor's boats slid along the shore. And then I saw the headlamps of Owen, Tucker and Nelson through the trees below us. As the rest of the search team followed game trails up this steep slope, they remained in the area by the downed cedar, despite Jackson's instruction to fan out. Through the trees, I could see Tucker's headlamp shining on Owen's face as his father seemed to angrily gesture at him, and then all three of them resumed a search of the area around the felled tree, kicking and digging through the snow.

"What are they doing?" Noah asked. "Did they find something?"

*Did they find Ben?*

"I don't know," I said. But with hope surging through me, I plummeted back down into the dark, skidding and sliding in the snow. Noah followed close behind.

On the hill above us, Jackson shone his headlamp in our direction and called out, "Hey, what's going on?" And then there was the crackle of his radio as he talked to others on the team, telling them he was heading back down.

I reached the Boulders, and the felled old-growth tree, out of breath and just in time to see Owen stoop to fish an object from the snow, something that flashed, metallic, in the light from his headlamp. "Hey," I shouted. "Did you find something? Any sign of Ben?"

Owen stood up slowly, slipping the item into his pocket, then took his time rolling his answer around in his mouth. "Nope."

A choking lump of disappointment slid down my throat. "What was that, then?" I asked. "What you just picked up."

"My cigarette pack. I dropped it, then thought better of it. Figured you'd give me hell for littering."

"What are you doing down here, anyway?" Noah asked Tucker. "We're supposed to be searching the trails."

"You were looking for something," I added.

Owen snorted. "Your husband?"

"I mean . . ." I glanced from Owen to Nelson, who wiped his runny nose with his sleeve. "Why *are* you sticking to this area when Jackson asked you to move on?" And then the answer dawned on me. "You left something behind when you took down this tree, didn't you?" I asked Owen. "Something that would incriminate you, make it clear you're responsible. You just pocketed evidence."

"Evidence?" He laughed a little. "What do you think you are? A cop? This is a search, Piper, for Ben. This isn't a crime scene."

Jackson arrived, his headlamp skimming the tree branches over our heads. "You find something?"

Owen pointed at me. "I picked up my cigarette pack, and now she thinks I'm hiding evidence."

Jackson held his palm open. "Let's see it, then."

Owen pulled an empty cigarette pack out of his pocket. Player's Light. His brand. "There, happy?" It was wet, like it had been lying there for a while.

"You didn't just drop this here," I said. "You left it here when you cut down this cedar. But this wasn't what you were hunting for, was it?" It could be anyone's pack of cigarettes. Half the town still smoked. Hardly incriminating. "What did you leave behind?" When he didn't immediately answer, I said, "You haven't found it yet, have you? Whatever you left when you cut down this tree, it's still here." Hidden under this blanket of snow. "Was it your belt?" I asked. A logger's belt, with pouches that held plastic wedges used in felling, a felling axe, a saw file and wrench. I doubted he would have

84

left his chainsaw here, or his chaps. Maybe he forgot his lunch box or gas can, gloves or hardhat with its earmuffs and mesh face shield, items he might have taken off or put down to the side. Loggers, used to working in teams in the bush, put their names or initials on everything.

And then the question percolated up to the surface and was out of my mouth before I could rein it in. "Were you out here trying to find it yesterday, when Ben was scanning this area with his drone?"

Behind me, Jackson used my name as a warning. "*Piper.*"

"What are you saying?" Owen asked me.

Tucker and Nelson both took slow steps backward, as if afraid Owen was a bomb about to explode. Owen cocked his head at me, and as he spoke, he closed the distance between us. "If I was out here yesterday and saw Ben, if I had any idea where he was, don't you think I would tell you? Don't you think I would have taken you there? Just what kind of a man do you think I am?"

I glanced behind Owen at Tucker's swollen face, and the boy shook his head in his bobble-headed way, warning me to drop it, to back off, for his sake as much as mine, I was sure.

I lowered my head in deference to Owen. "Of course you would," I said. "I didn't mean to suggest otherwise. I was only wondering—"

But Jackson cleared his throat. *Just stop there.*

Owen spoke to him, not me. "Can we get on with the search? Or should me and Nelson and Tucker just go home?"

"Owen, we appreciate your help," Jackson said. "But out there on the trails, not down here. We've already searched the area."

Owen pulled out a fresh, dry cigarette pack and lit a cigarette, inhaling and blowing the smoke out the side of his lips. He shook his head at me before pushing past, cigarette in hand. Nelson and then Tucker followed, both of them keeping their eyes to the ground as they passed us.

Jackson stared at me, his headlamp bright on my face, but he didn't say anything. He didn't need to.

I held up both hands. "I know, I know. I should have kept my mouth shut."

"Let's save the accusations for after we've found Ben, okay?"

I nodded. "Yes."

Jackson unzipped his pack.

"Aren't we going back up the hill?" Noah asked.

"It's too dark," Jackson explained. "We'll never see anything in this forest. I'm going to set off a flare, get some light in here." He radioed his team that he was going to fire it off into the night sky, and then asked Noah and me to step back. We stood some distance away, not far from the Hourglass boulder. On the slope above, I could see the headlamps and flashlights of the SAR team bobbing between the trees. Snow fell and fell.

Jackson set off a parachute flare with a hiss of sparks and a bang, and it hung there in the sky over our heads, illuminating the forest with an eerie orange glow. And then, from behind me, I heard my name whispered. *Piper.*

I swung around and saw him on the snow-covered game trail, standing in front of the dense bushes by the Hourglass. In the glow of the flare, his figure, his *presence* was unmistakable.

Ben.

# 12

"Ben?" I cried out. My husband acted as if he hadn't heard me, though he must have at this distance. He just stared up at the forested slope above, dressed in his uniform, but without a coat or body armour.

"What is it?" Noah asked, hope flush on his face. "You see Dad?" Or was I just calling his name as the other searchers did?

In answer, I raced forward. "Ben!" I called louder.

But it seemed Ben didn't hear me. How could he not hear or see me when I was this close? I waved my poles above my head as I stumbled through the snow. It was deeper here, in this clearing in the canopy. "Ben!" But he didn't turn my way.

"Where is he?" Noah asked as he caught up to me.

I turned to call Jackson. "We found Ben! He's okay!" At least I thought he was okay. When I turned back, he seemed frozen, like a statue.

"Where?" Jackson called, bounding toward Noah and me as we struggled through the snow.

"There, there! The backside of the Hourglass. He's standing right there, near the base."

"I don't see him."

It was then that Ben turned to look at me, one of his eyes glazed, dead, as my father's had been in the dream I had just before his death. I took in a sharp, shocked breath. The flare drifted down and went out, and Ben disappeared. "Ben!"

As Jackson radioed our position to the rest of the searchers, I shone my flashlight over the spot where Ben had stood, a thick patch of rhododendron and boxwood at the base of the Hourglass boulder, then at the trees and boulders beyond, and caught the reflective eyes of something. I trained the light back. An owl flitted up and flew off into the trees. But Ben was gone.

"You really saw him?" Noah asked.

"Yes, of course. Didn't you?"

"Where is he?" Jackson asked as he came up behind me.

"He was right there!"

Jackson took the lead. "Ben!" he called out. "Ben, can you hear me?" He shone his much brighter flashlight over the whole area. "Was he hurt? Was he lying in the snow?"

"No, he was standing. He didn't seem to hear me. Then he looked at me . . ." No, *through* me. His eye was clouded, dead. I rubbed a wet gloved hand over my cold face. "He just disappeared."

"He walked away?"

"No. He just . . ." I paused. ". . . vanished."

"*Vanished,*" Jackson repeated. I lifted my hand to block the glare from his headlamp. Then he turned to Noah. "Did you see him?"

Noah glanced at me and shook his head.

"He *was* here," I said to Jackson. "Right here. I swear." I turned in a circle. "Where did he go?"

Jackson breathed out heavily as he watched Nelson and Owen slog through the snow toward us, the embers of their cigarettes brightening with every swing of their arms within the gloom. Behind Owen, Tucker was his father's shadow.

"You found Ben?" Owen called out.

"We don't know," Jackson told him. "He doesn't seem to be here, though Piper thought she saw him."

"I *did* see him."

Jackson lowered his voice to a near whisper, sparing me embarrassment in front of Owen, I imagine. "In the dark, it's easy to see things that aren't there, especially when we *want* to see them."

"The flare lit up everything. Jackson, I saw his face. It was Ben. His eye seemed, I don't know, injured." Dead.

Jackson trained his flashlight over the area again.

"I'm telling you. He's here."

"Dad!" Noah cried out. "Dad!"

We listened, called again, listened, but heard only the searchers making their way toward us. Once they reached us, Jackson set off another flare, and in the strange light we all combed the area in different directions, calling and calling.

"Why would Dad ignore us?" Noah asked me. "Why would he hide from us?"

"Ben!" I cried, my voice mournful in the snow. Finally, I went back to the base of the boulder where I had seen my husband, sank to my knees in front of the thicket and dug into the wet snow with my gloved hands. "Maybe there's a hole he fell into, a tree well." Tree wells, deep holes hidden in the snow around tree trunks, could suck a person down, cover him with snow, trap and suffocate him.

"You won't find a tree well there," Owen said. "There's no trunk for it to form around. Anyway, there's not enough snow yet for that, at least not down here." It was another story on the hills above, where snow had been accumulating over the last couple of weeks.

Noah took my arm, tried to lift me up. "Piper. Stop."

But I wouldn't stop, *couldn't* stop. I dug and dug in the wet snow, grunting with the effort of it, until Noah alerted Jackson and he hooked both hands under my armpits, hoisting me back to standing. "Piper. *Piper!* He's not here."

I was in tears now as I brushed the snow from my ski pants. "But I saw him."

"I believe you saw something, someone, and that you might even have seen Ben. It happens out here. We hear things, see things in the wilderness, things that aren't there."

"You think I hallucinated."

Nelson hacked out a phlegmy cough and pointed his cigarette at me from just up the trail. "That happened to me," he said. "I got turned around up near Hunter's Creek one afternoon. Couldn't find my way back to the logging road. Wandered around for hours until I finally got my bearings. Damned if I didn't smell bacon out there. Somebody frying bacon. I followed that smell all the way back to the road."

"A camper?" Noah asked.

"In the dead of winter?" Nelson shook his head. "There was nobody out there but me." He tapped his temple. "It was all in my head. Think it saved my life, though. The smell of bacon led me home."

"Bacon saved your life?" Tucker asked. "More likely to end it."

"I don't doubt that happened," Jackson said to Nelson. Then he turned to me. "When people are out here, especially when they're in crisis, their imaginations take over and they see strange things. The families I've worked with during these searches often think they hear or see their lost loved ones, when no one else does."

"They see ghosts?" Noah asked. "I mean, do people see the ghost only when the person is dead? Or do they see the ghost when that person is still alive?"

So Noah had seen Ben too. But when?

Jackson hesitated before replying. "Yes, sometimes when a

family member has seen the ghost of their missing loved one, we later find that person alive."

"A doppelgänger," I said.

"Exactly." Jackson waved a hand in a circle over his head as he rounded up his team. "Let's go, everybody, back to the search." Nelson, Owen and Tucker trudged back up the slope along with the other searchers. But Jackson stayed with Noah and me. "This is too stressful for you. I'm taking both of you home."

"Jackson, I *did* see Ben—"

He held up a hand. "And it's clear we'll cover more ground if you're not with us."

I nodded slowly. I knew that was true. "And if you do find Ben?"

"Then we'll radio you immediately. You'll know right away."

"Okay."

Jackson ushered Noah and me back down to the beach trail, and as he walked behind us, he radioed his team to let them know we were going. As we threaded our way through the giant cedars and boulders, Tucker lumbered down the trail behind us. "Hey, can I go back across with you?" He pointed at his leather boots. "I need to warm up. Can't feel my toes."

Owen boomed from the hill above him. "What the fuck were you thinking, wearing those useless boots? I bought you thermals."

Jackson ignored him and waved Tucker along, and we hiked down the remainder of the trail back to the beach and the SAR inflatable. We got in the boat as Jackson untied it, Tucker taking the seat up front as Noah and I sat together behind.

As Jackson pushed off, I leaned into Noah. "You've seen him, haven't you?" I asked. "Your dad. Your dad's ghost. Out here?"

"At home." He hesitated. "If we both saw Dad's ghost, that means he's dead, doesn't it?"

But before I could reply, Jackson started the engine, so, instead of yelling over the noise, I shook my head and squeezed Noah's hand. I had no good answer for him in any case.

We headed back across the lake through swirling snow. About halfway, Tucker called out, pointing. "What's that?"

I scanned the water ahead with Noah and Jackson, and saw something glint in the choppy waves, the rounded shape appearing and disappearing. It was an overturned aluminum hull, lifting and falling in the black water as snow fell through the dark all around. A boat.

Ben's boat.

# 13

Jackson immediately called on his radio for the other searchers to join us on the water as he swung his vessel toward Ben's upturned boat, focusing the searchlight on it. He manoeuvred alongside, cut the engine and then, together with Tucker, used his oars to raise one side of Ben's boat, though they couldn't flip it over. The skiff was empty. Everything that had been inside had drifted out. Most of Ben's things were likely now at the bottom of this deep lake. But was Ben? Our boat rose and fell under us as we sat in shocked silence.

*Oh god.*

Jackson pulled out his flashlight and swept the water, and then we all did, the stream of lights crossing paths, but we saw only the inky water, the choppy waves, the thick snowflakes.

"Ben!" I cried.

"Dad!" Noah called. "Dad?"

Jackson cupped his hands to his face and hollered. "Ben!" And Tucker echoed him.

Between each call, we listened for a response. But there was only the sound of Ben's boat bumping up against the hull of Jackson's inflatable, the slap of the waves against both vessels, and then the thunder of engines as first Chase and then Trevor swung their boats our way. Spots of light dotted the beach as searchers raced to their boats.

"Do you see him?" Noah asked, his voice barely a whisper.

It was hard to see much of anything. We were surrounded by a curtain of snow that swirled and danced in the early-morning dark, leaving me with the sensation that my world was flaking away.

My world *was* flaking away.

Ben wore a bright-yellow life jacket when boating. Had he put it on before leaving? I struggled to remember now. It seemed so long ago. But of course he would put it on. Wouldn't he? He was so cautious when boating, always lecturing Noah and me about water safety. "Ben!"

Tucker's flashlight cast a pool of light on the hull of Ben's boat. "He must have gone back out on the water after he launched the drone," he said.

"No." I didn't want to believe it.

"The controller would have fallen in the water when the boat capsized," Tucker added. "That's why the drone went home, to the place Ben launched it. It lost radio signal."

"He must have been in his boat when the storm hit," Jackson said. "Likely near the beach." Where the wind kicked the water against the rocks. "And after it capsized, the boat drifted out."

I imagined Ben, controller in hand, perhaps caught off guard as he turned sharply into a swell, pitching overboard as his boat took on water. He would have treaded desperately as he tried to pull himself up on the hull of the capsized boat. How long could he survive in the cold water? Not long, I knew, but longer than most people realized. If he didn't die of cold shock in the first couple of minutes, he might live for another half-hour or more, *if* he was wearing a life jacket. If not, he would lose control of his limbs quickly and, no longer able to swim, he would drown. He would have died before we even set out to search for him. I exchanged a panicked look with Noah, who seemed to be thinking the same thing, *must* have been thinking it.

"I shouldn't have pushed Ben to go out yesterday," I said.

"What do you mean?" Noah asked.

"Yesterday morning, your dad talked about putting off his trip across, for another day."

Jackson steered the inflatable in a wide circle around Ben's skiff, sweeping the searchlight over the water. Thick, wet snow continued to fall all around us, accumulating on our coats and in the bottom of the boat, and showed no sign of letting up. As the other boats approached, their lights shone beams through the dark.

"Maybe he swam to shore," Noah said. "And that's why you saw him over there."

"Maybe."

Chase, the youngest member of the search and rescue crew, swam across the lake nearly daily in the summer, as if it was a pool. He'd had Olympic aspirations at one time. I could tell, from the upright stance of his silhouette, that he was the one leading the flotilla of boats speeding our way.

Once they reached us, Chase and Trevor both immediately took up the search, circling the area with their searchlights. As the others arrived, Jackson fired off another flare, and it shot up into the night sky with a hiss and show of sparks, hovering above us on its parachute to light up the lake below. I squinted across the water with Jackson.

"Anything?" he called out.

"Nothing here," Chase called back.

And then Trevor: "Nothing here."

But then, from the boat farthest from us, Nelson's boat, Owen shouted, "Hey, there's something on the water. I see something."

"Is it Ben?" I called.

"Not sure. Something reflected the light." He paused. "There it is again."

Jackson eased us toward Nelson's skiff as Nelson leaned over to retrieve the floating object. I stood, hanging on to Tucker's seat in front of me, to get a better view as he lifted it, dripping, from the water. It was yellow. Bright yellow, with reflective strips that glowed.

Ben's life jacket.

A sick emptiness hollowed out my belly as I sank back into my seat.

"Is that it?" Noah asked me, his face crumpling in grief. "Is Dad dead?" Drowned.

In the seat in front of me, Tucker hugged his stomach, reacting to Noah's pain as if it were his own.

I thought again of Ben's body floating down into the dark water, his form fading into the black. No. It didn't feel right. That couldn't be what had happened. "When the storm hit, the waves could have pulled the boat back into the water," I said. "This doesn't mean Ben was out here when . . ." When his boat capsized.

Jackson shook his head slowly, as if I was only fooling myself. "Piper, it appears that Ben—"

"He didn't drown!" I said, too loudly. Owen and Nelson, Chase and Trevor, on the boats closest to us, stopped talking, the beams of their headlamps spotlighting me. "He didn't drown," I said again. I tried for a smile. "You all know Ben. Safety first. If he was in a boat, he was wearing a life jacket. If that jacket wasn't on him, then he didn't go back out on the water. He's still on land."

Jackson paused. "You might be right." Humouring me. "Let me take you home as the team continues the search on the water." I read his tone to mean, *You shouldn't be out here for this.*

I waved both gloved hands. "No, listen, Jackson, if we found Ben's life jacket out here, it means it was likely in the boat when it capsized, right? So Ben wasn't wearing it. He would have dragged the boat onto the shore like we all did tonight, but there isn't much in the way of a shore there." A rocky ledge that quickly dropped off into deep water. "The waves could have pulled the boat back out."

I looked to Noah for support, that I wasn't making this up, that Ben was almost certainly still onshore, where I'd seen him. Where I *thought* I'd seen him.

But Noah turned his angry gaze on me. "You shouldn't have bugged Dad to go out yesterday," he said. "It was his day off. You knew this snowstorm was headed our way. Now Dad's dead and it's your fault. This is all your fault!"

A shocked hush fell over the men in the other boats. They were watching. Chase, Trevor, Jackson, Nelson, Tucker, Owen—they were all watching. I set my eyes on the upside-down hull of Ben's boat, floating alone in the near distance as I felt the weight of guilt press down on me. I could have stopped Ben from going out. I could have encouraged him to linger in bed on his day off. Instead, I had insisted he go. Ben's disappearance *was* partly my fault. *My fault*. But those weren't the words that haunted me most. It was Noah's declaration:

*Dad's dead.*

# 14

In the early-morning light, Jackson slid the SAR inflatable up to our dock, towing Ben's capsized boat behind it. It had been nearly twenty-four hours since Ben left for the far shore. After we found Ben's boat, I had insisted on staying out on the water with Jackson. But beyond the boat and life jacket, we had found no more traces of Ben. Now that morning was on us, Jackson had finally brought Noah, Tucker and me home to warm up and get some rest. A fresh group of volunteers from the community had already deployed from our beach to pick up the search, some back on the far shore, many on the lake, and their vehicles were parked in our yard. An RCMP cruiser was parked there as well, and the officer waited onshore.

I had already given the RCMP all the information I could when we initiated the search from the water, so, as Jackson talked to the cop and the boys secured both boats and collected the gear, I made my way up the snow-covered shore and stairs of the deck. My limbs felt wobbly, unnaturally heavy, alien, as if I were an astronaut who had only just returned from many weeks in space. As I unlocked the door and entered the house, my home, too, felt strange, as if I had been away that long.

I dropped my keys on the kitchen table and listened, half hoping to hear Ben moving about, but the house was quiet, too quiet. There was still coffee in the pot from the morning before, coffee Ben had made. Although it was cold, I could still smell it. I closed my eyes and imagined Ben was in the addition, in his office, working up his reports before starting his day on patrol.

"Ben?" I whispered. Then louder, "Ben?" I held my breath as I listened for an answer. Then startled as Jackson's, Noah's, and Tucker's footfalls thumped up the steps of the deck and Jackson opened the kitchen patio door, allowing the wind, the smell of snow and the lake, to rush in. As Jackson and Tucker ducked inside, Noah closed the door behind them. There were blue half circles under Noah's eyes. He appeared exhausted, spent. But then neither of us had slept for twenty-four hours.

"Boots off," I reminded the three of them, out of habit, and kicked off my own, leaving a puddle of melting snow on the floor. I hung my jacket over a kitchen chair, near the register where it would dry off. As I stepped out of my ski pants, Noah peeled off his coat and headed straight for the bathroom.

Tucker slid off his jacket as well. "Hey, can I crash on the couch for a bit?" he asked as he hung it over a chair. "Maybe I can hang out here with Noah while they search." He waited until Noah closed the bathroom door and lowered his voice. "You know, keep him distracted until we get news?"

He was sweet about it. But my head throbbed, and the thought of Noah and Tucker playing video games across the hall from my bedroom felt overwhelming. The music and beeps and zings. I hung my ski pants over another chair. "I'm sorry, Tucker. Not right now. Another day, okay?"

"But you said I was welcome here anytime."

I rubbed my forehead, the piercing headache there. "With everything that's going on, we just need a bit of time to ourselves."

Tucker slid his coat back on and grabbed his boots, carrying them to the hall. "I get it," he said. "You don't need me hanging around." His voice was bitter with hurt.

*Shit.*

I followed him. "Tucker, wait," I said. "It's okay. You can stay."

"Forget it, all right? I'm sorry I asked."

"Tucker—"

His voice rose and he sounded, in his hurt and anger, like his father. "Just drop it!"

I glanced back at Jackson, watching from the kitchen. "What about your dad? You're taking his truck?"

He slipped on his boots. "Nelson will give him a ride when they get back."

I took in his black eye. "But will you be . . ." I paused. ". . . safe, at home, with your dad?"

Tucker's eyes slid back and forth, looking anywhere but at my face. There were times I wondered if he was on the spectrum. But no, I remembered withdrawing like that. I had learned from my dad to never make eye contact. To do so was to invite confrontation, or worse.

And then, for once, Tucker didn't lie. "Dad will be out there for a while," he said, "and bushed when he gets home. He'll have a couple of beers and fall into bed."

"You okay driving yourself home, then?" I asked.

"Yeah," he said, with attitude. "Why wouldn't I be?"

"The roads," I explained. "The snow."

"He's been driving the winter logging roads since he got his learner's," Jackson said as he came down the hall. He clapped a hand on Tucker's shoulder. "Working on his dad's crew. Haven't you, son?"

"Yeah." Tucker nodded at Noah as he left the bathroom. "Later," he said to him.

"Later."

Tucker banged out of the house without saying goodbye to Jackson or me as Noah slid into his room.

Jackson nodded after him. "He's a bit high-strung, isn't he?"

I turned back to the kitchen. "Tucker's a good kid in a bad situation."

"How about me?" Jackson asked as he followed.

"What's that?" I asked dimly, not understanding what he was asking. I rubbed my forehead again. I needed a painkiller. Or a drink.

"Okay if I stay, grab a nap here? I'll be heading back out again in a couple of hours. Makes no sense to drive all the way home and back."

"Yes, yes, of course. You're welcome to stay here during the search." As he often did when he and Ben had a couple of beers, stretching out on the short twin bed in the basement spare room, his large, socked feet dangling off the end. I sometimes wondered about that bed, if Ben's first wife, Shannon, had kept Noah's old bed for a future child she and Ben planned to have together, before the cancer ravaged her body. It was a question I had never asked Ben, perhaps because I was too afraid to ask. We hadn't yet talked about having children. And now it might be too late.

Was it too late? I felt the last bit of energy drain from my legs and slid into a kitchen chair so I wouldn't simply crumple to the floor. Jackson squatted in front of me, taking my hand in both of his. He spoke quietly, presumably so Noah wouldn't hear. "Piper, we will continue our search of the far shore and the lake for as long as the weather allows. But conditions are already tough, and we found Ben's boat on the water. You need to prepare yourself . . . You need to prepare Noah—"

"Ben didn't drown."

Jackson nodded slowly, then squeezed my hand. "Okay." He stood, turning to the stove. "You and Noah must be hungry. You haven't eaten since, what? Lunchtime yesterday? You didn't get supper last night, did you?"

My stomach rumbled at the thought of food. The night before, I had waited on Ben, finally putting a lid on the stew I'd thrown together for supper and sliding it into the fridge along with that crumble. I had no idea if Noah had grabbed something or not before we went out with Jackson to search. After the panic of the night before, I only now remembered the squares Maggie had packed for us.

"I'll make us some eggs," Jackson said.

He opened a bottom cupboard door and reached down for a frying pan, familiar with the house as he had spent so much time here.

I pushed myself to standing and took the pan from his hands. "I'll do it, Jackson. You've done so much for us already."

He watched as I put the pan on the stove and switched on the heat, reading me, I think. "It's natural to feel frightened right now," he said. "But we *will* find Ben, Piper. One way or the other, we'll find him."

I drizzled a pool of oil into the pan. *One way or the other.* Dead or alive. As I grabbed a carton of eggs from the fridge, I again envisioned Ben's body, weighted by his gear, drifting down into the black water, his face pale, his hair lifting and undulating in the currents.

I cracked the eggs against the edge of the pan and bits of shell slipped into the yolks. "Dammit." I tried to dig them out with the spatula, but my hands shook.

Jackson took the spatula and wrapped his arms around me, his slender, angular body against mine. His jacket smelled of smoke, from the stove in his living room. He heated his house with wood. "I know it doesn't feel like it, but you *can* handle things, as they come." He squeezed my shoulders as he let go. "Right now, you need to rest. Go get changed into some dry clothes. I'll have this ready by the time you come back out. Okay?"

I nodded wearily. "Thank you."

"Toast?"

"Sure."

"Hey, Piper?" He lowered his voice. "Noah," he said. "He'll be thinking of his mother."

Of course. Noah wouldn't just fear that his father had drowned. He would be reliving the loss of his mother.

I shuffled out of the kitchen, feeling dissociated from myself, numb, and stopped at Noah's room. I held my hand up to Noah's door, hesitated as I summoned the energy, then knocked.

"Yeah?" he said, from inside.

I spoke into the door. "You dressed? Mind if I come in?"

"I guess."

When I opened the door, Noah was sitting on the edge of his bed with Ben's drone in his hands. He'd changed into sweats and a hoodie, his feet in the socks Ben had given him for Christmas, wool to keep his feet drier on our treks into the wet wilderness. Ben had packaged those socks together with a Swiss Army knife. The knife sat on Noah's desk now.

"Jackson's making us something to eat," I said.

Noah spun a rotor on his father's drone.

"How are you weathering this?" My words sounded stiff and rehearsed, like a therapist's, but I plowed on. "I imagine all this— the search—is bringing up painful memories, of your mother, her death. If you need to talk . . ." I paused, my eyes scanning the objects in his small room: the many programming manuals on his book- shelf, the electric guitar he practised on nightly leaning against the wall. There were socks, candy wrappers, sheets of homework scat- tered across the floor. "You *should* talk about it," I said. "With me, if you like."

He stood, holding the drone. "It's shit, all right? What do you want me to say?"

I had no idea. I didn't know what to do for him, other than be here.

I eyed Noah's tall, thin frame in that oversized hoodie, the back of his head, the dark curls there. "Do you really blame me for . . ." For Ben's death. If he was dead.

Noah shook his head. "I was just mad."

"That he was missing. That we hadn't found him."

Noah nodded, then glanced sideways at me. "Before, you asked . . ." He hesitated. "I saw Dad's ghost last night. Before the search. Here in my room. He called my name."

"Just before I tried to take the kayak out, you mean, before I called Jackson?"

Noah nodded. We'd had the same experience at the same time. "I saw him then too," I said.

He flicked the rotors around and around, and then he said what we were both thinking. "What if that was when he died?" he said. "If we both saw his ghost . . ."

I took the drone from him, setting it on the dresser so I could hug him. "We don't know that. I won't believe that, not until . . ." Not until we found Ben's body. "We won't stop searching until we find him."

Noah started to cry. I rocked him because I didn't know what else to do. I wept and rocked myself as much as him.

After a time, we parted awkwardly, and Noah wiped his face. He was suddenly tall again, the man and not the boy, or nearly a man.

"Listen, is it okay if I keep that drone in my room?" I asked Noah. "I mean, keep it charged up there, in case—"

"In case Dad has the controller and activates it?"

I picked up the drone again, spun a rotor. "I know it's a long shot."

When he sank his hands into the pockets of his sweats, I pointed a thumb at the door. "Jackson is cooking eggs. We should go eat."

"I just need a minute," he said.

"Yeah, sure."

I left the room, closing the door behind me, and carried the drone into our bedroom, placing it on my dresser beside the wedding photo Jackson had taken of Ben and me on the beach, with the lake behind us, both of us laughing, our noses red as it had been unseasonably cold that day. What the picture didn't record was the crowd, almost the whole village, who were on the beach to celebrate the day with us. I had felt like I belonged, perhaps for the first time in my life. I had found a community, home, here in Moston.

I quickly changed into pyjama pants and a T-shirt before retrieving the drone's charging station and cord from Ben's office and setting it up on the dresser. Silly as it seemed, I wanted the drone close so I could keep an eye on it, even as I tried to get some rest. If Ben did have the controller, then there was a slim chance he might activate the drone, because its radio link could cover fifteen kilometres. He couldn't pick up cell reception over there, and he might have dropped his radio. If so, this was one way he could let us know he was alive.

I leaned down, with both hands on the top of the dresser, to look the thing in its one glossy black eye.

"Ben, where the hell are you?" I gulped back a sob. "Are you in that lake?"

Everything in the room around me was exactly the same as it had been the morning before. And yet everything was different. Smaller, emptier, lonelier. Twenty-four hours ago, Ben had stood right there in front of the patio door in a towel. If only I could wind back the clock, reach back there and take his hand, tell him to forget about going out on the water, to wait until the storm had come and gone before checking on that poached tree. Then he would be here now. He would be here, alive.

"Ben?" I whispered. "Ben, are you there? Can you see me?" Could he see me on the screen of his controller, the image this drone sent to him? Maybe, if he had the controller on him, if its batteries were charged, if he was in range, if he was on the shore on the other side of the lake, and not in the water, if he was alive.

"Ben? I love you. So very much." I touched the drone, this strange, alien machine that seemed, nevertheless, alive. "Please tell me where you are. Show me you're still out there. Just—*move*." If Ben had the controller, he could make that eye move, up and down, right to left. But the eye on the drone remained still, staring back at me blankly.

# MONDAY

# 15

*Piper. Piper, wake up!*

I woke with a start, my name echoing in my ears as if someone had called me. Not someone. *Ben.* I opened my eyes, disoriented. Where the hell was I? The room seemed so strange, so unfamiliar. Then I rose enough from dream to realize it was the charging light on the drone throwing a green hue over the wall above the dresser that made the room seem so odd. The drone's glossy eye stared back at me from the gloom. But there was something else, a shadow lurking by the dresser.

"Ben?" I said, groggily. "Is that you?" Passing by the bed on his way to the bathroom, as he so often did just before dawn. But then I woke more fully and remembered: dozens of volunteers had swept the waters and the shores of Black Lake yesterday, Sunday, and hadn't found any more signs of Ben. Jackson was certain, now, that my husband had drowned.

I sat up just in time to see a dark figure, silhouetted against the window, skitter around the foot of the bed and out the door. *Was it Ben?* His voice had woken me. From the morning twilight, I guessed it was an hour or more before dawn. I threw off the covers and leapt out of bed to follow, but when I stepped into the hallway, it was empty. "Ben?" I called out.

There was a bang and scuffle from the addition, and the sound of a window sliding up. I rushed to Ben's office. There was no one there, but the window was open, letting in the cold winter air. His laptop shed a blue light over the dark room.

I leaned out the window in my T-shirt and fleece pyjama pants and searched the snowy yard for him. "Ben!" I called, and then again, much louder, "Ben!" There was frost on the sill. The sky had cleared, and the stars sparkled; the predicted cold front had moved in after the snow, bringing even colder temperatures. Goosebumps rose on my arms. "Ben!"

From the basement below, I heard a thump and the sound of the door to the spare room opening, Jackson's footsteps sprinting up the stairs. He had stayed over, as he planned to get an early start on the search today. Now he raced down the hall, flicked on the office light and stood at the doorway in the borrowed T-shirt and sweats he had slept in, his hair pushed up one side of his head, his moustache wild, his eyes dull from sleep. "What's going on?" he asked, squinting. "I heard you calling. Are you okay?"

"There was someone here," I said, my voice rising in excitement. "I think it may have been Ben."

"*Ben?*"

When I saw the expression on his face, I knew how ridiculous I must sound to him. "He woke me," I said, realizing at once that telling him this was also a mistake. "I mean, his voice woke me. Someone ran out of the bedroom. Then I heard a noise here, in the office. He must have jumped out the window."

I stepped back as Jackson leaned out over the frame to peer outside. It was still dark, but a haze of light had started to creep up over the mountain ridge as dawn approached. "I don't see anyone," he said.

"Someone *was* here," I said.

I went into the hall and slipped my bare feet into my boots. Jackson followed, grabbing his search and rescue parka on the way. "Why do you think it was Ben?" he asked as I slid on my coat. "I mean, why would he come here only to jump out the window? It makes no sense."

"I don't know," I said, feeling even more foolish now. "Maybe he came back to get something."

"Like what?"

"I don't know!"

I opened the front door to jog down the steps, gasping involuntarily as the chilled air hit me. The trucks belonging to members of the search and rescue team and other volunteers who were currently searching the far shore were parked behind ours, and the snow in the driveway was muddy from all the traffic, though, now, that mud was frozen stiff. Frozen puddles glistened in the morning twilight.

Jackson trailed behind, shining a flashlight over the snow around the house. The many footprints of the volunteers crisscrossed the yard. "It's hard to tell if there's a fresh trail from that side of the house or not," he said. "Did you actually see the guy jump out the window?"

"No."

"Did you get a good look at him?"

I paused. "No."

"Then it could have been anyone." Jackson cast his light on me. "You just woke, from a dream by the sounds of it. Could it be you were still dreaming when you saw the figure in your room?"

"There *was* someone in my room, Jackson. I followed him into the office."

"None of us got much rest over the last couple of days, and you're under considerable stress. Maybe you were still half-asleep. As I said at the Boulders, in a crisis situation like this, in grief, people often see their lost loved ones, or think they hear them."

I rubbed my face with both hands. God. I *had* seen Ben's ghost, his doppelgänger, over the weekend. Was I just seeing things now? "I didn't hallucinate that open window," I said.

"Then maybe you opened it yourself?" Jackson asked. "I had a cousin who did bizarre things while sleepwalking. He drove his car to work in the middle of the night. Woke up at his desk in his pyjamas with the janitor cleaning the office around him."

"I wasn't sleepwalking. I'm telling you, Jackson, there *was* someone here." I tried to remember details, but my memory of the event was already fading, like a dream. "I distinctly heard Ben's voice, waking me." The urgency there. "It was like he was warning me—"

"*Warning* you?"

"Waking me, anyway, like there was something he wanted me to see. *Someone* he wanted me to see. Maybe he was warning me someone had broken into the house, our bedroom, that I was in danger."

And then I realized what I was really saying: that Ben's ghost had warned me there was an intruder. Some part of me was already starting to accept that Ben was dead.

# 16

Jackson and I stomped the snow from our boots as we stepped back into the warmth of the house. As he hung his parka on the coat rack, Jackson hesitated as a thought struck him. "Your intruder couldn't have been Noah, could it? I mean, he wouldn't try going out on his own, would he?"

"Through the office window?"

"I don't know. Maybe he was trying to sneak out without waking you?"

Our bedroom doors were right across the hall from each other. I rushed to open the door to Noah's room and switched on the light. But Noah was still there, in bed, his dark curls sticking out from under his red comforter. He rolled his head to the left, to the right, then sat up suddenly. His eyes were wide open but confused, like those of a much younger child still partly submerged in dream.

"What?" he said, squinting, his voice gravelly from sleep. He glanced past me, at Jackson standing at the threshold. "What's going on? Have you found Dad?"

"You weren't just out here?" I asked him. "In my bedroom? Or Ben's office?"

"What? No. Why?"

"I think someone broke into the house. Stay put."

But he had already thrown back his covers and was grabbing some clothes from the floor as I left the room.

As Jackson opened closets and checked corners to make sure the intruder had, in fact, left, I walked through the house to see if anything was missing, stolen. Everything appeared to be in order. If it had been some kid hunting for cash, they would have grabbed Ben's raku change bowl in the bedroom. My purse was hanging on the back of the bedroom door, where I'd left it. My phone was still on the dresser, alongside the drone. Surely a thief would have taken the expensive drone, if a quick resale was what they were after. Or maybe that *had* been the thief's goal and I'd scared him out of the room, the house, before he had the chance to grab it.

I heard Noah banging around in his room as I met Jackson back in Ben's office. Jackson closed the window. "Anything missing in here?" he asked.

"Not that I can see." Ben's home office was housed in what appeared to have been a porch in the past but had been framed in decades before for more interior space. There was tacky wood panelling on the walls, a water stain on the ceiling, the faint smell of mildew rising from the grey carpet. Officially, Ben's government office was in Clifton, but most days he was either out in the wilderness or worked from home. Ben had pieced together his home office with used furniture he'd accumulated over time. A cheap eighties desk and ragtag office chair, a heavy green filing cabinet that he must have gotten from an army surplus store. A large map of the region was thumbtacked to the wall. Other than Ben's laptop, there really wasn't much to take. The PC was open, though. He usually closed it when he wasn't using it.

"Ben's laptop was lit up when I first came in," I said. "Like someone had just tried to access it." I moved the mouse to bring the screen back to life. The login box popped up, empty.

"It likely wasn't Ben who came in here, then, was it?" Jackson asked. "He would have logged in if he were using it. Or he would have taken it with him."

I breathed out a heavy sigh. Of course, the whole idea that Ben had broken into his own house, only to flee, was ludicrous. But then who had I seen? "Who would break into Ben's work laptop?" I asked. And then I immediately knew the answer. "Owen," I said.

"Owen? What would he hope to find on this laptop?"

"Ben's files from work, the case he was building against him."

"I can't see Owen breaking into a house like this."

"He's stolen things before. He has a record."

"He stole lumber from the mill he worked at years ago. Breaking into someone's house—that's different."

"Is it?"

Jackson gestured toward the window. "If there *was* an intruder, it could just as easily have been the Green Man. Now that the summer cabins are closed up, and the fridges in them are empty, he's scrounging for food in *our* houses. He did the same thing last winter. I woke up one night to find he'd made a pot of mac and cheese on my stove and ate it at my kitchen table. I managed to sleep through the whole thing. And he even—"

"Left the pot for you to clean. I know." Jackson had told the story to Ben and me, to everyone, several times. "But whoever broke in here didn't take anything, Jackson. If it was the Green Man, surely he would have made off with something."

"Have you checked the fridge?"

"Not yet. But I've run into this guy in the forest before. The Green Man is quiet, stealthy. He knows how to hide, escape detection." I held out a hand to the window. "This guy, whoever broke in, was noisy, an amateur, or big. Too big to get through that window gracefully." I crossed my arms. "I'm betting it was Owen. He came back here and figured he could get Ben's file on him or delete it."

"Or maybe it was a kid looking for something to sell," Noah said. We both turned to find Noah at the door, dressed in jeans, a T-shirt and a hoodie. "Hen and Archie said some middle school kids broke into their place last month," he said. "Stole Pizza Pops and freezies they had in their freezer for their grandkids."

"Again, that sounds more like the Green Man," Jackson said. "He doesn't appear to have a sophisticated palate."

"Kids would have taken Ben's laptop," I said. "And what would the Green Man want with it, out in those woods? Why would he try to access it? No, I'm thinking it was Owen. At least he didn't have the password."

Jackson shook his head slightly, indicating I should watch what I said in front of Noah. What Ben had said: I shouldn't make accusations against Owen without proof. "You could both be right," I said wearily. "I guess I really have no idea who it was." I slumped in Ben's office chair. "I just wish I knew what the hell happened to Ben, where he is."

"Maybe we can access the photos he took from the drone," Noah said.

I groaned at my own thoughtlessness. "Why wasn't that the first thing I did?" I asked.

Jackson patted my shoulder. "Don't be so hard on yourself. You're exhausted and stressed to the limit. In any case, *I* should have thought of it. But we figured we knew where Ben was, or where he was supposed to be. And then we found his boat in the water." He paused. *And what happened to him*, he implied.

We had found Ben's boat. And I knew the odds of finding Ben alive now, after he had spent two days in the winter wilderness, were slim. "But what if he wasn't in the boat when it capsized?" I asked.

Jackson nodded. "Okay, how do we access the images?"

"We can get the photos off the SD card," Noah said, "but if we plug the drone into the laptop, we can also download all the mission data, not just the photos but the drone's GPS route. Dad showed me how. Get me the drone and I'll take care of it." He nudged me to get up, and took over the chair to sit in front of Ben's laptop.

"But we don't know Ben's password," I said.

"Yes, we do." Noah quickly typed in a password to Ben's laptop to unlock it.

"How do you know that?" I asked.

"When Dad teaches me stuff, I watch him log in. Sometimes I use his laptop when you guys are out. It's way faster for gaming."

"He'll be pissed," I said. "That's his work laptop."

"If we find him, I don't care."

"I'll get the drone." I grabbed the drone from its charging station on my dresser and brought it back to the office. Noah set it up, plugging it into the USB port, and, opening the drone mission planning software, quickly downloaded the photos and GPS coordinates. Within minutes he'd created a map of the drone's route, with the photos it had taken embedded as dots on the map. If we clicked a dot, the photo taken at that location popped open in a viewer.

"Where should I start?" Noah asked.

"From the beginning of his route, I guess."

He clicked on each dot on the map in progression and we watched as, in stills, the drone rose up from the shore and hovered over Ben, his kind, bearded face. I put a hand to my mouth as I felt the sting of tears. "*Ben.*"

Jackson wrapped an arm around me.

"Dad programmed the drone to stop and snap a photo at regular intervals on a grid search," Noah said, "but he would have seen everything the drone saw in between the photos too, on the controller screen."

As the drone steadily rose in the series of photographs, we got a clear view of Ben's boat pulled partially onshore and secured with a rope to a boulder. His life jacket hung over a seat within the boat.

"So he did land onshore," I said. "I mean, his boat didn't capsize on the way over."

"But he must have gone out again," Jackson said. "Or we wouldn't have found the upturned boat in the water."

"Unless, again, the storm waves simply washed the boat out." I tapped the screen. "You can see his life jacket in the boat. If he went back out on the water, he would have been wearing it."

In the images on the screen, the drone swivelled and shot off over the stand of old-growth cedars and the huge boulders that stepped up the base of the mountain, flying a preprogrammed flight path over the forest, clicking still images as it went.

"There, there!" said Jackson, pointing at the screen. "That's the old tree that was cut down, before it was covered in snow." Near the towering Hourglass boulder, where I had seen Ben standing so strangely, looking through me, before he vanished.

Noah clicked through the images and stopped on one that gave us a clear view of the felled ancient cedar.

Jackson pointed out the newly bucked rounds, the blocks of wood. "They were in the middle of hauling, likely trying to get as much out as they could before the snow hit."

"See the tracks through the mud there?" I said. "Jump ahead a bit. Maybe we'll see the poachers." Owen, I thought, and likely Nelson, and maybe Tucker since it hadn't been a school day.

Noah skipped over a number of photos as the drone rose high above the trees. Ben had evidently hoped to get a good look at the surrounding forest for signs of the poachers, and how they had gotten into this remote section of the forest. As the drone flew its grid search, it caught a few images of the many winding game trails high up the mountain. In one of the photos there was a flash, light hitting something large and metallic on the ridge above. Noah clicked on the next image.

"Go back," I said, then, pointing at the metallic flash, asked, "What is that?"

Noah clicked through several more photos and stopped on an image with a clear view of the ridge, which was already covered in snow at the time.

"That's a four-wheeler." I tapped the screen. "There, that's proof. Owen is one of the few people left here who own quads. He *was* out there yesterday."

"But there *are* others who own four-wheelers," said Jackson. "And it could just as easily have been someone from out of town." He squinted at the photo. "It appears it was just parked there, nobody in it."

"But someone was definitely there at the same time as Ben," I said.

"Or the poachers got stuck in the snow," Noah added. "Left the four-wheeler behind."

"Where is that exactly?" I asked Jackson.

"The ridge above Miners' Ravine," he said. "The other side goes straight down into a gully, a creek bed, Silver Creek. That game trail the ATV is on follows the ridge and then leads all the way back to the old logging road that runs past Hunter's Creek. It's one of the few ways to get down to that beach from the town side of the lake. Or to that old-growth cedar they cut down."

Noah continued to click on the photos on the map, one after the other. The drone, programmed to perform its grid search, flew high over the trees, snapping image after image. An eagle lifted from the top of a tree and soared below the drone for several photos before disappearing out of the frame. Then the drone appeared to swing around to carry out its grid search in the opposite direction, back to the lake.

"There's the ATV again," Noah said. "It's still just sitting there."

I pointed at the screen. "What's that?" I asked. "There. That figure." Dark, tiny under the branches of a tree, as if the person were hiding there, pressed against the trunk. It was hard to see, as the drone had been flying so far above and there were branches in the way, but it was definitely a human form. "Someone *was* there," I said. "Hiding from the drone. I bet it was one of the tree poachers." Owen.

Jackson squinted, leaning toward the screen. "Maybe." He didn't sound convinced. "It could have been the Green Man. He camouflages himself, green clothes, green face paint. That figure definitely blends into the surroundings. You can barely see him." He stepped back. "Owen told me he thinks the bushman's hideout is somewhere in that area. At least, he seems very protective of this whole slope, from the Boulders up to the ridge above Miners' Ravine. He took potshots at Nelson and Owen in that area, trying to scare them off."

"When was this?"

"Not sure. Sometime over the last couple of weeks."

"Owen admits he took down that cedar, then?"

"It was Nelson who told me. He only said they were over there when the Green Man shot at them."

Noah clicked on several more photos.

"Look! There's Ben." Jackson pointed him out. "There, under that branch. He's making his way up the slope through the Boulders."

"Maybe toward that four-wheeler on the ridge," I said. "He could have seen the ATV on the controller."

"Oh, he did see it," Noah said. "He would have seen that flash of metal better than we did in these stills as the drone flew over it."

"How long would it take to get up to the ridge on foot?" I asked Jackson.

"An hour. Maybe more. Even if he wasn't wading through snow."

"The drone would run out of juice way before that," Noah said. "It would have returned home to its launch point after fifteen minutes or so."

"So Ben was likely up on that ridge long after the drone flew back to the beach." I looked up at Jackson. "That means he wasn't in the boat when it capsized."

"Unless he changed up the batteries and took the drone out a second time," Jackson said. "Or he left the drone on the beach for some reason while he took the boat out."

"*Is* there a second drone route?" I asked Noah.

He quickly skimmed through the data. "No," he said.

"Skip ahead in the photos. Any sign of Ben? Where does he go?"

Noah clicked through the images as Jackson and I stood on either side of him, leaning into the desk, squinting as we tried to find Ben, small under the dense canopy of giant old-growth forest.

"There he is," I said. "He's following that game trail." I took the mouse out of Noah's hand and clicked on a photo icon farther up the map. I clicked again and again, scrutinizing the photos for any sign of Ben. "There, there he is again."

"He *is* climbing toward that ridge." Jackson tapped the screen. "If he made it that far, it's a steep trail along the ridge, and narrow. Beautiful as hell, but I wouldn't drive a four-wheeler on it, or even send a hiker there. I nearly slipped to my death into the ravine one time I hiked over it. If Ben went up there to check out that ATV—"

I stood back. "In the wet, in the snow and mud, he could have fallen into the gully."

"Wait," said Noah. "What's that?" A huge shadow on the trail behind Ben. Noah zoomed in.

"Oh my god," I said. "A grizzly."

"Click ahead," Jackson said.

Mouse in hand, Noah filed through the images until the drone returned to the trail and there, in one clear shot, was the cinnamon-coloured sow, the bear that had mauled the young honeymooning couple, killing the woman, the year before. It was the grizzly that had stalked Ben, the one Ben and Jackson had been trying to trap, to remove from the area.

Jackson swore under his breath. "That bear was on Ben's trail, on the hunt. It was stalking him."

I felt suddenly chilled. None of us moved or spoke for several moments as the shock of it set in.

"Look through the rest of the photos," I said.

We all scanned the remaining photos, looking for any sign of the bear or Ben, but the trees were in the way.

"We know Ben carried bear spray and a bear banger," Jackson said. "He would have protected himself."

But there was doubt in his voice, and I knew he was thinking the same thing I was, because he and Ben and I had discussed it in the past: would the bear banger and bear spray be enough to deter *this* grizzly? It was aggressive and had already hunted humans. It had killed and eaten that poor woman, clawed her husband.

"Maybe Dad climbed a tree," Noah said. "And escaped the bear. Maybe he couldn't get back down." He was remembering a story Ben told about a tourist who had gotten himself in just that predicament.

"Or maybe he's only injured," I said. "If the bear attacked and he used the spray, if he escaped . . ." He might be bleeding out in the cold right now. The husband of the young woman this grizzly had killed had survived a couple of days in the forest with his injuries until Ben had found him and called in the SAR helicopter from Clifton to airlift him to the hospital. "If he didn't get back to the water, then he's up by Miners' Ravine. He was hiking in that direction." To the four-wheeler.

"Maybe." Jackson stepped back from the desk. "But Piper, you need to understand that we *will* keep searching the water." He held eye contact to make sure I did, in fact, understand. He still believed Ben had drowned in the lake. "But this is worth a shot. As long as this break in the snow holds, we'll get the SAR helicopter from Clifton to do a flyover of the ravine. But when it comes to a ground search, that area around the ravine is difficult to access and a bigger search area than we originally planned for. We'll need more volunteers, and searchers on snowmobiles."

I stood. "Then we better get to work."

# 17

That afternoon, I hung on to Jackson as he steered one of the volunteers' snowmobiles through the snow, sidehilling us up the slope through the trees toward the ridge and Miners' Ravine, roughly following the game trail we had seen Ben hiking in the drone images. This far up the slope, the cedar and hemlock forest that dominated the lower elevations had given way to spruce and fir, and the snow was deeper.

Behind us, another volunteer gave Noah a lift up on his machine. On either side of the trail, searchers on snowshoes, skis or snowmobiles combed the mountainside, even as others in boats continued to hunt for any sign of Ben on the lake below. Jackson, Noah and I had spent the morning and early afternoon searching the trail we had seen Ben on in those drone images, but we'd found no sign of him, or the grizzly for that matter. But then the snow hampered our search, covering everything in a thick blanket. Now we were heading back up to the ravine, as the SAR helicopter from Clifton was due to arrive any moment, later than we had hoped because low cloud cover had made visibility poor throughout the region earlier in the day.

Once at the foot of the ridge, Jackson followed the same narrow game trail the four-wheeler would have driven in those images the drone captured, and parked at the peak overlooking the ravine. A number of searchers had been up here all morning, and I saw now that Nelson, Owen and Tucker had joined them, arriving on their snowmobiles. It was the first I'd seen of Owen since the break-in at our house that morning.

We dismounted and removed our helmets to stare down into Miners' Ravine. It wasn't all that far down to the creek, but the grade was very steep, heavily treed and tangled with broken rocks and fallen trees from slides over the centuries. On Jackson's instructions, none of the searchers had ventured down. One false step and a person could fall to their death into the Silver Creek drainage, hitting trees or rocks on their way down. I had read that a few prospectors had met their deaths that way in Moston's pioneering days, leading to the ravine's name.

"The tree cover is so thick down there," I said, tucking my helmet under my arm. "Is the helicopter team going to see anything from above?"

"Maybe, maybe not," Jackson said. "The heavy snow may have helped us out on that front, tamped down at least some of the vegetation, made Ben easier to spot against the white."

"If he's not buried in it," Noah said. His brows were furrowed as if he was about to cry, and I put an arm around him. We both knew the reality. Experienced hikers went missing every year in the wilderness, and were never found, or their remains were discovered years after they disappeared. Still, after seeing those images on Ben's drone, I had to hope that he was somewhere on this mountain, and not in the water.

"He's *not* buried," I said, to myself as much as to Noah. "Not unless he built himself a snow shelter." And up here, in this deep snow, he could have. As long as he could stay dry, a cave dug into the snow would insulate him against the cold.

Noah nodded, but wiped his eyes, his nose, with his sleeve.

"There's Tucker," I said, to distract him. I waved the boy over, and he waded up to us through the snow, bundled up in snow-mobile gear, a blue monosuit that was obviously too small for him now. Like Noah, he had grown so much, so fast, in the last year. The bruise around his eye was now a deep purple.

As we waited on the helicopter, I offered the boys hot chocolate laced with tiny marshmallows and chocolate-covered granola bars, sugary stuff Maggie had sent along that I couldn't stomach myself when I was anxious. Even as a teen, I had regularly thrown up after eating cake at birthday parties. But Tucker asked for seconds and then thirds of both. And then, as he downed the last of the hot chocolate, he held his hand over his eyes as if spotting something in the air.

"There they are!" Jackson called out, pointing as the beat of a helicopter echoed against the mountain face. We watched together as the bright-yellow SAR helicopter from Clifton flew low over the water and then, as it reached the shore, lifted over the tree line, scaling the mountain slope until it hovered over our heads.

I leaned into Jackson and raised my voice over the noise. "The cloud cover is so low on the mountain. That's dangerous to fly in, right?"

"As long as the pilot can fly above the trees, we're good," Jackson shouted back. "The clouds may actually help us out, as strong shadows cast on a sunny day would make it harder to see Ben from the air." He looked up at the cloud hanging over the moun-tain above us, obscuring the view of the trees at the peak. "But obviously we're watching the weather. We're expecting more snow, and visibility will be poor again later this afternoon. Today's search will likely be short. We mostly want to get a good look into the ravine before we risk sending anyone from our team down there." He lifted his radio from his vest as he nodded up to the helicopter above us. "I've got to check in with them."

Jackson stepped away to talk with the team in the helicopter. I waited to the side with Noah and Tucker, watching, our heads tipped back, as the helicopter team conducted their initial search of the ravine and surrounding area, circling and then circling again. The helicopter flew so low, I could see that one member of the team had the door ajar so he could look straight down into the gully.

I caught Jackson's eye. "They see anything?" I shouted.

"Nothing yet. But then, as you said, the tree canopy is pretty dense."

He radioed back and forth with the team in the air as they circled again. The boys and I stamped our feet in an attempt to stay warm. The cloud cover sank down the mountain as the minutes ticked on. Snowflakes began to fall.

Then the helicopter abruptly veered toward the lake.

"What are they doing?" I called to Jackson. "Are they leaving already?"

Jackson waded back toward me. "I'm sorry, Piper. As you can see, the weather front has moved in earlier than we thought. The helicopter team needs to head back to Clifton before the cloud cover is any lower or the snow gets heavier. They can lose their way, get disoriented in this. As it is, they'll have to fly low on the return trip."

"Will you get them back here tomorrow?"

"If the weather gives us a break, we may try for an overflight of other areas. But there was no sign of Ben down there."

"There are so many trees. Maybe they missed something." I watched the helicopter fly off over the lake. It seemed to fade as it moved through the low cloud cover.

"So, what now?" Noah asked Jackson.

Jackson scanned the many volunteers. "We've got a lot of cold, exhausted people out here. And we've been all over this slope." He squinted up at the snow that was already falling more heavily now. "I think we need to call it a day, at least up here. Regroup."

"But no one has gone down into the gully yet." I picked up my backpack. "You said yourself if Ben made it up this far, he could have fallen into the ravine."

Jackson put out a hand. "Whoa. There's no way I'd let you go down there. You could easily fall yourself and get hurt. Then we'd have to rescue you, putting my team in danger."

I raised an eyebrow and exchanged a look with Noah. "Yes, I know," I said. I unzipped my bag. "But a drone could fly down there easily."

"Our team doesn't have one," Jackson said.

I pulled out the drone. "That's why we brought Ben's."

On seeing the drone, Tucker's eyes opened wide. He clearly coveted the thing. When all this was over, I would have to get him one so he and Noah could fly them together. Toy drones weren't all that expensive.

"But you don't have Ben's controller," Tucker said.

Noah retrieved his drone controller from his backpack. "Yeah, but I have mine," he said, holding it up. "Same company as Dad's, same software. Dad paired the controllers to both drones so we could fly them with either controller."

"You think you can navigate those trees?" Jackson asked.

"Noah's a good pilot," I said.

"Fair," Noah corrected me. "I'm still learning."

"And the snow?" Tucker asked. He held out a gloved hand to the flakes circling down. "Can you fly a drone in this?"

Noah took Ben's drone from me. "It's better to fly in snow than rain," he said. "Dad bought this drone because it's more resistant to moisture."

"Okay," Jackson said. "You think you can handle flying that thing through the ravine, you go right ahead."

Noah, buoyed by the task, placed the drone on the seat of a Ski-Doo. He turned it on, setting the rotors whirring, and it lifted above our heads, then flew down into the ravine. Almost as soon as Noah had started the thing, Owen made his way up to us in his monosuit, with Nelson following behind. He stopped a few metres away to watch the drone. I leaned into Noah, along with Tucker and Jackson, to view the video being transmitted from the drone to the screen on his controller. Noah piloted the machine through the trees and rocks, zigzagging progressively lower into the gully.

"What are we looking for, exactly?" Noah asked. "I mean, I know I want to see Dad."

Jackson shaded Noah's controller with a hand to better view the screen. "Ben would have tried to signal us," he said. "He might have used nearly anything to flag his location. So, a reflective vest or maybe a foil emergency blanket."

"Anything shiny and bright," I said, echoing advice Ben had given Noah and me.

"And if he was badly hurt?" Noah asked.

Jackson paused. "Then we're hunting for anything that appears to be a human form under the snow. Or a boot, a glove."

We all squinted as we watched the images on the screen of Noah's controller. Tree branches, rocks jutting up through snow. Snow. More snow. A crow that flew so close I thought the drone would collide with it, but of course the drone was programmed not to. Noah flew the machine back and forth down the wall of the ravine and then across the gully bottom, following the winding path of Silver Creek, the snow-covered logs that had fallen at all angles over the ribbon of churning water. But there was no sign of Ben.

"Can you turn back?" Tucker asked.

Noah thumbed the controls. "Where?"

"Under that tree," Tucker said. "There, there. That clearing under the canopy, where you can see ferns. That boulder shaped like a giant egg."

Owen sauntered nearer as Noah manoeuvred the drone down low so we could see beneath the branches of a spruce that sheltered a clearing in the snow.

"Closer," Tucker said.

Owen slid on his businessman glasses to take a look at the screen. "What did you find?" he asked. Behind him, Nelson sucked on his cigarette.

"There's nothing," Noah said. Just the egg-shaped boulder and ferns peeking out from beneath drifts of snow. "Dad didn't fall into the ravine."

"But I was sure—" Tucker bent over, his hands on his knees.

Noah glanced back as his friend choked and spit as if he were about to throw up. He hit home on the controller, to bring the drone back, as he turned to his friend. "You okay, man?"

"Hey, take that over there," Owen told his son. "I don't want you throwing up on our boots." He stepped back to stand with Nelson, to light a cigarette. *Asshole.*

I eyed Owen as I put a hand on Tucker's back, to soothe him. "Hey, what's going on?"

"I don't feel so good." The boy's face blanched. "Can I get a ride home?" he asked Jackson.

"Of course."

And then I *knew*. I had bent over and spit up like that the day my father was hauled away in that ambulance. What Tucker was experiencing wasn't the sudden onset of an illness. It was guilt and fear.

I lowered my voice to a near whisper as I glanced first at

Owen, who had turned away, and then at Jackson. "Tucker, if you know something, anything, about Ben's disappearance, you need to tell us."

He wiped his mouth with his glove. "What? I don't know nothing," he said. But a look of panic washed over his face. He *did* know something.

"You and your father were out here Saturday, weren't you?" I asked, quietly. "When Ben was here?"

But Owen heard. "What was that?" he bellowed, swinging around.

Tucker licked his lips. The whine of the drone rose up as it flew back automatically from the gully below.

Jackson stepped in. "We saw a four-wheeler on this ridge in the photos on Ben's drone," he explained to Owen.

"Was that you?" I asked. "Were you up here Saturday?" As Ben hiked the slope to investigate.

Owen ran a finger under his nose. Then he nodded at the mountain slope below us, the many searchers in their brightly coloured winter jackets dotting the landscape. "I'm out here searching for Ben same as you, same as everybody here. I risk my neck for you, for Ben, and you accuse me of—of what, exactly?"

Jackson held out a gloved hand. "I'm sure Piper is only wondering if you have any information you might want to share. Isn't that right, Piper?"

I nodded, uncertain. What was I saying exactly? That Owen had hurt Ben? That he'd *killed* him? The drone continued to hover, stationary, over our heads as we stood too close to the seat of the Ski-Doo, its landing spot. The miserable whine of the thing.

"If you were up here on Saturday, you might have seen something that could help us find Ben." Jackson crossed his arms as he regarded Owen. "*Do* you have anything you'd like to tell us?"

Owen swung his head away, a bitter grin on his face. "If I had anything to offer, don't you think I would have told you by now?"

Jackson studied him for a long moment, then turned to the boy. "Tucker?"

"I don't know nothing," Tucker cried out again. He flung his hand at me. "I was just feeling sick and she started grilling me, like I know something. When I don't. I had too much chocolate, that's all."

"Shut it," Owen said to his son, then he pointed a finger at me. "I've had enough of your bullshit! You and your kid better stay the hell away from me and my boy. You hear me? Stay away." He grabbed Tucker's arm and hauled him down the slope toward their snowmobiles. Nelson flicked his cigarette butt to the snow at my feet before he skidded downhill after them. Tucker turned to glare at me as his father dragged him off, anger and hurt hot on his face. He felt I had betrayed him. I took a shaky step back, away from the snowmobile, and the drone finally landed on the seat. *Plunk.*

*Had* I misread the boy? Tucker had had several cups of hot chocolate, several chocolate-covered granola bars. Maybe he *was* simply ill from an overload of sugar. And yet—

"He never answered your question," Noah said, staring after his friend. "Neither of them did."

"No, they didn't." Were they up on this ridge Saturday when Ben was here?

Was Owen somehow responsible for Ben's disappearance?

He was brash, belligerent, a petty criminal and undoubtedly abusive when drunk. But a *killer*? The word, unsaid, curled like a maggot on my tongue.

And did I really believe Ben was dead?

I refused to believe it.

Didn't I?

# TUESDAY

# 18

I sat on the floor, wedged between the bed and the wall, fiddling with the silver necklace Ben had given me and drinking wine. Hiding. Over the last few days, Jackson had set up a temporary headquarters in Ben's office to coordinate the search and rescue operation as his team led more than a hundred volunteers in a search of both the lake and the mountains above the far shore. Now there was a constant stream of chatter from the radio Jackson had installed there, volunteers reporting in or asking for direction. That morning, after a conversation with officers at the Clifton RCMP detachment, Jackson had expanded the search to the game trails above the Silver Creek drainage. Others had taken snow-mobiles to search the trails leading off the old logging road that led to Hunter's Creek and beyond, though it was unlikely Ben would have made it that far in either direction on foot. Jackson had put many more boats on the water, concentrating the search on the lake, making it clear he still believed Ben had drowned. Earlier, I'd heard the *whump-whump* of the search and rescue heli-copter circling the lake several times before finally heading back to Clifton. While we had had a brief reprieve in the weather today, the forecast was for yet another dump of snow this evening. Now, in late afternoon, as the light started to fade, snow was already fall-ing heavily. I could barely see past the beach, much less to the far side of the lake.

For the past half-hour, sitting here on the floor half-drunk, I had tried to remember Ben's middle name and couldn't, and that tortured me. It was like my memory of Ben was already starting to fade. I thought of asking Noah, but it seemed like an odd question to ask at such a time, and I didn't want to worry him.

I got up from the floor, stopping to regain my balance as a wave of dizziness ran through me, then refilled my glass from the wine bottle on the little table by the patio door where Ben and I had shared morning coffee on the weekends. I stood there, drinking, gazing over the snowy scene in the T-shirt and underwear I had napped in, not caring, anymore, if anyone saw me. I had come to feel a strange sort of intimacy with the searchers over the past day, the kind one might find with roommates. A steady stream of volunteers used our small yellow bathroom upstairs, or the blue one below, or warmed themselves by the gas fireplace in the basement as they readied to leave or returned. Jackson's SAR team and others now regularly entered the house without knocking and tramped down the hall to talk to Jackson in Ben's office. Last night and earlier today, these members of my community, my friends, had offered me hugs when I ventured to the basement in my sweats to thank them. Despite my grief and the deep ache for Ben that I carried in my belly, I also felt a part of something, something big and urgent: a communal effort to find my husband. Still, there were moments, like now, when it was all too much.

"Piper?" Jackson's voice reached me from the hall. "Piper, you in there?" He knocked on my bedroom door, then opened it without waiting for a response. When he saw me standing there in nothing but my underwear and T-shirt, he turned away. "Sorry."

"It's okay," I said. "Can you hand me my bathrobe?"

His face reddening, he grabbed my mustard robe from the hook on the door and held it out with his back to me. "Did I wake you?"

"No." Though I had slept on and off throughout most of the day, lying on Ben's side, breathing in his earthy scent, which still lingered on his pillow. In the panic of the last few days, sleep had been evasive at night, and intrusive in the day. The night before I had lain on the bed staring at the ceiling in the dark, my mind racing through the many horrific possibilities of what might have happened to Ben, but then today exhaustion caught up with me and I found myself nodding off at the kitchen table. I finally stumbled to the bed for a nap that, when I woke, left me feeling wrecked, confused.

I closed the robe and tied it, picked up my glass again. Only then did Jackson take in the wine bottle and sniff the air as I wavered on my feet.

"You've been drinking," he said.

"A bit."

"A lot." He took the glass from me. "You never drink like this. Not anymore."

Jackson knew something of my history. Although I hadn't drunk much since moving to Moston—just a beer or two on poker night—alcohol had often been my best buddy before I met Ben.

Now Ben was gone.

"Don't look so worried," I said. "I'm fine."

Jackson appraised my dishevelled appearance. We both knew I was anything but fine. "Get yourself dressed," he said, tossing me a pair of jeans that had been draped over a chair. "Quickly."

"For what?" I asked, letting them fall to the floor at my feet.

Jackson picked up the half-empty wine bottle and left the room without answering. "You need coffee," he called back to me. "I'll put on a pot."

I closed the door behind him and sat stiffly on the bed, trying to get my bearings. Then I wobbled to the dresser to grab a pair of joggers and slid them on under my bathrobe. Below me volunteers disappeared under the deck as they got themselves coffee from Maggie's warming station. Where was Maggie? I hadn't seen her for a couple of hours, but she'd been here almost non-stop yesterday evening and today, doing the dishes, making our meals, trying to get me to eat. She had even done some laundry. After using the bathroom earlier, I found my clothes neatly stacked on my bed. At any other time, her assumption that she could take over my household chores would have annoyed me. But now it was a relief to let go of responsibilities. Nothing mattered except finding Ben.

I staggered across the hall to the bathroom and rinsed my mouth with Scope, as I couldn't drum up the energy to brush, then I leaned against the sink to stare into the mirror at the deep-purple crescents under my eyes, my dry, pale skin, the vein visible at my temple, my orange hair that stuck up at all angles. I felt no connection to that person in the mirror, as if she weren't me. It wasn't the first time. I had grown up feeling that disassociation. In my life with my father, it was necessary. But in recent years, with Ben, I had come to identify with, even like, the person I saw in the mirror. Now I felt nothing again. I patted my hair in an attempt to tame its unruliness and shuffled into the hall. Then I just stood there, my exhausted, tipsy mind bewildered as to what to do next. Why was I out here? I could hear Jackson banging around in the kitchen, smell the coffee brewing. Right. He had told me to dress, to get ready for something. But for what?

Before I could join him in the kitchen, there was a knock on the front door. More volunteers, or neighbours bearing casseroles and painfully considerate words. I closed my eyes, gathering the strength to be social, and tried for a slight smile before opening the door. But then, on opening it, my smile fell. The woman in front of me was as petite as I was, smaller. Similar green eyes to those I saw in the mirror each morning (though hers were carefully made up with eyeshadow and liner), a similar haystack of orange hair (though hers was worn longer, chin-length, and was dyed now). She carried a leather travel bag and wore a camel coat with a green scarf thrown jauntily around her neck, along with fashionable leather boots that would not keep her feet warm in this climate. "Surprise!" she said.

"Libby." My mother. I ran a hand over my forehead as a new wave of fatigue washed over me. "What are you doing here?"

"That should be obvious, I would think." Libby loosened her scarf. "You know how I found out about Ben? On the *news*."

Behind her, Maggie, bundled up in a red puffer jacket and toque with a pompom, smiled an apology. She must have driven my mother here from the diner, the gas station where the bus dropped off passengers. "Should I leave now, then?" Maggie asked. "I should leave." But she didn't. The door was still open. Cold air rushed in, raising goosebumps on my arms.

"I guess I should have phoned," I said to Libby.

"I *did* phone," she said. "I texted. But somebody wasn't picking up." My mother eyed me. Those piercing green eyes, so like my own.

"The reception is poor here," I said.

"I'm sure it is." She put down her bag to tug off her leather gloves. "But I can see you still have a land line." The old beige phone hanging on the wall in the hallway. "Then Maggie here phones and I get the details from her. A total stranger calls me, but not my own daughter. Do you have any idea how that makes me feel?"

Trust my mother to make Ben's disappearance all about her.

As she pocketed her gloves, I looked past her at Maggie. "You phoned Libby? How did you get her number?"

Maggie grinned and held up both hands. *Don't put this on me.* I heard Jackson's steps coming down the hall behind me, and I knew the answer to my question before he gave it.

"You've mentioned your mother a time or two," he said, standing next to me.

Libby smirked as she unbuttoned her coat. "I bet she has."

Jackson held out his hand. "Libby," he said. "I'm Jackson."

My mother cupped his hand in both of hers warmly, suddenly a different woman. It was always like this when an attractive man entered the room. "I understand you're the one who orchestrated my visit," she said.

"About that," I said, turning to Jackson.

"I'll just step outside, then," Maggie said. "Let you get your mother settled."

"We'll talk," I said to her, smiling a little. "Later."

She grinned guiltily at me. "I'll be in the basement if you need me."

She turned, but I put a hand on her arm to stop her. "I do appreciate your time, Maggie," I said. "Thanks for arranging this."

She glanced between my mother and me, raising an eyebrow, and I knew I'd have to fill her in about Libby later. "My pleasure," she said, then backed out the door. I lifted a hand to her as she closed it behind her.

My mother hadn't bothered to thank her, or even look in her direction. "I had to *bus* here," Libby said to me, as she hung her coat on a hook. "Can you imagine? Isn't there an airport somewhere around here?"

"There is one," Jackson said, "just outside of Clifton, but it lost its passenger flights during the pandemic."

Noah peered out his partially opened door at us.

"And who is this?" Libby asked, smiling.

"Noah," I said. "Ben's son. Noah, this is my mother, Libby."

"I guess it's *Grandma* to you," my mother said.

Noah gave her a squinty look that said, *Really?* "Is she staying with us?" he asked me. He sounded slightly horrified. Or perhaps I was just projecting.

"Where *are* you staying?" I asked Libby.

"I thought here."

Noah slowly closed his bedroom door, eyeing us before he disappeared.

"We really don't have the space," I told my mother. I gave Jackson a wide-eyed look, pleading for his help. I did *not* want my mother staying here. "Maybe Jackson knows of a cabin you can rent for a few days. Oh, or Maggie has a room above the diner." Maggie rented out an apartment there occasionally, as an Airbnb.

My mother snorted. "You want me to stay at a gas station?"

"It's a nice apartment," I said, though I'd never seen it.

"You don't have a spare bedroom? What about in the basement?"

"Jackson is using it right now."

She looked Jackson up and down. His walrus moustache on his handsome face, his socked feet under jeans. "*Really.*"

"Just during the search," he said. "But I'll be out of here tonight. The spare bedroom is all yours."

I gave Jackson another look that said, *Thanks a lot, buddy.*

"Where's the bathroom?" Libby asked, as she picked up her travel bag. "I refused to use that disgusting bathroom at the gas station. Have you seen that thing?"

"You just passed it," I said.

She took in the yellow tub and sink, the yellow linoleum floor, the daisy-patterned tiles. "Huh," she said. "Quaint."

Once she had closed the door to the bathroom, I pulled Jackson into the kitchen. "What were you thinking?" I asked. "Bringing her here?"

"You need family, Piper, especially now."

"You didn't think to ask first?"

"Would you have said yes?"

"No!"

"Piper, I just don't think you should be alone right now."

I glanced at the many people outside, the volunteers warming themselves by a burn barrel on the beach. "I'm hardly alone."

"You need family," he said again.

"You don't understand. My mother is—" I put my hands on my hips and bowed my head as I struggled to think what to say, how to explain, without giving too much away. "Okay, so, one day I came home, for reading break. I was, I don't know, maybe twenty. Libby was sitting in her living room, drinking with some college kid about my age. I mean, they were both hammered."

"A guy?"

"Yes, a man. A very young man. She'd hired him to create garden beds, even though she would never do any gardening. And the guy never did any work. My mother hired him so she could drink with him all afternoon."

"She was lonely."

"She was a drunk."

Jackson raised an eyebrow, reminding me he'd just caught me drinking alone in my bedroom.

I lowered my voice. "My dad and Libby drank together like that before he died. And after he died, she just kept on drinking." At least until I left home for good. Then, only then, did she finally get help.

"Okay, so she wasn't there for you. Neither of your parents were there for you. I get it. But maybe she can be here for you now."

"You don't understand. Dad was an angry drunk. I was so scared of him, Jackson. He would yell and throw things. He would shake me, hit me. Libby didn't protect me." At least not until the end.

We both listened to the water pump click on as my mother flushed the toilet in the bathroom.

Jackson ran a hand through his greying hair. "This was a mistake. I shouldn't have presumed to bring her here."

"You didn't know."

"I knew enough." From our beer-fuelled conversations about our families on poker night: Ben's father, who had pissed off when he was a kid; Jackson's mother, who had spent more time with her horses than with Jackson; and then there were my drunken father and mother, though I hadn't told Jackson or Ben the half of it.

"Do you want me to find a cabin for her to stay in?" Jackson asked. "Or get her back on the bus?"

"The next bus back won't leave until tomorrow afternoon."

"I guess she could stay with me."

"I wouldn't inflict Libby on you, or anyone else."

"I'm so sorry, Piper. I just wanted to make sure you had someone here when—"

But before Jackson could finish, my gaze shifted past him to the view beyond, and I stepped up to the patio door. On the lake, emerging one by one through the haze of heavy snow, were the boats, all the boats, all the men and women in the boats, the searchers making their way home.

# 19

I gestured at the flotilla of boats sliding over the black water toward us, snow falling all around them. "Why are they coming back in?" I asked Jackson. When he didn't immediately reply, I said it again more firmly. "Jackson, why is everyone coming back in?"

"You want coffee?" he asked. He held up an empty cup.

"No. I want to know what's going on."

He poured himself a cup as my mother joined us in the kitchen.

"Libby, you want anything?" Jackson asked.

"Maybe later. After."

"After what?" I looked from my mother to Jackson. "Tell me what's happening! Why is everyone coming in?"

He and Libby exchanged a glance. This wasn't the first time they had spoken. Jackson had been talking to her over the phone. "I waited until I was sure Libby was on her way to the house before I called everyone in," he said.

"What do you mean?" I pressed my fingers to the table. "Jackson, what are you doing?"

He put his cup on the counter, tapped a spoon against his hand. "Piper, the snow is too heavy and will only get worse—"

"You're stopping for the night? But if Ben's still out there in that—"

"It's not just for tonight, Piper."

"What are you *saying*?"

He gave me a sorrowful look. *You know exactly what I'm saying.*

Libby wrapped an arm around me. But I kept my eyes on Jackson. "You're not calling off the search."

"I've asked the volunteers to stand down, yes."

"Jackson, you can't—"

Jackson raised a hand. "Piper, please understand this was the most difficult decision I've ever had to make." His face twisted in anguish. "Ben was like a brother to me. You know that. I would never give up on him if I thought there was a chance of finding him alive. But we've already covered all the ground that we could safely reach. Today the warmer temperatures turned the snow to mush. We were postholing up there." Sinking knee-deep into the soft snow, he meant. "Everyone is worn out. We've been at it twenty-four hours a day since Saturday, in tough winter conditions, on steep, rocky terrain, even though we found Ben's capsized boat on our first night, even though we know what happened to him."

I shook my head. "We don't know for sure he was in his boat. The drone footage showed him—" I ran both hands through my hair. "For god's sake, he's only been missing four days. We can't give up now."

"Piper, we found Ben's radio floating on the lake this morning."

"His radio?" Ben's work radio was waterproof and floated, as he spent so much of his time on the water. He wore it fixed to his vest or belt.

"And then, this afternoon, we found his coat in the water."

I sank into a chair and covered my mouth as panic rose up my torso. "*What?*"

"Chase found it."

"No, no, you're wrong. He didn't drown. He must have just taken off his coat, left it in the boat. He—he didn't have his life jacket on.

And he would have if he was on the water. And he left the drone onshore. He would have picked it up if he was coming home."

"Or he was in a hurry to check something out and jumped in the boat, thinking he'd come back. Everything points to that. His capsized boat. His life jacket and coat in the water. He kept his radio on him at all times. The only way his radio was in the water was . . ." If he had been in the water too.

"But when I saw him at the Hourglass—"

"What do you mean, you saw him?" Libby asked.

Jackson shook his head in exasperation. "Piper, we've talked about this. Ben wasn't really there."

"No, hear me out." I touched my fingers to my lips. "I've been thinking. The way Ben looked at me. Like he was telling me something."

"You mean, his *ghost* was telling you something?" Libby asked. "Like where his body is?" She put a hand on my arm. "Piper, do you hear yourself?"

"We've been over and over that area," Jackson said. "We found nothing."

"I know. But I've got this feeling." I tapped my chest. "I know he's still out there."

"We've searched farther than Ben could have possibly gone on foot. I'm sorry, Piper. But we've done all we could."

"But what about the break-in?"

"Someone broke into your house?" Libby asked.

"There's more going on," I said. "I know it."

Jackson put out a hand. "Now, you're not going to start blaming Owen—"

"Owen?" Libby turned to Jackson, lost. "Who's Owen?"

Jackson sighed heavily through his nose. "Piper, I understand how hard this is. When people go missing, their families often come up with all kinds of theories to explain what happened to them. But I'm convinced the answer is simple: Ben's body is in the lake. We found his capsized boat, his life jacket, his radio, his coat." He paused. "I'm absolutely certain now that he did drown."

"No," I said, shaking my head rapidly. "I know he didn't drown. His drone was on the shore. We saw him climb that hill. You can't call off the search."

"We've scoured every inch of the mountain from the Boulders to the ridge and beyond. He's not there."

"Then we'll search again!"

"With the accumulation of snow in the search area, I can't justify putting my crew and the other volunteers at risk when we know Ben was lost in the water."

"You're wrong."

Jackson took me by the shoulders. "Piper, please, just listen to me."

I pushed him out of the way and slid open the patio door to the deck. Then I waved my hands over my head at the volunteers who had started pulling their smaller boats onto shore. "You can't stop!" I cried. "Ben is still out there. You need to go back." But as Jackson came out behind me, an unsettling silence fell on the volunteers. No one said a word. Over their heads, a raven circled.

Maggie stepped out from below the deck. "Piper," she said sadly.

"You can't stop!" I cried again. "You've got to keep searching."

Jackson wrapped an arm around me. "We've already put these men's and women's lives at risk. With another storm coming on, we can't ask more of them."

I shook both hands beside my head. "He's over there some-where, on land. I know he is. I saw him on the beach, and again at the Hourglass."

"You saw *someone*, or *something* on the beach," Jackson said quietly. "As for what you saw at the Boulders—"

"Jackson, *please*, we can't give up on Ben."

"Piper, the time has come to accept—"

But I pulled away from him. "He's not dead! Ben's not dead. He's out there. He needs us. We have to find him!"

"We won't stop looking. But Piper, the next step in the search . . ." His voice shook a little. "The RCMP URT arrives tomorrow."

"The *what?*"

"The underwater recovery team. They'll search the lake with sonar. It's a recovery mission now, for Ben's body."

"No. No. No." I stumbled down the slippery steps of the deck toward the crowd of volunteers standing silently on the beach, pushing them out of the way, barely aware of the snow under my bare feet.

"Piper!" Jackson called after me.

One of the volunteers tried to stop me, but I pushed past him into the water, to drag one of the aluminum boats off the beach, my feet numb now with the cold. I jumped in the vessel just as Jackson reached me, grasping the side of the boat to stop me from going out farther. "What are you doing?" he asked.

"Going out to find Ben."

"In bare feet?"

I looked down at my reddened feet in the floor of the boat.

"And no jacket," he added.

It was only then that I became aware of how I must look, how distraught, how lost. I felt suddenly woozy, a red cloud covered my vision, the world slid north, and Jackson, standing calf-high in freezing water beside the boat, caught me as I fell.

"He can't be gone," I whispered. "He can't be. He's not gone."

"Shush now," he said, as he would to a child. He lifted me from the boat and carried me back across the beach to the deck. I wondered if he had picked up his dying wife like this, when she was cancer-riddled, her body wasted. As one of the volunteers pulled the aluminum boat back to shore and secured it, the crowd of men and women turned away from Jackson and me as they might from an intimate act. This private moment of grief.

Jackson took the deck stairs slowly, labouring a little under my weight. His wet socked foot slipped on ice, and I clung to him as he tottered before regaining his balance. Libby slid open the patio door of the bedroom. "Put her down on the bed," she told him.

"I need to talk to Noah," I said. "I need to let him know."

"I'll do it," Jackson said. "It's probably better coming from me in any case."

He was likely right. Noah had known Jackson far longer than he'd known me, since the boy was small. Jackson was an uncle to him. And I knew I was in no shape to offer my stepson the care he needed right now.

"You can talk to him later," Jackson added. "Pull yourself together first."

Jackson rolled me onto the bed, and I curled up, my head to my knees.

Libby patted his arm. "I'll take care of her," she said. "You go take care of Noah."

Jackson hesitated by my side. "I'll arrive at about eight in the morning tomorrow," he said, "before the dive team gets here. So you don't have to deal with them directly."

"I appreciate it."

"It's the least I can do." He left, closing the bedroom door behind him. I heard him knock on Noah's door, and then their muted voices before Jackson closed that door too.

A wave of pain coursed through my body, and I heaved it up in great, soundless sobs, my face contorted, my mouth wide open. Libby brought me Ben's ugly green sweater, perhaps thinking it was my own, and I clutched it as my mother sat beside me on the bed. She took my hand, cupping it in both her own. My mother's older, veined hands.

"You *will* survive this," she told me. "It won't feel like that now. But you will survive." She put a hand on my forehead, as if offering a blessing, then ran her hand over my hair, something she had done after my father's drunken rages. Outside, there was the hum of many voices, the rumble of trucks as the volunteers lined up at the boat launch to collect their vessels. They were leaving, giving up. They believed Ben was dead.

# WEDNESDAY

# 20

I slept fitfully, sliding in and out of dreams. Dreams of water, of sinking, drowning. I woke gasping and sat up. The room was dark, though the drone on my dresser glowed green, indicating it was charged. I threw back the blankets to sit on the edge of the bed, thinking I would use the bathroom. But as I stood, I saw a dark figure silhouetted on the deck outside, a shadow, the black shape of a man. I knew him immediately.

"Ben?"

He just stood there, staring across the lake to the far shore.

I slid open the door, expecting he would disappear, as he had in my past visions, but he remained.

"Ben."

He looked at me over his shoulder. "Find me," he said, his eye glazed, dead, as my father's had been in the dream I'd had so many years before. Then he was gone. Just gone.

I sat up in bed and gasped, my heart hammering in my chest. I half expected Ben to be there, on the deck, as he had been in my dream. It all felt so real.

*Find me.*

I flung off the covers and staggered over to the patio door to step, barefoot, out onto the snowy deck where Ben had stood in my dream. His presence was so tangible that when I closed my eyes, I *knew* he was with me.

"Ben," I said out loud.

Was he still alive? Or was his spirit simply asking me to find his body?

Or was I losing my mind?

The sky, just before dawn, was clear and crisp, the air achingly cold. The stars above shone so brightly over the snow-covered landscape. An idyllic winter scene. But in a few hours the RCMP dive team, the *recovery* team, would be here to do their grid search of the lake, using a boat equipped with sonar, scanning for Ben's body. His *body*. The truth was, I didn't want them to find Ben's body. If they didn't find him, then I could believe he was still out there, alive. I knew, now, that the thought was irrational. Jackson, the other members of the search and rescue team, the RCMP, the whole community believed Ben was dead. I had seen his ghost. So why couldn't I shake this feeling that he *wasn't* gone?

Denial, my mother had told me. A stage of grief. That's all.

And yet, Ben had said *Find me.* I had seen him at the Hourglass. He was there, somewhere.

I marched back inside, closing the patio door behind me, and clicked on the light to dress quickly, gearing up in my thermal underwear, my wool sweater, snow pants and jacket, and pocketed my ski gloves.

I put on a pot of coffee, threw together a few snacks and hastily scribbled a note for Noah and my mother: *Searching the Boulders again for Ben. I'll be back before dark.* Always leave a travel plan, Ben had told me. I knew they would send Jackson after me. But maybe I could put in a few hours of searching before he arrived to stop me.

I packed a Thermos of hot coffee and my snacks into a backpack and quietly left the house. The engine for Ben's aluminum boat had been trashed when the boat capsized. It would have to be flushed and the oil drained and changed. I suspected it might never work again. So I slid my hiking poles and gear into my kayak and dragged it across the snow and down to the water. Then I climbed in and pushed off, breaking the thin sheet of ice that had formed around shore overnight.

I followed the path of moonlight across the lake, paddling in near silence, hearing only the hush of water as my boat cut through it. This wasn't the first time I had kayaked at night. Ben and I often took the boats out after dark, even in winter, revisiting our honeymoon, when we had kayaked side by side through the bioluminescent phytoplankton off the Sunshine Coast, the tiny creatures' fanciful blue glow stirred up by the movement of our boats and paddles through the water. An aura of blue had surrounded our kayaks, and Ben and I had grinned at each other over and over, giddy in the wonder of it. I'd been travelling through the stars of the Milky Way, through eternity, with my love. Now, on this winter night, I felt Ben's presence almost as keenly, as the snow-covered mountains glowed in the moonlight and the universe was reflected in the still lake. Once again we were paddling together through the stars.

As I approached the far shore, the pink of first light peeked over the mountain, and as if I had willed him there, I saw a dark figure, a man, standing at the edge of the forest.

"Ben?" I called. Then louder, "Ben!" My voice bounced back to me from the face of the cliff, as Ben's had the day he asked me to marry him. *Ben, Ben, Ben.*

I listened, but there was no reply, except for a coyote's howl. The figure loped into the bushes like a sasquatch. It was the Green Man, then.

A chill ran through me. I would be all alone in the forest with the bushman. And no one yet knew I had left the house. I started to turn the kayak, to head home, but then the thought occurred to me: the Green Man would know this forest better than Jackson or Owen or the SAR crew. And he was always watching. If anyone knew what had happened to Ben, he did.

I swung the kayak back to shore and, after easing into the rocky shallows, I got out and pulled it onto the thin strip of snowy beach, tied it to a boulder. Then, carrying my backpack and hiking poles, I searched the shoreline in the early-morning twilight for footprints until I found them. A man's footprints, from large boots. I stuck my poles in the frozen snow and cupped my hands to my face. "Hello!" I shouted, my voice ricocheting off the cliff face above. "I saw you standing on the shore. I know you saw me. I just want to talk to you."

Somewhere close, an owl called back. *Who, who.* Otherwise, there was only silence.

I adjusted my backpack, took a deep breath as I summoned my courage and launched forward using my hiking poles, following the footsteps up the treed and rocky slope.

"Hello?"

It was so much darker here, under the forest canopy. I pulled a headlamp out of my pack and put it on. The steep slope was blanketed with snow, but I doggedly followed the footsteps up the trail through the boulders and trees, stopping every few metres to call and listen for a reply, on alert also for any sign of the grizzly, her large, clawed footprints or scat. As I climbed, the sun also rose, setting the sky aglow, and still I followed the footprints ever higher up the mountain. I hadn't anticipated following the Green Man, so I hadn't thought to bring snowshoes. As the trees transitioned from the cedar and hemlock forest to fir and spruce, the snow grew deeper, more difficult to navigate. Still, I pushed on and on, up the slope, stepping into the bushman's footprints, eyeing the ridge above me, calling for him. But I saw no one through the trees.

And then the trail ended.

Where had he gone? Had he doubled back? Or slipped off the trail I followed without me noticing?

"Hello?" I called out. "Anyone here?" I was far up the slope now, high above the Boulders and giant cedars and the thin stretch of beach below. I could only catch glimpses of the lake through the trees, the hill was so heavily forested. "Hello?" I called again.

Hearing nothing but the chatter of chickadees, I doubled back, following my own trail, and the trail of the man I'd seen, back down the slope.

Then something caught my eye, a glint in the forest off the trail. I navigated around the trees, hanging on to boughs as I worked my way through the snow to get a better look at it.

Bizarrely, in the middle of this snowy wilderness, and tucked beneath the protective canopy of a large fir, a much smaller spruce was freshly decorated in garish silver garlands and silver and red Christmas decorations. There was even a small string of white LED lights on it, battery powered. A shaft of sunlight slid through the trees onto this small section of the forest, and this Christmas tree. Fine crystals of frost drifted down on it, sparkling. A scene from a Christmas card. Forgetting, for an instant, my task at hand, I laughed in wonder, pulled out my phone and took a photo of it. Then I pushed forward through the snow to the Christmas tree and lifted a glittering silver ball from a branch. It appeared to be freshly decorated. Why would anyone put this here, where no one would see it?

I experienced a childish flood of magical thinking, grief thinking. *It was Ben*, I thought. Ben had put this tree here, for me, to make up for everything. For disappearing on me.

But then my foot hit something hard, shaking away the snow, and, looking down, I found a cross built of rock, fairly recently constructed, I thought, as it had no moss growing on it. I brushed the remaining snow from it and found a glittering silver necklace with a cross hanging from it. I pulled more snow away and found a teddy bear.

And then that feeling of being watched slithered up my neck.

I swung around. "Hello?" I called again. "I just want to talk. About Ben, my husband, Ben. The man the searchers were looking for?" The bushman must have seen them all, heard them talking about Ben, as they invaded his forest. "Have you seen Ben? Do you know what happened to him?"

But on the slope above me, the huge, dark shadow that rose up wasn't the Green Man. A grizzly stood on her hind legs to sniff the air. The cinnamon sow. She must have returned immediately after the search ended the day before. Startled out of hibernation by that felled cedar, she was very likely hungry. There wouldn't be much for her to eat out here this time of year.

Except maybe Ben. And now me.

The bear huffed and dropped heavily to her feet, shuddering the snow from the small trees surrounding her, and then, head down, ears back, she barrelled through the snow down the hill, directly toward me.

"*Shit.*"

I checked my hip for the bear spray. But in my groggy state and haste to leave the house that morning, I hadn't thought to bring the spray or banger. They were tucked into the holster I usually wore in the bush, hanging in the hallway. I was defenseless against this animal. I couldn't outrun her and there was no time to climb a tree. In any case, a grizzly could, in theory, climb up after me. I had my hiking poles, but did I really think I could fight off a bear with these sticks?

Panicked, I did exactly what Ben had always told me not to do: run. I turned my back on the creature and bounded awkwardly down the slope, but the snow was so much deeper here and I lost both my footing and my grip on my hiking poles, tumbling and then skidding, sliding downhill on the slippery fabric of my jacket and ski pants. A younger fir loomed in front of me as I skidded toward it feet first. But instead of hitting it, I slipped down into a cavity in the snow at the base of the tree, where branches had shielded the space around the trunk from the heavy snowfall. As I fell in, the snow from the tree above tumbled down on me. A tree well. A death trap. I would sink deeper and deeper until I suffocated in snow, just as I would in water. It would be almost impossible to rescue myself. Nevertheless, I floundered within the tree well, trying to escape as I hung on to a lower branch, but I only sank farther.

I was trapped and sinking deeper.

And the grizzly was right behind me.

# 21

I struggled to pull myself out of the tree well, but with every movement, the snow only sucked me down, collapsing over my chest, so that my legs and torso became even more confined.

On the hill right above me, the bear huffed and barked as it charged toward me like an enormous dog. I whimpered in fear and panic.

And then I heard it.

*Hug me.* Ben's voice, from behind me, right at my ear. *Breathe deep to calm yourself.* I stopped moving, listened, hoping to hear his voice again. Then I hugged the tree trunk to keep myself from sinking. Within the embrace of the tree well, as in Ben's hug, I took a deep breath and purposefully relaxed my body. The sinking stalled and I hung, suspended, in the tree well.

Trapped facing the lake, I could hear and smell the bear right behind me. People think a bear will smell foul, rank, or at least like a dog. But they don't, most of the time. They smell sweet, like grass, as their diet is mostly vegetation and berries. But this grizzly, forced to eat what she could find, had nosed her way into carrion, and her breath was foul with death.

She had eaten something already dead.

Had she eaten *Ben*?

I clung to the tree and held my breath as the foul stench grew stronger. The bear woofed within only a metre of me.

I slowly looked over my shoulder to see her there, right there, eyeing me. *Don't make eye contact,* Ben had told me. I quickly averted my gaze. But the bear sniffed my hair, clawed the sleeve of my jacket, trying to get to me under the low-hanging branches.

*Oh god.*

And then a rifle shot rang out in the forest and the grizzly startled. Another shot cracked, buzzing the foliage of the next tree, and the bear grunted and bounded away. A third shot and the sow was gone, lost in the dark brush of the forest.

I clung to the tree, gasping. *Hug me,* Ben's voice had said. *Breathe deep to calm yourself.* I hung on to the tree and breathed deeply until my heart settled.

But who was out there with a gun? The Green Man. It had to be him.

"Hello?" I called tentatively. Then louder, "Hello?"

There was a hush as snow shimmered to the ground from a branch above.

"Are you there?" I cried. "I slid into this tree well. I can't climb out. Can you help me?" I paused. "Hello?"

But after repeated calls, I got no answer.

I rocked my body back and forth within the tree well as much as I could, hoping to open a gap in the snow, to free myself, but the motion only knocked more snow into the well, brought more snow from the tree above down on my head. I let out a sob. The rough bark bristled against my face. Minutes ticked by and my pleas for help became more and more desperate. As the morning sun slid up the sky, chickadees sang their lonely winter song. A crow landed on a nearby spruce and peered down at me, curious.

I knew as temperatures rose the snow would only become wetter, the mass above me more likely to slide down, engulfing me. I could be buried alive before Jackson found me.

I craned my neck to check for any sign of the grizzly, and then I saw a green form standing to the side of one of the trees on the slope above me. The Green Man. He had likely been there all this time, watching me. Dressed in camouflage, his face painted green, his hair stuck with twigs and leaves, he blended right into the foliage around him. I could barely make him out. The same form I had seen in the mist up at Hunter's Creek just before Ben met me there. I wondered how close he'd been when I was out in the forest. There must have been times when I looked right at him but couldn't see him. But this time, there was a glint of dark metal in his hands. A gun.

*He's dangerous*, Ben had told me. But then, the Green Man had shot at that bear to protect me. And stuck in this tree well, what choice did I have other than to ask for his help?

"I can see you," I said. "Can you give me a hand?" I paused. "I could die here."

The figure hesitated, then slid the rifle into a shoulder holster, tossed a snowboard to the snow and slid down the slope toward me, too fast. He was an adept snowboarder. But in his camouflage getup, with his bush of messy hair and beard, he seemed almost comical, like a sasquatch on a snowboard.

He skidded to a stop right in front of me, throwing up a wash of snow crystals. Ben's and Jackson's descriptions of him matched what I saw now. Green camouflage pants and jacket, green face paint. Ferns and twigs of boxwood and salal stuck out of his long hair and his ragged, earth-caked clothes. With his face concealed by the face paint and leaves, he did, in fact, look like the Green Man sculptures found in European churches, images of the forest spirits that lingered into medieval times from a pagan past.

I flinched as he pulled the rifle from his holster. Did he intend to threaten me with that gun? But then he turned the rifle on end and used the butt to pull snow away from me.

"Is that grizzly still around?" I asked.

He didn't answer.

"Did you hit it?"

When he spoke, his voice was younger than I would have expected. He was still in his twenties, I realized. "Not going to shoot her," he said. "A female, likely pregnant." Then, under his breath, he whispered, *"Pregnant, eggplant."*

"I guess I should thank you for scaring her off," I said. "I don't think I would be alive right now if you hadn't."

He stopped digging, the butt of the rifle hovering over the snow, then bent back to his task.

"The tree poachers disturbed that bear, didn't they?" I asked. "They brought her out of hibernation when they felled that tree. Her den was close."

The Green Man dug on as if I had said nothing at all. This close, he gave off a musky odour. I imagined he hadn't bathed since the weather turned. In warmer weather, there had been reports of him bathing in the lake, with soap, the bubbles churning in the water along this shore. His camouflage was rubbed with dirt, and it seemed he had purposefully stuck leaves and twigs in his wild mass of curly brown hair. The green face paint covered the entirety of his face and made the whites of his eyes and his teeth seem that much whiter. The Green Man. Already a legendary figure in the region. But now that I was this close, there was something familiar about his face.

"Do I know you?" I asked, squinting at him.

The question seemed to set him off. He shook his head rapidly and scratched his matt of messy hair. "No, no. No one knows me. No."

"Okay."

His eyes slid everywhere but at me as he rocked back and forth on his feet. Finally, he seemed to settle and went back to digging.

I watched him for a few minutes before I tried again. "Did you decorate that Christmas tree?"

His eyes flicked to me and away. "She liked Christmas," he said. "She put up the tree early every year, in November. *Ember. Dismember.*"

She. She *liked* Christmas. Past tense. "You built that memorial. The things there, the necklace, the teddy bear—who did they belong to?"

He pointed a dirty finger at me. His nails were chewed to the quick. "You leave that alone!" he shouted. "You don't touch that."

He eyed me until I nodded, and then he bent back to pulling the snow away. "That's Andrea's," he mumbled.

"Andrea." Who was Andrea? Then I remembered. "Andrea Peterson. She was killed here, while she was bouldering." Killed on her honeymoon by that grizzly Ben and Jackson had never been able to trap, the sow that had just come after me. The bear had also taken several swipes at her husband, Elijah. I had accompanied Ben on one of his trips to the hospital to see the young man. The Green Man, the bushman who had been haunting these woods, was Elijah Peterson, who had lost his bride to the bear in this forest during their honeymoon. He had not only watched his young wife die, he had watched the grizzly eat her. How does anyone escape something like that in one piece?

They don't.

He had been a paramedic before the bear attack, and his wife a nurse. He had abandoned everything, his life, to squat on Crown land, to live where his bride had been killed. Did he see her ghost here, I wondered, as I had seen Ben? Was that what kept him here? Given everything I had gone through over the last several days, I knew it was. Grief had trapped him here, in this forest, where it had happened.

Was that what was happening to me?

The snow beneath me shifted suddenly, and I momentarily lost my grip on the trunk as I slipped down into the tree well. Elijah's digging immediately grew more laboured and desperate. He began to attack the snow with the butt of the rifle, grunting as he did so. I turned my face, worried he would accidently hit me with the gun.

"Stop." I raised my voice. "Elijah, stop!"

He stepped back, holding the rifle in both hands as if he was about to use it. "Don't call me that name," he said, his voice angry now. "No one is supposed to know who I am."

"They call you the Green Man," I said.

"I heard that."

*Where?* I wondered. Did he have a radio stolen from one of the cabins? Had he listened to a local news report during one of his many break-ins?

"Green Man," he said, apparently echoing me, and then, not bothering to whisper his word salad anymore, he said, "He Man. Masked Man. Bat Man."

"Do you remember me?" I asked, cutting him off.

Still holding the gun in one hand, he reached out, hesitated, then ran his fingers down my cheek. They smelled of shit. I recoiled and he snatched his hand back. "You're the wife," he said, and went back to digging.

"Yes, I'm Ben's wife," I said. "The officer's wife. He found you following the grizzly attack."

Elijah stopped. "He took care of me, after—"

"He got you to the hospital."

"He visited me."

Ben had arranged to pick up a few things from Elijah's apartment, to make his hospital stay more comfortable, and he made regular visits to Elijah until his release. I had gone with him the one time, bringing flowers and chocolates, but then Elijah had stared out the window and told us how, as a child, he had watched his older brother die in a car accident, caused by his father's drunk driving, and how similar his brother's body and his wife's had appeared at their deaths, broken and bloody, their faces torn beyond recognition. He stated it all in a matter-of-fact tone, with little emotion in his voice, and in far too much detail. The skin of his brother's cheek pulled back, exposing bone and teeth. His wife's torso ripped open by the grizzly.

"I ran," Elijah had told us. "I ran and left her there."

"You were injured," Ben had said. The bear had clawed Elijah's chest, his thigh. "And Andrea was already dead. There was little you could have done."

"I ran," Elijah said again, staring out the window. "I should have saved her."

I had put a hand to Elijah's arm and squeezed, but then excused myself and rushed to the bathroom across the hall to spit up into the toilet. Then I went outside to wait for Ben in the truck. I didn't go back to see Elijah after that. His story, and the aging hospital corridors and rooms, had brought back too many bloody memories of my own.

During Ben's later visits, Elijah stopped talking to him or the hospital staff. He only stared at the photograph of himself and his wife on his wedding day. He seemed to have shut down completely. But Ben continued to visit anyway, chatting about the news, or the animals he'd seen with his drone while out on patrol. I objected once to the time he was taking out of our lives for this stranger, worrying that Ben was perhaps in some way reliving the long hospital stay his first wife had endured before her death. Ben didn't try to counter my argument or explain himself. He said only, "This young man lost the woman he loves. He lost her in the worst possible way, and now he has no one."

On his release from the hospital, Elijah had disappeared. When

166

Ben stopped in at his apartment, the building manager told him that Elijah had abandoned the place, leaving behind almost everything he owned. Ben, worrying over Elijah's mental health, had phoned Elijah's place of work and was told the young man had never gone back. He had no family, no forwarding address. Ben had to abandon his search for him, assuming he had moved away. Given Elijah's mental state, Ben had sometimes wondered if the young man had ended up on the streets.

Now here he was, saving my life in this forest, digging me out of this hole.

"Ben took care of me," Elijah said again. "I owe him."

"He's missing."

Elijah kept on digging.

I said, "You must have seen the searchers hunting for him."

He glanced briefly at me, acknowledging he had, of course, seen them, even though they hadn't seen him. He was a master at hiding. He'd managed to elude the RCMP searches for him.

"Have you seen Ben?" I asked. "Or any trace of him?" I paused to scan his face. How far gone was he? Had Ben stumbled onto him in the woods? If Elijah didn't want to be found, to be known, had he harmed Ben to keep his identity a secret? "Maybe you know what happened to him?" I asked.

He stopped digging and his eyes drifted past me, to the forest beyond. "There are so many bears," he said. "Bears' hairs caught in snares."

My heart skipped a beat. "What do you mean? Did that grizzly attack him? Elijah? Look at me."

His eyes slid up to my face and away again.

"Did the grizzly kill my husband?"

He shook his head over and over, repeating himself as he went back to digging. "So many bears. So many bears. So many bears."

Bears. What did he mean by *bears*? Did he mean dangers? There were so many dangers? His rhyming, nonsensical speech was clearly a symptom of disordered thinking. Was he undergoing a psychotic episode? He must be, to live like this out here. I knew that trauma, whether in childhood or present-day, was a risk factor in schizoaffective disorder, and he had witnessed the horrific deaths of both his brother and his wife.

"Elijah, if you know anything about Ben, please tell me."

But he shook his head. "No. No. I won't tell. I won't tell a spell." He eyed me. "I saw you. You were out here with the bear. You know the bear. You were plotting with the bear. No, no. Can't tell."

*Plotting* with the bear? "Is the bear a man?" I asked, scanning his face. "Do you mean you saw me with the man who hurt Ben?"

Owen.

He nodded repeatedly, though I wasn't sure if it was in response to my question or a nervous tic. "I won't let the bear hurt anyone else," he said. "It's my job, to take care of people. Bob's job. Heartthrob."

"You were a paramedic," I said, trying to make sense of what he was telling me.

He dug furiously. "It's my job and I didn't save her."

His wife. He didn't save his wife. Did he feel this was his penance, then, to live in this forest and protect others? Perhaps he *had* been watching over me all this time.

"But you do know what happened to Ben, don't you?" I asked. He shook his head. "I won't let it happen again. Won't. Won't let it float, float in a boat."

"Ben's boat?" I asked. "Elijah, what won't you let happen again?" Elijah stopped digging and stood up straight. He listened.

"What is it?" I asked. "Is it the grizzly?" And then I heard a boat engine making its way across the water. I squinted to see what

I could of the lake through the branches. Was it Jackson? *Please let it be Jackson*. And then the boat came into view, the RCMP search boat. If I called, they would never hear me at this distance or over the engine, but surely Jackson was on his way to find me. Unless he never went inside the house, and Noah and my mother were still sleeping.

Elijah gripped the rifle and glared at me, his face tense with anger. "You brought more bears here," he said, as if I had betrayed him. *Bears*. Not cops. So, to Elijah, the word *bear* did mean any kind of danger.

"No, they're not after you," I said. "That's the recovery team. They're using sonar to scan for Ben's body in the water."

He slung his rifle into his holster and slipped his feet into the bindings on his snowboard.

The snow shifted under me, and I slid down again, undoing the work Elijah had done to free me. "Wait, Elijah. Please, you've got to tell me. What happened to Ben?"

But Elijah took off sideways down the hill on his snowboard, away from the trampled path, and quickly disappeared into the bush. Why the hell was he rushing downhill, toward the Boulders, toward shore, if he wanted to avoid the cops?

"Elijah!" I cried out. But he was gone.

I watched the RCMP boat do a slow turn on the water and head back across the lake, scanning the water with sonar in a grid search. They weren't coming to rescue me from this tree well. I struggled again, trying to loosen my torso from the snow's grip, but I only slid down farther. I craned my neck to look all around me, panic rising.

The grizzly was still out there.

# 22

The minutes ticked by. I had no idea how long I waited in the tree well, listening for the grizzly's return. Every rustle through the trees sounded like the huffing of the bear, and snowfall from the branches above seemed to mark her approach. I startled over and over again, terrified. Somewhere close by, two trees rubbed against each other, generating a shriek.

And then I heard another boat, the engine smaller, with more whine, and finally saw it far down below through the branches. The SAR inflatable speeding toward the beach. Jackson. *Oh, thank god.* And someone was with him. Likely Noah. But would they find me up here? As Jackson cut the engine and slid the boat silently to the rocky shore, I lost sight of them. I called and called, but I was so far up the mountain.

After what seemed like hours, there was a sharp crack and bang as Jackson set off a bear banger. I squirmed within the snow, desperately trying to reach a dead branch to bang a nearby tree in response, to let them know where I was, but before I could reach one, I settled even farther down the tree well. *Shit.*

"Jackson?" I cried. "Noah!" I had a whistle on me, in the pocket of my coat, but it was under the snow that gripped me. I held the trunk of the tree tighter, and called and called, until my voice grew hoarse.

Just when I was about to give up hope, I heard Jackson shout. "Piper?" And then, echoing him, Noah called my name too.

"Jackson, Noah! I'm here! Up the slope. But I'm stuck in a tree well. I can't get free."

"We're coming," Jackson called back. "Hang on."

Within this tree well, my arms around the trunk of the tree, hanging on was all I *could* do. I called periodically and Jackson and Noah called back, reassuring me they were hiking in the right direction. And then, finally, I saw them both through the trees on the slope below me, Noah's blue toque and Jackson's orange-red search and rescue jacket flashing between branches.

"Jackson, Noah! Up here!"

I could tell from the set of Noah's shoulders that he was angry with me. I had worried him. I imagine I had worried Jackson and my mother too.

On reaching me, Jackson threw his backpack on the snow and unzipped it. His nose was red. Frost covered his walrus moustache. Even though Noah was bundled up in his ski suit, his cheeks were red from the cold.

"I can't tell you how glad I am to see you," I said.

"Are you hurt?" Jackson asked.

"No." Just cold and scared.

"You seriously freaked us out," Noah said. "Your mom went into hysterics when she found your note. What were you thinking, coming out here by yourself? Especially after . . ."

Especially after the way I had acted the day before. Jumping into that boat barefoot in front of all the volunteers, demanding that they continue the search. I felt mortified thinking of it.

"I didn't mean to frighten you."

"Well, you did."

To express his own disappointment, Jackson simply gave me *the look* as he pulled out a collapsible shovel. Then he traced Elijah's efforts with its blade. "Someone was digging here."

"The Green Man. Jackson, he's Elijah Peterson. His wife was Andrea."

Jackson started digging snow away from me, from the slope below. "Huh. That explains a lot."

"You're lucky he didn't hurt you," Noah said as he dug alongside Jackson with gloved hands. "I heard he's armed now."

"He is, but he used the rifle to scare off the grizzly."

"The Cinnamon Girl?" Noah asked. The name Ben had given the bear. Worry replaced the anger on his face. "She attacked?"

"I was running from her when I fell into this tree well." I showed him the claw marks on my sleeve. "She nearly had me too. Elijah fired off a few shots to scare her, and then he tried to dig me out before the RCMP boat scared *him* off. Jackson, he saved my life." Still holding the trunk, I put one hand to my cheek, remembering the Green Man's unsettling touch. I shivered it off. "He has a memorial up there, to his wife," I said, pointing behind me. "He even decorated a Christmas tree for her. He didn't want me anywhere near it. He's been living out here all that time, to be near his wife, I think. Where she died."

"Is that why you came out here?" Jackson asked. "To be near Ben?"

"No, I came to *find* Ben. Or some clue as to what happened to him."

Jackson dug deeper, tossing the snow down the steep slope. "What did you hope to find that the searchers haven't?" he asked. "We've gone over every square inch of this mountainside."

"We missed Elijah's memorial to his wife. During the search, no one stumbled across the stone cross he made. And no one ran into

Elijah either. When I saw him, I thought maybe he might know something. That's why I followed him up here."

Jackson held my gaze as he continued to shovel snow, his face grim. "Promise me you won't go out into this forest alone to look for Ben again," he said. When I didn't immediately answer, he stopped digging and repeated himself. "Promise me you won't do anything stupid."

I felt a sting in my stomach. That was what Ben had said to me up at Hunter's Creek before I marched off to confront Owen at the diner, starting the cascade of events that had led to Ben's disappearance. *Don't do anything stupid.*

"Promise me," Jackson said again.

"I'll try my best," I said.

Noah stopped digging and stood back. "I can't lose you too. You're the only family I have now."

I grinned to take the edge off. "I'm not your only family. You have Grandma now too."

Noah made a face. "*Grandma?* Can't I call her Libby?"

"I do," I said.

"She's not, like, going to live with us, is she?"

I laughed a little. "No."

"Good."

Now that they had shovelled enough snow away to expose my torso, Jackson and Noah each took one of my arms and pulled me free from the tree well, sliding me headfirst down the slope toward them like a seal slipping into the water. Then Noah helped me up.

"You okay to make the hike back down?" Jackson asked me.

I stood, my legs shaky, and fingered snow out of the tops of my boots, shook it from my toque, the back of my neck. "Yeah, I think so." I glanced back up the hill. I sure as hell wasn't going back for my hiking poles. Not today.

173

Jackson packed his gear and then, keeping an eye out for the grizzly and Elijah, he led us back down the steep trail through the trees to the beach. I leaned on Noah much of the way, as my legs kept giving out, and stopped frequently to take a rest. Once we reached the SAR boat, Jackson got me seated and wrapped a blanket around me. Noah climbed in beside me and spun open a Thermos, offering me a cup. I wrinkled my nose at the smell. Chamomile tea.

"Libby—*Grandma*—thought this would be better for you than coffee right now," he said. "She said it would ease your nerves."

*Funny*, I thought. *She used to say the same thing about a shot of whiskey.*

Jackson tied my kayak to his boat. Then he pushed us out, jumping into the SAR inflatable with wet boots. He started the engine.

As we returned home across the lake, I huddled under the blanket, nursing the hot cup of tea, shivering. We all lifted a hand as we passed the RCMP boat. Would they find Ben's body with sonar, a hazy grey but unmistakable image of a human form on the bottom of the lake? Jackson seemed certain of it. Everyone had already accepted that Ben had drowned.

So why couldn't I?

# 23

Once the SAR boat was secured, and as Noah dragged my kayak onto shore, Jackson supported me as I stumbled, shaky, up the shore and steps to the house. I was trembling. I had never felt so cold.

Libby slid open the kitchen patio door and stepped back as Jackson helped me inside. She hadn't put on makeup and her face appeared raw, red-eyed, from crying. She'd been crying over me? "Thank god you're all right!" she said. "What the hell were you thinking?" Then she grabbed me in a fierce hug.

"Maybe we can save the interrogation for later," Jackson said, smiling a little. "Right now, Piper needs to get warmed up. Can you help her into a hot shower?"

But the effort of taking one more step seemed too much. "I need to sit for a minute," I said, sinking into a kitchen chair.

"Of course."

After closing the patio door behind him, Noah kicked off his boots and shrugged off his coat. "I'm going to get changed," he said, carrying both down the hall. His ski pants rustled as he walked.

My mother placed a cup of tea in front of me, and I slipped off my gloves to feel the heat of the mug in my hands.

"Tea?" she asked Jackson.

"No, I'm fine. I've got a Thermos of coffee with me."

Libby sat at the table across from me. She had dyed her own hair, I only just noticed. It was all one colour. No highlights. A flat orange, similar to her natural colour, to cover the grey, but one that left a residue of colour on her scalp.

Jackson placed a hand on my shoulder. "Are you sure you're all right?" he asked. "Maybe I should drive you to Clifton, get you checked out at emergency."

I put my hand on his. "Honestly, Jackson, I'll be all right. You've done enough. You don't have to stay."

"I'll take care of her," my mother said.

"You're sure?" he asked Libby, not me.

"I'm fine," I said, smiling. "Go!"

"Then perhaps I'll head back out onto the lake, check in on the dive team's progress. See if they've found anything. Anything that might help you find closure." He squeezed my hand and let go. "Try to get some rest, all right?"

He slipped out onto the deck, closing the door behind him. I watched as he made his way down the stairs and to the dock. The snow-covered beach was empty. After the uproar of boats and people over the last several days, it seemed *too* empty, lonely.

Libby tapped the table. "*Now* do you want to tell me what the hell you were thinking?"

I turned wearily to my mother. "Please, not now," I said.

"This isn't just about you, you know. Noah needs your help to get through this, to grieve for his father."

"I *know.*" I knew that better than my mother, who had rarely been there for me.

"How can he grieve if you cling to this fantasy that Ben is somehow alive?"

I rubbed my forehead. The dull ache there. "Can we talk about this later?"

"You're in denial. You've got to move on, start to mourn. Piper, you need to accept that Ben is gone."

I pressed my lips together. "I'm not sure I can do that." Not until I saw a body. Not until I knew *exactly* what had happened to him. "I just can't shake the feeling that we're missing something."

"You said you saw his ghost, more than once. Noah said he did too. Doesn't that tell you Ben is gone?"

A part of me knew Libby was right. Even if Ben hadn't drowned on the lake, there was almost no chance that he had survived several nights out in the cold, in winter storms. I needed to let go of this idea that Ben was alive. For me. For Noah.

"I can't remember Ben's middle name," I blurted out.

"What?"

"His middle name."

Libby took a sip. "Oh, well, grief and stress make us stupid," she said. "Forgetful. After your father died, I found my slippers in the fridge. I had a habit of putting them on this wire shoe rack he had set up in the closet. The closet door was white, and the wire shoe rack kind of looked like the rack in the fridge. I must have gone on autopilot, put my slippers in there like I would the closet. I had no memory of doing it. In the months following his funeral, I found objects in weird places all over the house. I thought I was losing my mind."

It was partly the drink in her case, but it was good to know I wasn't alone in this strange mental decline. Still. "Ben's been gone less than a week and I can't remember his middle name."

"Get some rest and you'll remember."

I turned and turned my mug. "Ben really is gone, isn't he? He drowned in the lake."

She looked at me sadly. "I suppose we should start planning a funeral," she said. "Although, I guess it's not a funeral if there is no body. A memorial, then? Something to remember Ben by." She paused. "I just wish I'd met him."

"I'm not ready for that," I said. "A memorial."

"Is there a church here we could use?" she asked. "Or perhaps a community hall?"

I shook my head. "When the time comes, *if* the time comes, I don't want anything big. Just something for Ben's closest friends. More like a wake. A party, a celebration of his life, here, in the house."

"Ben was well known, Piper. You'll want a community event. A memorial isn't just for you and Noah. The town needs to process this." She waved a hand as if dismissing a fly. "Oh, I know planning a memorial can seem overwhelming right now. *Everything* seems overwhelming when we're grieving. I sure as hell felt overwhelmed when we buried your father. Honest to god, dealing with all those people offering their condolences was harder than coming to terms with his death."

I didn't believe that. My mother had spent the weeks following my father's passing drunk.

"But don't you worry," she said. "I'll help you plan things. You won't have to handle this by yourself." She stared at me pointedly. "Remember, I'm a widow, like you. I do know what it's like to go through this loss. I won't let you go through it alone."

A *widow*. The word hit me like a blow to the stomach. I was *that* woman, the *widow*. Ben had a habit of saying "This is the wife, Piper," like some old-timey farmer, rather than "This is *my* wife." Perhaps he was being ironic, as I hardly fit the mould of a stereotypical wife. But now I was no longer *the wife*. I was *the widow*. No, I wasn't even that. Without a body to put in a casket, without a funeral to mourn his loss, I was thrust into an agonizing limbo where I was not the widow, but the *almost* widow, unable to properly grieve or perhaps even put Ben's affairs in order.

I twirled my thick wedding band that seemed almost too big

for my hand, but was small enough to nest inside Ben's, as his fingers were so much bigger than my own. His ring. His ring was lost, as he was, to the lake. I felt the tears well up and pushed away from the table. "I'm going to grab that shower," I said.

Libby stood, arms out. "Here, let me help you."

I steadied myself, hanging on to the back of the chair. "No, I'm good. I can do this."

As I limped down the hall, my legs like Jell-O, my mother called after me. "If you need help—"

I lifted a hand as I leaned against the wall for support, then carried on. Once in the bedroom, I slumped down onto the bed to strip off my wet jacket and ski pants. I felt numb, inside and out, not just from the cold and exhaustion, but disconnected from myself, the world, as I so often had as a child when my father came home late, drunk, banging from wall to wall, knocking things over, and I hid in the closet of my room, hoping, wrongly, that he wouldn't think to look for me there. Then, as now, I prayed someone would come to save me, rescue me. But there was no rescue from this. I would have to rescue myself or end up like the Green Man, Elijah Peterson, trapped in grief, living with a ghost in the forest.

Ben was dead.

Dead.

Ben was dead.

If I said it enough, thought it enough, perhaps I could come to believe it was true.

And yet his clothes still hung in the closet, his slippers were there, just under the bed, his latest novel and his favourite mug were on his night table. I grabbed Ben's green sweater from the bed, where I had slept with it, and threw it on. His favourite, he said, as I had knitted it myself during the worst of the pandemic. It was crayon green, the sleeves were too long, and it was full of holes.

Still, Ben had made a point of wearing it in the evenings, saying it was the most comfortable thing he owned. Liar. The wool was rough and scratchy to the touch. He wore it to please me. I loved him for that.

Ben's smell, his comforting earthy scent, permeated the sweater, the room, and was strongest on his pillow, the pillowcase I refused to wash. I felt his presence so keenly that he could be in the room with me right then. I could turn to find him standing there in front of the window.

But he wasn't.

I heard a light mechanical *zit*, and thought I caught movement out of the corner of my eye. Had the camera lens on the drone just moved? I bent over to stare back into the glossy eye of the drone. "Ben?" I willed it to move, but it didn't. I stood back. My imagination had tricked me again, no doubt. As my mother had pointed out, this stubborn belief that Ben was still alive was only magical, wishful thinking, brought on by a grieving mind in denial.

Nevertheless, I stared into the drone's eye, willing my message to reach him. "Ben, sweetheart, what the hell happened to you?"

# THURSDAY

# 24

I stood at my bedroom patio window within a swath of late-afternoon sun, hugging myself as I watched the RCMP underwater recovery boat sweep the lake for Ben's body. His *body*, under all that water, cold and alone on the lake bottom. The lake had already begun to freeze over. A thin crust rimmed the shore of this horseshoe bay. Jackson had told me the team would likely have to suspend the search as of the end of the day, because yet another snowstorm was forecasted for this evening. Heavy grey clouds hovered over the mountain already. He wasn't sure yet if the URT would return afterward or not. So much depended on the weather. Come spring, we might have to bring in a volunteer team that specialized in searching for drowning victims. It could be months, maybe even years, before we finally found Ben's body.

His *body*. Ben was dead. *Ben was dead.* I had to accept that I was a widow.

I was a *widow*.

And then it finally hit me: Noah was an *orphan*. My mother was absolutely right: I had made Ben's disappearance about me, about my loss, and not Noah's. I needed to step up, be there for him, be the person Ben had asked me to be on that terrible morning when he left for the far shore.

But how could we mourn Ben's passing without a body? As Libby had pointed out, we couldn't have a funeral for Ben yet, but we needed some kind of ritual to mark Ben's death. We would have a large memorial for the community later, but for now, Noah and I needed a way to say goodbye to Ben. But what? I thought of Elijah's memorial, his stone cross adorned with his beloved's teddy bear and necklace, likely the necklace she had been wearing when the grizzly attacked.

I padded across the hall to Noah's room, stopping to take down the framed photo of Noah and Ben that hung on the hallway wall. I ran a thumb over Ben's kind face before hanging the picture back in place. I knocked. "Noah? Okay if I come in?"

I heard a muffled "Yeah."

I opened the door to find Noah lying on the bed in jeans and a blue T-shirt, with a pillow over his head. "Were you sleeping?"

"No."

"Am I disturbing you?"

He didn't answer.

I sat at the foot of his bed. His long, slender feet were a little dirty from walking around the house barefoot. Ben had always been after him to wear slippers or at least socks. Noah always gave him the same reply: *They bug me.*

"Okay if we talk?"

"I guess."

I waited until he pulled the pillow off his face. "I wanted to say, first, that I'm sorry, about yesterday, for taking off like that, scaring you. I'm truly sorry for how I've been acting." I fiddled with the corner of his comforter, worrying it between my fingers. "I suppose I've been having trouble accepting that Ben is gone."

He was quiet for a moment. "Yeah, well, I can't believe Dad is dead either."

I put a hand on his heel, then took it back as the gesture felt too intimate, like that of a mother. But then, that's what I was to him now, a mother. "It's hard to say goodbye when we don't know what happened, when we don't have a body to bury." I paused. "I have an idea, though. Maybe a small way we *can* say goodbye."

"You're not going to have a funeral?"

"We will. But I thought we could have a private memorial, for just you and me."

He sat up, hugging the pillow. I pushed on.

"On the mountain, I mentioned I'd come across a memorial the Green Man, Elijah, had built for his wife. I thought maybe we could build a memorial like that for Ben."

"You mean like one of those roadside crosses that mark where somebody died in a car accident?" Adorned with fake flowers, teddy bears or balloons.

"I was thinking more like an inukshuk. We could build it on the beach here, in front of the house." Where Ben and I had gotten married. Where he had shouted across the water to ask me to marry him. Where we had spent so much of our time together as a family, eating suppers or launching our boats. "Is that silly?" I asked.

"No."

"You want to do that now?"

"*Now?*" He glanced at his laptop, a little dubiously. He had likely planned to disappear into his games for the day. "I guess."

I stood. "Get dressed and meet me outside."

Once we were geared up in our parkas and boots, Noah and I collected the biggest rocks from the beach and started building our cairn, a figure with blocky legs, a barrel chest, rock arms aimed toward the water, and a round boulder for a head. A structure not quite as tall as Ben, but one that nevertheless suggested Ben's large build. It was fitting that it should be made of stone, I thought, as Ben had been the rock that anchored me. He had so often held me firm, helped me contain my emotions so they wouldn't wash me away. I knew he had done the same for Noah. I would have to do that for both of us now. The inukshuk pointed the way to the far shore, to where Ben lay, whether in the water or on land.

"What do you think?" I asked, standing back.

Noah stared at the thing for a long time, his eyes watering. "I miss him," he said.

I wrapped an arm around his waist and rested my head on his shoulder. "I miss him too."

"It doesn't feel like he's gone, you know?"

I did know. But then, Libby was right. I had to help Noah find his way through this. "Listen, Noah, there are five stages to grief—"

He rattled them off. "Denial, anger, bargaining, depression, acceptance."

I forgot. Noah had been through this before. Ben had sought grief counselling for them both after his mother's death.

"I get it," he said. "I'm still in denial."

As I was, I knew.

He tapped his chest. "But I can still *feel* that he's alive," he said. "I don't know how to explain it."

I didn't either and yet I also felt that connection to Ben. That thread between us hadn't been broken. In the same way I knew when someone was watching me in the forest, I could sense Ben's presence.

"Have you seen him again?" I asked.

Noah touched the stone hand of the figure we'd built. "At first it was just flashes, something out of the corner of my eye, and I'd *know* he was there. I heard him a few times, calling my name. Then he—" Noah stopped, grinned a little in embarrassment. "He was at the end of my bed the other night. But when I turned on the light, he wasn't there. It felt like he was trying to get my attention, like he wanted something." He hesitated. "Like he wanted me to find him."

The snowy beach seemed to shift under my feet. In my bedroom and again in my dream, Ben had said, *Find me*.

But I knew hanging on to the fantasy that Ben was still alive was unhealthy. "I read somewhere that any one of us hallucinates something like five times a day," I said. "Hearing voices in the whir of a fan, that kind of thing. And that's when we're not grieving. The dying often feel they are visited by family or friends who have died before them; they seem as real as you or me."

"Is that what you think is happening?" Noah asked me. "We're hallucinating?"

"That's my guess."

His feet kicked snow. "I don't know what to do now."

I laughed a little in recognition. "Me neither." That was exactly what I was feeling: adrift. I took his hand and swung it a little. "But we'll figure it out together," I said.

Noah's body started to shake as he sobbed silently, and I found myself crying with him. I put an arm around him, and he hugged me back, hanging on somewhat desperately. This tall, slim kid.

"We're family," I said. "You understand? We'll always be family. I love you."

"I love you too." Although he had always been affectionate with me, that was the first time he'd said it out loud.

He wiped his eyes and we both stood there, staring at what we had made together, this blocky, awkward thing.

Then I undid the silver necklace Ben had given me, slid off my engagement and wedding rings and ran the chain through them, refastening the necklace around the neck of the stone figure. "You got anything you want to leave here?" I asked Noah.

He thought about that. "Maybe." He jogged back inside and brought out the jackknife Ben had given him and placed it on the hand of the statue. "To keep him safe out there," he said. Something Ben had said when he gave Noah the knife for Christmas.

"That's good," I said. "Perfect."

We stood there together in silence as the sun slid below the mountain, casting the valley in shadow. Even though we had built the inukshuk and left our small offerings, our little ceremony seemed flat, not what I'd hoped for. I hugged myself as I watched the underwater recovery boat circle for another pass over the lake, likely the last of the day, or perhaps the year.

I turned back to Noah. "Did you want to say anything?" I asked.

"Like what?"

"I don't know. Maybe say goodbye?"

Libby slid open the patio door. "Noah," she called. "Your friend is here."

Noah turned to go. *So much for our touching memorial*, I thought. But maybe it was good enough for now.

# 25

I followed Noah into the kitchen, where Libby was washing dishes, and took off my boots and coat.

Tucker stood awkwardly in the hall, underdressed for the cold in black jeans and a hoodie. He gripped the handles of a plastic grocery bag. "Hey," he said to Noah.

"Hey."

"Tucker?" I grinned. "It's so good to see you."

He moved his head in something between a nod and a shake, and then, as if it caused him pain, he touched his injured eye. The swelling had gone down, and the bruising had started to turn yellow as he healed. But the white of his eye was still bloodshot.

"Listen," I started, sliding my hands into my armpits. "About what went down on the mountain—"

"Don't sweat it," Tucker said. "You lost Ben. You were upset. But I swear, Dad wasn't up on that ridge Saturday. And I don't know nothing about what happened to Ben."

He was so earnest. I nodded slowly. "Okay."

"Peace offering," he said, as he held out the grocery bag. "From Dad and me."

I took the bag from him, held both handles open to peer inside. A rectangular freezer cake, chocolate, its rows and rows of small rosette icing like the waves on Black Lake.

"Owen sent this?"

"Well … he doesn't know I'm here." A shy grin slid up his face. "But Dad's sorry about Ben too. He really is. Ben was a good guy. He was always so nice to me."

"I appreciate it," I said, closing the bag. "Thank you."

"It's your favourite," he said to Noah.

"You mean it's *your* favourite," Noah said.

Tucker shrugged.

"Ah," I said, smiling. "So, *you'd* like a piece, would you?"

Tucker shook his head, embarrassed. "I bought it for you guys, really."

"Let me cut you both a slice." With the boys following, I took the cake to the kitchen counter and popped open the plastic cover to carve out two pieces of cake, handing them each a slice on a plate with a fork. Noah carried his to his room, expecting Tucker to follow. But Tucker lingered in the kitchen, plate in hand.

"Was there something else?" I asked him.

He ducked his head, shaking it back and forth in that strange way of his. "No. Nothing. I'm just sorry about Ben." He lifted one shoulder. "I wanted you to know." Then he turned heel and ate his cake as he wandered to Noah's room. He wore no winter boots, only runners, on this winter day, and left wet footprints down the hall.

"Tucker," I called after him. "Are you all right?" I asked. "I mean, is everything all right at home? With your dad?"

He hesitated, chewing, then nodded, bobble-headed. So things weren't all right.

"You can stay for supper, and overnight if you want. Hang with Noah. You'll have to sleep in his room, though. Libby's in the guest room. I've got an air mattress and sleeping bag you can use."

"I don't know." He hung his head. "Dad doesn't want me here."

"If you need to get away from things at home—" I stopped

there as Tucker's gaze slid to my mother. He didn't want me talking about his situation in front of this stranger, and rightly so. "Anyway," I said, "you're welcome to stay the night."

His eyes on the floor, he mumbled a noncommittal "Thanks" before disappearing into Noah's room.

"Poor kid," my mother said, drying her hands on a dishtowel.

I shot her a heated look but didn't respond. I had been that kid, and my mother had done little to protect me.

She sat at the table. "That's the son of that bastard you hate, right?"

I shushed her, looking back at Noah's door. "I never said I hated Owen."

"You didn't have to."

"I guess I feel sorry for Tucker," I said. "He has a hard go of it at home, like—" I stopped there.

Libby sat back, crossing her arms. "Like you did," she said.

I put the plastic lid back on the cake and put it away in the freezer, then reconsidered and peeled the lid back off. I cut myself a slice of the cake. When the piece seemed too small, I cut a second. "You want some?" I asked, licking the icing from my finger.

My mother shook her head, her expression grim. "You must remember some good times too," she said. "After, I mean. When it was just you and me?"

I didn't answer. Instead, I looked out at the lake, at the RCMP boat slowly travelling over water that now reflected the pink of sunset. I remembered Libby screaming at me because I had broken a bowl, her breath heavy with whiskey. I remembered waiting and waiting for her after school for pickup, until one of the teachers gave me a ride home. There, I found my mother passed out in the La-Z-Boy.

"I stopped drinking, for you," she said.

But by then, it was too late. I was in fourth year at university, living on my own.

I found a fork in the drying rack and took a bite of the cake. The icing was greasy and nearly tasteless. Nevertheless, I stuffed the cake into my mouth, not really enjoying it, but craving sugar.

"I did try," my mother said. "I tried to take care of you, to stop him. Was I really such a bad mother?"

"Libby, I just can't do this right now," I said, my mouth full of cake.

My mother got up, favouring a knee. "It's never the time, is it?" She limped down the hall, then closed the door to the basement behind her. I heard the steps to the basement creak as she followed them to the guest room.

A drink. I could use a drink. I rinsed the plate and fork, then grabbed a wine bottle from the stash of host gifts we had collected and opened it, but stopped before pouring myself a glass. This was how my mother had once coped with loss, with grief, with guilt: with a bottle. But I didn't have to. I poured the wine into the sink and slid the bottle into the recycling bin. I made myself a cup of chamomile tea and carried it into my bedroom to stare down at the stone figure, my less-than-stellar attempt at a memorial for Ben. We hadn't even gotten around to saying goodbye.

I turned to the drone. I had kept it charged all this time, hoping, foolishly, that Ben would activate it to tell us he was alive. It occurred to me now that this drone, seated in front of our wedding photo, served as a shrine of sorts, a memorial. Maybe it offered me a way to say goodbye.

I put my cup on the small table and leaned down to peer into the eye of the drone. The thing stared back at me, black and shiny, vacant. "I miss you," I said to the drone, to Ben. "I promised you I would take care of Noah, and I will." The drone sat there, its lights blinking. "I love you, Ben. I love you so very much."

I stood back and laughed a little. "Well, I guess that's all I have to say. Here I am talking to a stupid drone." I wiped the tears from my eyes, wiped my nose with the sleeve of my hoodie. "Maybe you can stop by sometime if you're in the neighbourhood. I mean, you visited me before." His silhouette at the patio door, his voice that woke me in the night, the vision of him at the foot of the Hourglass boulder, his whispers in my ear when I was trapped in the tree well.

"Goodbye, Ben," I said, and reached for the off switch on the drone.

But the eye moved, humming. *Zit, zit.*

Shocked, I took a step back. "Ben?" I looked into the eye of the machine. "Ben, is that you?"

The drone's eye moved up and down, as if in reply.

# 26

I crouched in front of the drone. The camera eye on it moved again, seeming to focus on me. "Ben?" I asked it, as if it could respond. "Is that you? Can you see me?" I laughed, cried a little. "Where are you?"

The camera on the drone moved left to right, the rotors started whirring, and the drone lifted off the dresser. The machine whined as it hovered right in front of me. I took a step back, then another, as the drone flew from side to side, rocking in the air like a drunken crow, and as I stepped back again, I bumped into the table and sent my cup of tea crashing to the floor, where it broke into pieces.

"Piper?" I heard Libby's voice from the basement below, and then her steps up the stairwell. "Piper, are you all right?" she called from the hall.

"The drone!" I cried. "Someone is flying the drone."

"What?"

She charged in, ducking as the drone careened overhead.

"It just started up. Someone has Ben's controller." *Maybe Ben,* I thought.

"Can't Noah fly that thing with *his* controller?"

Of course, Noah. Ben had paired the controllers to both drones, so they could fly the machines with either controller. I pushed past Libby and rapped on Noah's door.

"What?" he called from inside. But it was Tucker who opened

the door, headphones dangling around his neck. Noah was at his desk, playing a game on Ben's laptop.

"You weren't working the controller?" I asked Noah. "Flying Ben's drone?"

He pulled down his headphones but spoke with his eyes on the screen. "No." Then he registered what I was asking and finally paused the game. "Why? What's going on?"

"The drone. It just activated. It's flying around my bedroom."

"*What?*" Tucker ducked out the door to see, and Noah and I followed.

Inside my bedroom, my mother faced off with the drone. When she took a step toward it, the thing backed up automatically.

"Give it some room," I said. "Let's see what it does, what he wants."

"*He?*" Libby asked.

Noah's eyes grew round. "You think Dad's flying it?"

Libby snorted. "What, like his ghost?"

*His ghost.* I shook my head. "No. I don't know. I mean, it's not Noah's controller flying that thing, so it must be Ben's."

"*Could* Dad be alive?" Noah asked, his eyes glistening.

"No," Libby said firmly.

The drone hovered near the patio door, like a cat waiting to be let out. "Then tell me, who is piloting it?" I asked.

Tucker swung his head away, as if he was embarrassed for me, or overhearing something he shouldn't. This would all get back to Owen, of course, and then, from him, to the rest of the community.

"Someone must have found Dad's controller," Noah said.

"That means Ben must have dropped the controller on land," I said. "Like we thought."

I slid open the patio door.

"What are you doing?" Noah asked.

"I'm going to find out who's flying that thing. If they did find Ben's controller, then maybe they can give us some idea of where he is, what happened to him."

The drone zigzagged haphazardly outside. The boys bounded after it, excited, as it veered around the corner and to the yard where the trucks were parked. Once I saw the direction it was headed, I grabbed my purse and coat from the hook on the door and pulled out my truck keys.

"You're going to chase after it?" Libby asked.

I slid on my boots. "Got a better idea?"

As she hugged herself at the door, I jogged down the front steps to the truck with my eye on the drone. It hovered above the road, as if waiting for me, before zipping down Lakeshore. I jumped behind the wheel as Noah got in the passenger side. Tucker slid into the crew cab behind us.

I wavered down the gravel road, leaning forward to keep my eyes on the drone above me. It clipped along at its top speed, maybe thirty kilometres an hour, keeping to the road as if leading the way, then, as the road opened up to the shoreline, it swerved out over the lake but kept close to the shore, its image reflected in the water.

"What if the person who's flying that thing is—" Noah stopped there, but I knew what he was thinking. What if the person holding the controller was the one who had hurt Ben?

Or killed Ben?

"If I think we're in danger, I'll call Jackson." I glanced at Noah, barely able to contain my excitement. "But what if this guy can tell us where he found the controller? Or he knows where your dad is?"

I gripped the wheel and drove the snowy road past the turnoff into town as I followed the drone, past cabin after cabin along the lake, some of them bunched so close together a person could hold their arms out and touch the rough cedar siding of both buildings. The last of the red light of sunset slipped away, casting the valley in an early twilight.

And then, after rounding a corner, the drone disappeared from view.

"Where is it?" I asked Noah. We drove on for a time, both of us leaning forward to peer through the windshield at the sky, the snow-covered trees, the plowed road ahead.

"Do you see it?" I asked. "Did we drive past it?"

"I think we lost it," Tucker said from the crew cab.

Noah leaned forward, squinting into the darkening sky. The seconds ticked on, and disappointment started to settle in the seat between us. "There, there!" Noah said, pointing.

It zoomed low over the water, nearly touching the waves, as whoever was piloting it started to get the hang of the controls. Not Ben, then, I realized, unless his hand had been injured and he had difficulty negotiating the controls at first. But then why would he fly it down Lakeshore Road in the first place? Unless he was leading me somewhere, to his location. To him. I felt my heart flutter at the thought. But why would he be on this side of the lake?

The drone rose up again, higher now, well above tree level. I squinted to keep my eyes on it, nearly running over a cat that zipped across the icy road in front of the truck. The drone disappeared from sight again, then, as we rounded a corner, Noah pointed. "There!" It hovered and then slowly lowered to the pebbled beach. I put my foot to the gas to get to the spot before whoever piloted it did.

And then a large green shadow skittered across the road right in front of me. I swerved and braked, skidding on a patch of packed snow. All of us were thrust forward in our seats as the truck shuddered to a stop on the beach side of the road.

Noah held the truck console with both hands. "Is that—?"

"The Green Man," Tucker said. He sat back in the crew cab as if disgusted.

I opened the truck door to jump out. "Stay here," I told the boys.

Tucker remained in the truck, but Noah said, "No way," as he got out.

I stepped forward cautiously. The Green Man—Elijah—stared at us as he tried to gauge, I imagined, what we would do next. He was, as always, dressed in camouflage. Green face and hands, twigs and leaves in his hair and beard. With Ben's drone controller in hand, his body was bent forward, tense, as if he was about to bound back across the road and into the forest.

"Where did you get that controller?" I pointed at the device in his hand. "Did you find it on Ben?" Had he found it with his body?

Noah said, "You shouldn't get too close. Dad said he's dangerous, delusional."

Elijah scowled at Noah. "He's not supposed to be here." And then, to me, he said, "You were supposed to come alone. Alone, alone. Bone on bone."

"You *led* me here?" I asked, squinting at him. "You *wanted* to meet me?"

"You're the wife," he said, as he had on the mountainside.

Tucker got out of the truck. "Be careful," he said. "The guy's nuts. He fired on Dad and me."

Elijah pointed at him. "You, you—you, you—" Then he bolted for the other side of the road, the forest, the controller still in his hand.

"Wait!" I shouted as I ran after him. "Please, wait!" When he halted in the snow piled on the far shoulder, I stopped too, in the middle of the road, so I wouldn't spook him any more than I already had. "You wanted to talk to me, so let's talk." Or *was* it talk he wanted?

He glared past me, at Noah and Tucker, as he repeated himself. "No, no. You were supposed to come alone."

"Why?" I asked. What did he have planned for me? All at once I felt grateful for Noah and Tucker's presence, these two very tall young men. And then a sick realization dawned on me. "Just how long have you had the controller?" I asked him. "How long have you been watching me through the drone, Elijah?" When I dressed, undressed, as I slept. As I talked to Ben through it, confiding my love, saying goodbye. "How *long*?"

"He was watching you all this time?" Noah launched forward angrily to, what? Punch Elijah? I couldn't see him ever doing that, though I appreciated his bravado, his attempt to take over from his father as the man of the house. I grabbed his sleeve to pull him back, as I expected he knew I would.

Elijah edged away, shaking his head over and over, mumbling, "No, no, no . . ." His eyes wild, bloodshot, confused.

Tucker spit to the side in a habit he had picked up from his father. "Freak."

"Okay, that's enough," I said. "I'm sure Elijah just wants to tell us where he found Ben's controller. Isn't that right, Elijah?"

Elijah cowered, his eyes flitting between the three of us.

I took a tentative step toward him. "If you have that controller, you must have seen Ben use it out in the forest. You saw him out there, didn't you? I know you did." I held out both hands, pleading, begging. "Please, we just need to know where you found it."

"I bet he found it on Ben," Tucker said from behind me. On Ben's body, he meant. "I bet he took it from him. Maybe even killed him for it, for the drone."

I had thought the same thing, but now that Tucker had thrown the words into the air, I realized the idea made no sense. "Then he would have picked up the drone from the beach," I said over my shoulder. "We wouldn't have found it."

The bushman ran his teeth over his bottom lip as he watched

Noah bend down to retrieve the drone and brush the snow from it. His lip, his gums seemed unnaturally red against the green face paint.

"Where *did* you find the controller, then?" I asked.

"I can't . . ." Elijah hugged the controller closer. "I can't tell you."

"Why not?"

His eyes slid to Noah and Tucker, and I waved the boys back to the truck, though they didn't get inside.

"Please, Elijah, if you know anything about what happened to my husband, about Ben, you've got to tell me. You owe him at least that much."

Elijah tilted his head to eye me, like a crow. "He saved me," he said, as he had at the tree well.

"Yes, he did."

"I owe him." Then he repeated himself over and over as he madly scratched his bushy hair. "I owe him. I owe him. I owe him."

I held out my hand. "May I have Ben's controller?"

Elijah cradled the thing and kept on scratching his head, mumbling.

"Elijah? *Elijah*, can you look at me?"

His eyes met mine.

I tried for a smile. "You see, the controller is the last thing—" I stopped to compose myself. "Ben would have been holding that when—" When he drowned. When he fell. When he was killed. When whatever happened to him happened.

"I bet that freakshow *killed* Ben," Tucker said from beside the truck. "He's acting guilty enough."

Elijah's green face became distorted with pain.

"*Did* you kill Dad?" Noah asked, joining me on the road.

Elijah pointed at him. "You don't know—" he started, his voice anguished. "You think you know, but you don't." He backed into

200

the early-evening shadows under the trees, and his camouflaged form became almost indistinguishable from the dark foliage around him. I stepped into his footprints to follow, holding up both hands. "I only want to know how my husband died. Please, tell us where you found that controller."

He glanced at Noah standing some distance behind me, at Tucker waiting by the truck. Then he scuttled toward me to whisper in my ear. I wrinkled my nose at the stench of his unwashed body. "The bear," he said. "I found it in the bear's den."

*Oh my god.* That cinnamon sow had dragged Ben's body into its den, and the controller, perhaps in his backpack, with it. But then, we didn't see Ben's remains in that den, and Elijah hadn't said *the grizzly*, he'd said *the bear*. When he tried to dig me out of the snow well, he'd used the word *bear* to mean danger, any danger, and then he had said he had seen me with the bear, as if he was referring to a specific man. I lowered my voice to match his whisper. "You found the controller at Owen's place, didn't you?" I asked. "You stole it from his house."

Elijah nodded, and his gaze slid past me to focus on Tucker. We both looked at him. Beyond Tucker, the clouds carrying the forecasted snow rolled across the lake toward us. A few flakes fell on us now.

When I turned back, Elijah was gone, as if the forest had pulled him into itself.

I leapt into the snow after him. He couldn't disappear again. He couldn't. I had to get Ben's controller back. I had to know more. I pushed past the cedar boughs and into the gloom, the dark beneath the canopy, calf-high in snow, stepping into Elijah's footprints until, almost miraculously, the trail disappeared, as if he had ascended.

"Where did he go?" Noah asked, catching up to me.

"I don't know."

Tucker joined us to search the snow, the foliage, for any sign of the Green Man. I half expected Elijah to stare back down at me from the trees above, his face covered in moss, lichen and leaves, old man's beard, like the stone images of the Green Man of medieval churches.

"Elijah?" My voice echoed through the dark forest, quieting the winter song of chickadees. Noah, Tucker and I scanned the foliage, listening, trying to gauge where he had gone. But we heard only the groan and creak of trees rubbing against each other in the wind, the shimmer of snow falling from a cedar bough, a crow's caw.

# 27

The boys and I trudged through snow back to the road, to my truck. As we buckled our seatbelts, I glanced back at Tucker in the rear-view mirror. "Hey, have you had a break-in recently? Anything in the house go missing?"

He blinked back at me. "I don't think so."

"Are you sure?"

"I guess. I don't know."

"Why?" Noah asked.

I had been to Owen's house just once, with Ben, shortly after I moved to Moston, to arrange for firewood. His place was a disaster, stuff everywhere. Owen might not yet know Elijah had taken the controller. But he *would* know where he'd found it.

I started the engine and, instead of going home, continued down Lakeshore Road, the headlights illuminating the falling snow within the growing darkness. I imagined the crew of the URT boat would be packing up onshore by now, if they hadn't already left.

Noah clutched Ben's drone in his lap. "Where are we going?"

"Owen's place," I said.

"Did I do something wrong?" Tucker asked, his voice rising in worry.

I smiled at him through the rear-view mirror. "No," I said. "Nothing like that." But perhaps his father had. "I just need to speak with your dad."

"My pack is at your place. I left the truck there."

"This won't take long."

"Can you drop me off here?" Tucker asked. "So it doesn't look like I'm with you? Maybe you can pick me up on the way back?"

I turned on the windshield wipers to clear away the falling snow. "You're not dressed for walking in this." His hoodie and runners.

"But if Dad sees me with you guys—" He stopped there. His frightened face. His bruised eye.

"Stay in the truck," I said. "He doesn't have to know you're here." I lifted my chin. "But, Tucker, if you're that afraid of your father, should you be living with him? Like I said, you can stay with us tonight. You can even stay with us until you graduate, if that's what you want."

"Seriously?" Noah asked me. He seemed delighted.

"Or we can help you find someplace else to live." I paused, my eyes on the snowy road ahead. "Where you feel safe."

"You would do that?" Tucker asked.

"Yes, of course."

"Why?"

"Because you're our friend. Because I see things are hard for you, that you're hurting."

"But you don't owe me nothing."

"That's not the point."

Through the rear-view mirror, I saw Tucker's eyes shift from side to side as if he were thinking that through.

We reached Owen's house, the rusting trucks and equipment that filled his yard, broken-down machinery and projects he'd never get around to fixing. One busted window was newly patched with plywood, evidence of Owen's very recent angry outburst. The white paint on the siding was flaking off, revealing the grey boards beneath. It was clear no woman lived there.

I parked behind Owen's pickup and turned to the boys before getting out. "Both of you, stay in the truck, okay? And Tucker, stay out of sight." There was no argument from him. He flopped over, lying on the seat.

I jumped out of my truck and strode to the rundown house, the icy gravel crunching under my feet. The door was grey, unpainted. I knocked, listened, knocked again. From inside the house, there was the crash of glass falling and breaking, Owen swearing, his heavy footsteps. "Just a fucking minute," he called out. So he'd been drinking.

He opened the door with his chest bare and hairy under an open shirt, his paunch hanging over his underwear, a beer in hand. He'd been watching the game. The light of a television flickered in the darkened room beyond. Owen squinted at me as if he couldn't quite believe what he was seeing. "*You*. What the fuck do you want?"

Never look a bear in the eye, Ben had told me. They'll see it as a challenge and charge. But don't run either or they'll chase you. Stand your ground.

I stared at Owen's socked feet. His bare legs were hairy, covered in white scars, cuts and injuries from logging. The smell of onions, garlic and fried steak wafted out of the house. He had supper on.

"I understand you found Ben's controller," I said.

"His what?"

I eyed the thread that threatened to unravel the fabric of his right sock. "The controller for his drone. Elijah stole it from your house—"

"Elijah?"

"The Green Man."

Owen straightened, laughed a little. "So, you're on a first-name basis with that bastard now? You two make a perfect couple. You'll be very happy together, living in that park of yours."

If a bear charges, Ben told me, curl into a ball.

I lowered my gaze again, tried to ignore Owen's taunts. "As I said, Elijah had Ben's controller. He told me he took it from your house. Where did you find it?"

"I never found anything of Ben's, except that life jacket."

I squeezed my eyes shut in frustration. "Owen, can we please just drop the lies? I know you took down that old tree on the far shore. Everyone knows. I know you were over there on Saturday—"

"Now *that's* a lie."

"And I know you found Ben's controller. Please, just tell me where, so I can find my husband."

Owen shook his head a little, his voice softening with something like sympathy. "Piper, what the hell is this about?"

"Dad wouldn't know a controller to look at it," Tucker said.

I turned to find him standing by my truck, the crew cab door open.

"And I already said, he wasn't out there Saturday."

Owen squinted at him. "Tucker? I told you to stay away from these assholes."

"Well, he's staying with us tonight," I said.

"Like hell he is." He pointed at Tucker. "You lied to me about where you were going?" He flicked his thumb at the house. "Get in here."

Tucker closed my truck door before walking slowly to the house through the falling snow.

I held out a hand to stop him. "Tucker, just get back in the truck. *Please.*"

But Owen roared at the boy. "Get in the fucking house right now!"

"It'll be okay," Tucker whispered to me as he passed. "I'll be okay."

I took Tucker's elbow. "Your father has been drinking," I said. "You *won't* be okay."

"What about your truck, your stuff?" Noah called out through his opened window.

"I'll come by with Nelson tomorrow, pick it up," Tucker said.

"*I'll* drive you," Owen said.

"Please, just come home with us," I said.

But Tucker shook me off.

Owen turned to the side as his son slid past him into the house. Then he stepped back himself and slammed the door shut, locking it.

Tucker pulled a sheer curtain back to peek out the kitchen window. The boy was locked inside that house with a caged bear. I banged the door one more time. "Owen, don't you lay a hand on Tucker," I shouted. "You hear me? You hit him again and I'll make sure you face charges."

Tucker let the curtain fall back in place. And shortly after, I received three texts from him.

**Don't.**

**Pls, just go.**

**Or he'll get worse.**

*Shit.*

I texted back. **Call if you need help. Any time, day or night.**

As I got back to the truck, I pulled out my phone and dialled Jackson's number.

"You think Owen does know where Dad is?" Noah asked. "I mean, if he found the controller?"

"I don't know." I pressed the phone to my ear as it rang. "But maybe that doesn't matter, for now. Elijah had Ben's controller. And it works. Whether it was Owen or Elijah who first found it, it wasn't in the water—"

207

Noah finished the sentence for me. "Or the electronics would be trashed."

"Whoever found the controller must have found it on Ben and on land," I said.

I clicked out of the call as it went to voice mail. Jackson rarely ate supper at the diner, preferring to cook his own. He was usually at home at this time of day. I was sure I'd find him there.

"Okay, so now what?" Noah asked.

"Now," I said. "We restart the search."

# 28

I backed out of Owen's driveway and we snaked along the narrow road that followed the lake until we reached Jackson's log home, which he'd built here on his arrival many years before. I parked next to his truck.

"I'll only be a minute," I said to Noah as I unbuckled my seatbelt. "Wait in the truck."

I left the engine on, the heater running. Heavy, wet snow hit the warm hood over the engine and melted almost immediately. We'd have another dump of snow this evening.

I knocked and waited, then knocked again, glancing in the adjacent window. A pot and a pan were burbling on the stove and the door was unlocked, so I stepped inside. The smell of cooking tomatoes hit me as soon as I opened the door. He was making a spaghetti sauce, from scratch. "Jackson?"

The log home was cozy, more of a cabin, really, with two small bedrooms, one serving as Jackson's home office. There was an open floor plan in the tiny kitchen and living room, with butcher block countertops and hardwood floors throughout. He kept the place tidy, and there were more throw rugs and pillows than one would expect of a man living on his own. A stack of photography books and magazines sat on the coffee table. I'd always felt at home here, but we didn't visit often. Jackson usually came to our place for barbecues and poker nights, staying over if he had a couple of beers or glasses of wine. He wasn't a big drinker but was cautious about driving after drinking, something I appreciated about him. My own father had driven me home from volleyball practice drunk, after stopping at the bar first. He skidded into a tree once.

"Jackson?" I called again, kicking off my boots.

I peered out the window over the sink to see Jackson walking from his compost toward the house, a tin bucket in hand. Several crows were perched in the tree above, waiting for him to leave before flocking to the vegetable waste he'd left. I stepped back as he opened the back door into the kitchen.

"Piper!" he said, smiling. "What are you doing here?" He rinsed out the compost bucket in the sink.

"I'm sorry to barge in. I knocked, but—Jackson, we need to restart the search, right away. Elijah told me he took Ben's drone controller from Owen's house. That means Owen must have found it on—"

Jackson wiped his hands on a dishtowel. "Slow down," he said. "Explain it from the beginning."

I described my strange encounter with Elijah, my argument with Owen.

Jackson leaned against the kitchen counter as he listened. "Did Elijah actually say that he found the drone at Owen's?" he asked. "Did he use those words?"

"No, not exactly."

"What *exactly* did he say?"

I stared up at the ceiling as I spoke, because I knew how ridiculous I sounded. "He said he found it in the bear's den."

"The bear's den. You mean the grizzly's den?"

"He meant Owen's place. I'm sure of it."

"I don't understand. How did you get from *bear's den* to *Owen's place*?"

I wound a hand in the air. "It's how Elijah talks. Jackson, I *know* he found that controller at Owen's."

"The Green Man—Elijah—is mentally ill. I've had a few run-ins with him in the bush. He's paranoid, delusional. I don't think you can believe anything he says. And it doesn't sound like he was saying Owen was involved, in any case. You came to that conclusion on your own."

I shook my head. I *knew* I was right. But I held out a hand. "Okay, let's just put that to the side for the moment. If Elijah had Ben's controller, then it means whatever happened to Ben happened on *land*, on the mountain, not on water. Ben did *not* drown in the lake!"

"Piper," he said gently. "You *know* he did. All the evidence—"

"We have to restart the search!"

He ran a hand over his moustache. "I can't do that. If it was summer, it might be a different story. But you know as well as I do that even if Ben was lost on land, which I highly doubt, there is no way he could have survived all these days and nights in that cold."

"But—"

Jackson raised his voice to talk over me. "We've been through this. I'm not going to risk the lives of my crew or the other volunteers on what is undoubtedly a recovery mission at this point. Piper, you have got to let this go."

I pulled away, hugging myself as I turned to stare at my reflection in the window, my orange hair and green eyes, pale skin. I looked exhausted, haunted. "I think Elijah was watching me, Jackson, through the drone."

Jackson swore under his breath. "He's clearly fixated on you. He must have been the one who broke into the house, like I thought."

"I don't think so." Why would Elijah, normally so stealthy, make such a racket? And why didn't he take anything? He was known for stealing food, blankets, medicine, whatever he needed to survive in the woods. "Someone else was after the drone," I said. "Owen. He wanted the photos on it." Or more to the point, he didn't want us to see them.

Jackson didn't respond to that. "Have you had dinner?" he asked.

With my back to Jackson, I shook my head.

"Want to stay for spaghetti? I have more than enough."

"Noah's waiting in the truck."

"I'll invite him in. We can talk more about this over supper."

I swung around. "So you'll consider starting up the search again?"

"Now, Piper, I didn't say that."

"But you'll hear me out?"

The muscles in his jaw clenched. "We *will* talk," he said. Though apparently not about restarting the search. "Make yourself at home. I'll be right back."

As Jackson slipped on his boots and went outside, I shrugged off my coat and walked around the cabin, viewing the framed photos that Jackson had taken. The magical landscape of the Boulders. An eagle in flight. Caribou. There were more photos in his office, and I stepped inside, carrying my jacket. It was a room he had kept closed during our recent visits, and I wondered why. The walls were also covered in photos he'd taken while out in the wild, stunning images of the mountains, the mossy old-growth forests, salmon swimming upstream with a grizzly swiping at them. I recognized a few of the photos as ones he had provided for pieces I wrote in promotion of the park proposal, the town, his guiding business.

His worktable, a woodblock countertop that spread the length of the wall, was covered in shots that he'd printed off from a large professional printer parked in one corner. I picked up a few of the photographs, admiring them, and then, under a stack of pictures taken at the Boulders, I came across one of me. No, two, three, four—multiple images of me. All taken out in the forest, without my knowledge, apparently with a telephoto lens.

Jackson had been watching me, taking these photos from a distance. Was it *Jackson* who had been watching me in the forest all this time?

My heart skipped a beat.

But why?

I stumbled back out of the office and into the living room as Jackson and Noah stomped inside the house.

Jackson must have registered the shock on my face. "Is everything okay?"

I nodded. "Yes, fine."

He kept his eyes on me as he slipped off his boots. "You don't look fine."

"I'm just—I'm so exhausted."

"Of course." He pulled out a chair. "Here, sit. I'll serve up supper."

I threw my coat back on. "Actually, we have to go."

Jackson's forehead wrinkled as he raised his eyebrows. "You're not staying?"

Noah groaned. "Why? I love spaghetti."

"I'm just too exhausted to be social right now." I sank my hands into my pockets. "And I just remembered Libby said she was making dinner. Lasagna." Something Noah loved more than spaghetti. It wasn't a lie. One of our neighbours had dropped off a lasagna, and Libby had talked about heating it up for us tonight.

"I'm disappointed to hear that," Jackson said as Noah and I slid our boots back on. "I would have enjoyed your company."

I forced a smile. "Me too."

"Another time, then."

"Yes, another time."

Jackson hugged me goodbye as he had many times before, but I kept my arms to my sides. When he stepped back, he searched my face, puzzled. "We'll talk more tomorrow, all right?"

"Yes, tomorrow."

I ushered Noah back outside and into the truck. Jackson had turned off the engine and left the keys on the console. Once I had started the truck, I gripped the wheel as I stared through the window at Jackson serving up a meal for himself. He had been the first person I met in Moston, and a friend ever since. But now, after seeing those photos of me, photos he'd taken in the forest without my knowledge or consent, he felt like a stranger. A dangerous stranger.

"What was that all about?" Noah asked.

I put the truck into gear. "What do you mean?"

"You were acting weird. With Jackson."

"I'm fine. Everything's fine." Although I was contemplating going to the police about Jackson. But what would I say? *My husband's best friend took photos of me.*

"Is he restarting the search?"

"No." I backed out of Jackson's yard. I knew now there was no way I could talk Jackson into it.

"So what are we going to do?"

"I don't know."

"But if the Green Man or Owen found the controller, then maybe Dad didn't drown after all, and—"

"I *know*," I said, then, more gently, "I just need some time to think."

Noah shook his head and stared into the dark, at the black lake, the falling snow.

As I drove home, I tried to make sense of why Jackson had taken photos of me, why he had been watching me, his involvement in all of this. He had asked to stay with me during the search.

He had been there during the break-in. Had he slid the window up to make it seem like someone else had been there? He'd been quick to put the blame on the Green Man. But what would Jackson have been looking for?

He'd been after the drone, of course, and the images it might contain. He had been afraid the drone had captured *him*. When we'd viewed the drone photos, he had downplayed the idea that someone was up on the ridge with Ben. Jackson was the one who had told Ben about the felled old-growth tree. And now he didn't want to restart the search for Ben.

Was he working with Owen, making money off those poached trees? Maybe he had sent Ben out there to get rid of him when he felt Ben was getting too close to the truth. But then, Jackson had fought to create the park for years. He had everything to gain from it going through. His guiding business depended on the tourists who would come to see the rare pristine old-growth forest.

Was there something else going on here? There was a feeling of intimacy in the photos he'd taken of me, as if the portraits were of someone he cared deeply about. And this evening, he had seemed genuinely disappointed when I said we couldn't stay for supper.

I thought back to all the care he'd offered over the days since Ben's disappearance. He had been without a woman's company for years, and given the amount of time he spent at our house, I knew he was lonely. Or had he spent that much time at our house to be with me?

*Oh my god.* Had he harmed Ben, taken him out of the picture, to be with *me*?

# 29

As soon as we returned home, I put the drone back on its charger on my dresser, but I turned the thing off. Elijah would not be spying on me through its eerie eye again. When I stepped back out into the hall, Noah had already disappeared into his bedroom. I heard the blasts and music of his video game as I hung up my coat.

I found Libby sitting in the kitchen, waiting for me. Freshly showered, my mother wore my fluffy mustard bathrobe, as she hadn't brought her own.

"The lasagna is in the oven," she said.

I threw my keys on the table.

"Jackson phoned," she said. She closed the robe at her neck. "He told me about the bushman watching you through the drone." She shivered a little at the thought of it. "And about your confrontation with Owen."

I retrieved plates from the cupboard and put them on the table. "Jackson shouldn't have told you about that. He has no right."

"He's worried about you, Piper."

I collected cutlery from the drawer and set forks and knives by the plates. "Or he's worried I'm on to him," I said.

"What do you mean?"

I glanced toward the hall and lowered my voice as I sat opposite my mother. "I found a pile of photos Jackson had taken of me in the forest, when I didn't know he was there." I paused. "I think he might have had something to do with Ben's disappearance."

"Jackson? Why on earth would you think that?"

"At first, I wondered if he was working with Owen, and Ben got in the way. Or—"

"Working with Owen? To what end? To take down those trees? But I understand Jackson has led the effort to create the park."

"I know. But maybe all that was a cover."

Libby sat back in her chair. "A cover."

"Or maybe the reason he took those photos of me—" I glanced at Noah's door again and lowered my voice to a near whisper. "Do I have to spell it out?"

"You think Jackson has a thing for you? He's stalking you?"

I put a finger to my lips to shush her. "All I know is he was out there in the forest, following me, taking photos, when I had no idea he was there. Why would he do that?"

"There must be some explanation." Libby shifted uncomfortably in her chair like a broody hen settling over her fragile eggs. "Piper, this is exactly the kind of thing Jackson was worrying over when he phoned me. These theories of yours about what happened to Ben—"

I sat back. "You think I sound paranoid."

Libby smiled sadly. "A little."

"But think about it. Why would Jackson call off the search for Ben after only four days?"

"Because they found Ben's boat capsized in the water, along with his radio, life jacket and coat. And no sign of him anywhere on the mountain after an exhaustive search. Not to mention the terrible weather these men and women have endured day after day, night after night. Even if Ben did go missing on land, the chances of finding him alive now are—"

"I know." I leaned both elbows on the table to hold my head.

A pain started at my neck and fingered into my brain. I stood and rummaged for a wine bottle, poured myself a glass, took a long swig. My mother eyed the glass as I sat back down.

I let out a long sigh. "All through this, I haven't been able to shake the feeling that Owen had something to do with Ben's disappearance. When Elijah told me he found the controller in the bear's den, I was so sure Owen had taken it, that he knew where Ben was."

"And now?"

I stared down into my wine. "I don't know. Owen seemed confused, like he had no idea what I was talking about. Maybe he's just a good liar. But then I found those photos of me in Jackson's office . . ." I rubbed my forehead. "I know there's more going on here. I just don't know what, exactly."

"Maybe that's the problem, right there," Libby said. "You have no explanation for what happened to Ben. At least, not one you're ready to accept. You have no control over this situation. Believing that Ben is still alive, or that there is some kind of conspiracy involving Owen, and now Jackson—" She stopped to cup my hand in both of hers. "Maybe it's a way you can make sense of things, maintain control."

I sat back in my chair. Maybe. I did hold two conflicting theories in my head about Ben, that he was somehow alive and, secondly, that someone—Owen or the grizzly or the Green Man or, now, Jackson—had killed him.

I leaned back on the table to hold my head again. "Maybe you're right. Maybe I am losing it."

My mother stood to rub my back. "I see you're drinking again." She paused. "Have you been suffering from intrusive thoughts again too?"

"Intrusive thoughts?" I laughed a little, at myself. "Well, I'm thinking my husband is missing, and that somebody may have hurt him, and that someone broke into my house. Oh, and there's that graffiti on my truck, the window that was bashed in before Ben disappeared. So, yes, I guess I'd say I've been having a few intrusive thoughts."

"I mean, are you having dark thoughts about hurting yourself?"

"I'm not suicidal."

She patted my back. "Good, good." And I knew she was thinking of me, hooked up to an IV, groggy and ghostly after a suicide attempt when I was seventeen landed me in the hospital. An overdose of sleeping pills I'd found in my mother's medicine cabinet. I had never told Ben about that. I didn't want to scare him away.

I smiled wickedly, trying to lighten things. "I *am* thinking about offing Owen, though," I said.

"*Piper!*" My mother appeared genuinely alarmed.

I threw up both hands. "Seriously? I'm not going to hurt him, Libby." I pushed away my glass, then clawed it back, finished it up in quick, successive sips. The wine swam up to my brain, warming it, soothing it. The pain of grief, of guilt, lessened. No wonder my mother had lost herself in booze for so many years.

Libby sat again, facing me, her hand gripping my forearm firmly. "This obsession of yours that someone is responsible for Ben's death needs to end. Do you understand? You're chasing ghosts."

I laughed at that. "I *am* chasing ghosts," I said. "I see Ben. Sometimes he seems so real, solid, standing there. But at the same time, I can't shake the feeling that he's still alive." I looked up at the patio door that led out onto the deck, the snowy night sky beyond. "Even now, I feel like he could walk in that door any moment, stomp the snow from his boots." I glanced back at my mother. "*Am* I crazy?"

She sighed. "Crazy? No. But I always thought you were hard-wired differently. Even as a kid you seemed to see things that others didn't. Remember all those times you thought you saw your father after he was gone?"

I didn't think of it often now, or rather, I pushed those memories from my mind when they surfaced, as they did now. The ghost of my father at the end of my bed. Or standing outside the house on the lawn. My own mind at work, I knew, trying to process the guilt of what we'd done, what *I* had done.

"You never saw him, after his death?" I asked Libby. "You never felt haunted by him, by what happened?"

"Only when I was sober." So she felt haunted all the time, now. She leaned back in her chair. "It's still eating at you, isn't it? What happened to your father—I know what that can do to a person."

*What happened*—as if it had been an accident.

My mother gripped my hand. "Whatever happened to Ben, and what happened all those years ago to your father—I think they're all tangled up together in your mind somehow. If you just talk about it, you might be able to let go of Ben." She paused. "Are you seeing a therapist?" she asked. "I mean, through Zoom? I don't imagine there's a good counsellor around here."

"No," I said. "Not anymore." I hadn't for nearly a decade. The cost. And the therapist I had worked with had gotten too close to the truth, asked too many pointed questions.

Libby hesitated. "Did you ever tell your counsellor about it?"

I spun my wineglass. "She guessed I was holding onto something big, but no."

"Ben didn't know?"

"Have *you* told anyone?" I felt a sharp pang of fear. *Had* she told someone?

She shook her head. "But hanging on to this secret all this

time—maybe that is what's really going on here, the blame you're directing at Owen and now Jackson. Maybe Ben's death was the trigger. Piper, I worry that you've reached a crisis point."

I stood unsteadily. "I'm fine," I said. "I'm okay."

Libby visibly flinched at what should have been an innocent phrase. But I knew it wasn't, for either of us. Dad's last words to us were *I'm okay*.

"I wanted to tell Ben," I said. "But how could he stay with me, how could *anyone* stay, if they knew?" If they knew who I really was.

"What happened to your father—" She pulled a pack of cigarettes from her bag. "I wish I had found another way."

"You said there was no other way."

She put a cigarette to her lips, lit it. "There's always another way."

I waved to disperse the smoke, and she took her cigarette out onto the deck, closing the patio door behind her. I stood to pour myself another glass of wine.

Had there been another way? Maybe, but maybe not. When I was eight, Libby had tried to take me away, bustling me into the car while Dad was on the night shift, but he tracked us down in a glum motel through her credit card, and dragged us home. My mother had phoned the cops on him twice after that. But the officer who turned up at our door the first time knew him. Dad convinced the guy to drop the matter, saying Libby was overreacting. The second time, when I was ten, it was a female cop. Dad knew her too, but didn't even try to sweet-talk her. He told her the truth: he'd been out drinking in a bar after a particularly difficult shift, where he'd been forced to shoot a man, though not fatally, and when he got home, the stress, the pain of the matter, had gotten the best of him. When I gave him lip, he had slapped me. When my mother had intervened, he'd hit her.

He was charged with assault, diagnosed with PTSD and

required to go to regular counselling sessions with a therapist, like so many other cops and emergency workers. There was nothing new about his story, except that it was happening to us.

During and after the counselling, he still drank off and on. He still yelled. He still hit and pushed my mother and me around.

Until, when I was thirteen, Libby finally pushed back.

I heard them arguing in the kitchen just after Libby and I got home from shopping. I had carried in the groceries, but when I saw that Dad was home, and that he'd been drinking, I dropped the groceries on the kitchen counter and escaped to my room. His shouts and angry accusations began almost immediately. I could hear Libby's quiet voice trying to soothe him. And then I heard the smack of skin on skin, and my mother shrieking in pain. I rushed out just in time to see him take another swipe at her. But he was clumsy with drink, and when Libby pushed him away, he lost his balance, and the back of his head hit the corner edge of the granite counter with a sickening crack before he slid to the floor. He struggled to get up and slurred, "I'm okay," even though he clearly was not okay. Blood streaked down the side of his head from a gaping wound. "I'm okay," he said again, and then he slumped back down and was still.

Libby and I both stared down at him.

"What do we do?" I asked. "He's not moving."

"He'll be all right," she said, but her hand shook as she reached for mine and led me to the kitchen table.

"But Dad," I said. "He's hurt."

"I'll deal with it. Sit."

But she didn't deal with it. She poured herself a shot of whiskey and sat at the kitchen table opposite me. Her face, where he'd smacked her, raged red.

I stood. "I'm phoning 911."

"Just give it a minute." She took out a smoke, lit it. As I stood, to phone, she gripped my wrist, stopping me. "It's the only way," she said. "Do you understand what I'm saying?"

To stop my father. To stop him from hurting us.

"He's hurt. He's bleeding bad. We can't let him die."

"It's the only way," she repeated. "Just give it ten minutes. Ten minutes will make all the difference."

I pulled my wrist out of her grip and rubbed it as I watched the pool of blood grow on the floor. Was this really the only way out of the constant battles, the fear? It seemed so at the time, when the police and mental health system had done little to help us. I went back to my chair opposite my mother's and sat with my hands in my lap, staring at the clock above her head, watching the seconds tick by. After ten minutes had passed, Libby picked up the phone, called 911 and told them my father, drunk, had fallen and hit his head. "I only just found him," she said. "I don't know how long he's been out." She sobbed as she gave them the rest of the information.

I don't know if those ten minutes made a difference or if I could have saved him by phoning for help when he first fell. My father was still alive when the paramedics arrived. Libby didn't have to tell me to lie to the police. I simply repeated what she had told the paramedics. That my father was struggling with a drinking problem brought on by the trauma he experienced at work, that he'd been drinking more than usual recently. That we had come home from shopping to find him on the floor, bleeding out. The groceries were still on the counter. She had started the car again to make sure the engine was warm. They believed her. She was a police officer's wife, after all.

My father lived the remainder of his life, a matter of days, in a coma in a hospital bed, with tubes going in and out of him. Libby spent nearly every hour at his bedside, crying intermittently, drinking from a flask she kept hidden in her purse and holding my father's limp hand. And then, when he passed, and we were allowed to sit alone with his body for a time, she pressed his hand to her forehead, to her cheek, weeping.

I didn't understand her grief, not after what she'd done. And Dad had been so cruel to both of us. I felt nothing in that moment.

"You killed him," I said, quietly.

"I did not!" she said. "Why would you ever say that? He was drunk. He fell."

"We both killed him."

She carefully laid my father's hand on his chest and took mine instead, squeezing it so hard the pain brought tears to my eyes. "You didn't," she said. "Do you understand me? He was drunk. He fell." Then, still squeezing, she shook my hand. "Tell me, tell me again how your father died."

"He fell."

"He was drunk."

"He was drunk and fell."

"We phoned for help as soon as we found him." She nodded, encouraging me on.

"We phoned right away."

She let go and I nursed my bruised hand.

"You are not to blame," she said. "For any of it. Not his death. Not the way he hurt you or me. Don't take this on yourself, or you'll be plagued by guilt. You've got to find a way to let this go, Piper. If you don't, it will control you."

My mother had been right about that. She had been absolutely right.

# FRIDAY

# 30

I spent much of the night in a thick, intoxicated sleep haunted by vivid dreams of being trapped in a black space that smelled of earth, a grizzly den, perhaps.

But then I heard Ben's voice. *Piper. Piper!*

I woke with a start to an icy cold room, my heart hammering in my chest. The patio door was open and winter air rushed in. It had snowed heavily in the night. A heap of snow had collected on the deck. Heavy cloud obscured the early-morning light.

And there was a shadow in front of the glass, the silhouette of a man.

"Ben?" I sat up as the figure approached my bed. "Ben, is that you?" But this was no ghost. Whoever it was had opened the door. My voice rose up a notch as I recognized that bush of hair, the stench of unwashed human. "Elijah?"

I groped for the bedside light, knocking over my empty wine-glass in the process. It rolled to the floor, shattering. The Green Man, Elijah, stood there at the foot of the bed, only a metre or so away. He was dressed, as always, in camouflage and covered in green face paint, his hair and beard littered with leaves and twigs. He had a backpack slung over one shoulder.

I shifted back on the bed, yanking up the covers. "Elijah? What are you doing here?"

He held up Ben's drone controller, then placed it on the foot of my bed and stepped back.

"Tell me where you got that," I said. Then I raised my voice. "Please, tell me!"

"He told me to give it to you."

"Who?"

"You're the wife. Wife. Life. Happy wife."

When we both heard Noah step out into the hall, Elijah suddenly fled outside.

"Piper?" Noah asked through the door. "Are you okay? Who are you talking to?"

"Shit!" I sidestepped the broken glass and jogged out onto the deck, ankle-deep in fresh snow, to see Elijah racing toward the water. A second boat bounced on the waves at the dock, next to Ben's. "Elijah!" I called out.

Noah appeared at the bedroom patio door. "What's going on?"

I ran down the deck stairs, the snow cold beneath my bare feet. All around, snow fell in big, chunky flakes. "Elijah!" I called out. "Come back! Please, talk to me. Who told you to give me the controller? Was it Ben?" But he had already jumped in the boat. He started the engine and, after swinging the skiff around, careened across the dark water, disappearing behind the curtain of snow.

"Damn it."

Moments later Noah was out there with me, still in his pyjamas, but wearing his thermal boots. "Was that the Green Man?"

"Elijah. He was in my bedroom."

"Seriously? What did he want? Should we phone the police? Did he steal anything?"

"I don't know. He brought Ben's controller back." I started to head to the house, but then, remembering, stopped to wipe the snow off the inukshuk Noah and I had built, to make sure my necklace, engagement ring and wedding band were still hanging on it. Noah's knife, a gift from his father, was also still there. "Check your room," I said. "See if any tech is missing." Noah's gaming console, his phone and many gadgets.

Once back inside, I made sure my purse was hanging off the hook on the back of the bedroom door, and that Ben's change bowl and my few pieces of jewellery were still in place, though Elijah would have little use for money or silver earrings in the woods. The drone was still there, on the dresser. But something wasn't right: our wedding photo was gone.

I slid the dresser back from the wall, thinking the frame may have slid down behind it, but it wasn't there. I got down on my hands and knees, running my hand in the narrow space between the dresser's feet. There was nothing there but a layer of dust, and a toonie. I searched the whitewashed and scratched hardwood floor around it, the dust bunnies under the bed near Ben's slippers, behind the night table, stepping carefully to avoid the broken glass. But there was no sign of our picture.

"Noah," I called across the hall. "Have you seen the photo of Ben and me, our wedding photo?"

"What?"

"The photo I keep on my dresser."

He opened his door. "No. Why?"

"It's missing."

Where could it be? Something else was off, though it took me a moment to register what it was. Ben's nightstand was bare, but he always had a book there, to read before bed. His latest was a thriller with a man in red on the cover. And he had left his favourite mug there the day he disappeared, one Noah had given him. *World's Greatest Farter*. I hadn't moved it. I was certain I hadn't moved it.

The walls slid away from me in all directions as the sensation of déjà vu hit me. The wedding photo, the book, the mug. There was something oddly familiar about all this, like I'd lived it before. What was it?

"Noah?" I called again. "Did you borrow Ben's book?"

"What?"

"The novel he was reading. Did you take it?"

There was a pause, and then he stepped into my room. "No. Why?"

I put my fingers on Ben's nightstand. "It was here, where he left it." Then I pointed at the chair in the corner as it occurred to me what else was missing. "And his sweater was over the chair. I put it there."

"That ugly green sweater?"

I opened the lid of the laundry basket and rifled through the laundry in case I had absent-mindedly tossed it in there. Nothing. I rummaged through the closet, the drawers of his bureau for it. "Elijah. He must have taken it."

Noah cocked his head at me. "Why would he take *that* sweater?"

Or a crappy thriller. Or a novelty mug. Or our wedding photo. The feeling of déjà vu flooded back, and I finally remembered. When Elijah was in the hospital, Ben had taken him a novel to read, one of his thrillers, and he'd arranged with Elijah's landlord to get a few items from Elijah's apartment for his extended stay at the hospital: a sweater, as Elijah had complained it was cold in his room, a photo of Elijah and his young bride, taken on their wedding day, and his favourite mug, which read *Cavers Rescue Spelunkers*. Ben had thought the mug was funny, as anyone calling themselves a spelunker was an amateur, bound to get themselves into trouble underground. In the search and rescue world, cavers really did do the saving.

And then I *knew*.

I turned to Noah. "I think I know what really happened to Ben."

# 31

In the basement below our feet, Libby was rousing, awoken by our search for stolen items throughout the house. The flush of the toilet in the tiny, blue, mildewy bathroom downstairs. The bang of the door. She would be upstairs shortly.

In front of me, Noah blinked as if he too had just been roused from sleep. "What do you mean you know what happened to Dad?" he asked.

"All these missing items, Ben's favourite things, stuff that would remind him of home. Don't you see? Elijah just stole them from the house. He took them *for Ben*."

Noah nodded slowly as he understood. He had only just begun to grow a whispery beard and hadn't bothered to shave in days.

"I think he is trying to make Ben more comfortable," I said. "He's taking care of your dad, like Ben took care of him when he was in the hospital." After he lost his wife.

"So Dad *is* still alive?"

I paused. Could I really lift Noah's hopes again, just to have them dashed? I was convinced I was right. But then, I had been convinced I was right before.

"Maybe," I said carefully. "If Elijah gathered things for him, he's likely injured. Elijah was a paramedic before the bear attack on his wife. He'd be able to treat most injuries. But if they were serious—"

"Why wouldn't he get help for Dad?" Noah asked. "Why wouldn't he get him to a hospital?"

"Maybe he was afraid he would be caught by the police if he tried to get help. Or maybe he was afraid of something else. He kept talking about 'the bear' as if it were a man, a specific man that he was afraid of. I thought he was talking about Owen. If Owen attacked Ben, then maybe Elijah felt he was protecting him by hiding him in the forest." He was clearly delusional.

As Noah took that in, I heard my mother's footfalls on the stairs.

"So maybe Owen *did* hurt Dad?" Noah asked.

I hesitated. "I don't know. But I do think Ben got hurt somehow, and Elijah is taking care of your dad, in the way Ben took care of him."

"Where?"

I thought of the meticulous search of the forest. "I don't know. But Elijah just headed back across the lake. If we're quick, maybe we can track him."

"But it's snowing. By the time we get over there, his trail will likely be covered up."

"Then we'll go to the memorial Elijah built for his wife. It seemed like he watches over it. And we can cover a much larger area if we search with the drones." I glanced out the window at the snow in the morning haze. "Let's just hope this snow lets up. Get geared up and pack your drone."

Noah stepped into the hall. When he met my mother there, he dodged around her and rushed into his room, slamming the door behind him.

"What's all the banging about?" Libby said to his door. And then, when I brushed past her to grab my backpack from the hook in the hall, she asked me, "What's going on?"

I rushed back into my room, leaving the door ajar as I dug out a dry pair of thermal underwear and ski pants and threw them on the bed.

"Why is there glass on the floor?" My mother watched as I slipped out of my pyjama bottoms. "Seriously, what's going on?"

"Elijah was just here, in my room."

She put a hand to her mouth. "That bushman broke in?"

I slid on my long underwear before grabbing my ski pants. "I believe Elijah may have Ben."

My mother's face pruned in worry and disbelief. "Now you think the *bushman* has Ben? Piper, honestly."

"I'll explain it all later." Explaining now would only lead to an argument, as I knew she would find my logic far too tenuous. "Right now, we've got to track down Elijah."

"We?"

"Noah's coming with me. We're searching with the drones."

"You can't be serious about this, Piper. The man broke into your house. He stalked you through that drone."

"He's mentally ill."

"Yes, a traumatized man with a gun. Doesn't that sound familiar to you?"

Like Dad, yes. Dad aiming his handgun at my mother, and then me, to stop us from leaving. I didn't respond as I geared up.

"This is stupid," Libby said. "Beyond stupid. Dangerous. We already almost lost you to that tree well the last time you ran off like this. And not only is that bushman out there, but that grizzly too, right?"

Right. I went back into the hall for my holster that held the bear spray and banger. Then I carried my backpack into the kitchen to put on coffee. As the water was running through the filter, I grabbed the two-way radios from Ben's office and handed Libby one. "I'll check in frequently. And you can call on this any time."

When I started for the hallway to collect my boots and coat, she stood in front of me. "This is madness, Piper. At least tell Jackson what you're doing. Or get his help."

I pushed past her. "And if he *was* watching me in the forest, or is somehow involved in Owen's business?"

She watched as I put on my boots. "You don't really believe that, do you? He heads the search and rescue team."

"Even if there is some other explanation for those photos he took of me, Jackson has refused to start up the search again. He won't help me. He'll only try to stop me."

"As he should." My mother locked gazes with me, both of us stubbornly refusing to give ground. For once, she was the first to break eye contact. "What do I do if you don't come back?"

I slid on my coat. "We won't get lost."

"But Jackson said hikers get lost there all the time."

"I know the terrain." Some of it.

She followed as I went back into the kitchen. "At least tell me exactly where you're going, in case you do run into trouble."

"Elijah built a memorial to his wife on the slope above the Boulders. If I can't find Elijah's trail, we'll start there. We're going to use the drones to scan the area. Hopefully, we can talk to him, find out where he's hiding Ben."

"Piper," she said carefully. "You do understand how all this sounds." How nutty, how unhinged.

I zipped up my jacket. "Noah," I called. "You want to grab the snowshoes? I wish I'd taken them on my last hike up the mountain."

"Got it!" he called from his room. He disappeared out the front door to retrieve them from a shed where we also kept our skis.

"When will you be back?" Libby asked.

I poured the coffee into a Thermos and tucked it into my pack. "I don't know."

"Before dark, I hope."

"Libby, I need to do this," I said. I glanced at Noah as he returned with the snowshoes. "We both need to do this. If there is any chance, any chance at all, that Elijah has Ben, or knows where he is, I need to find him."

Libby nodded slowly. "You need closure. I understand."

I shouldered my bag. "No, I need to find my husband."

# 32

As soon as I had secured the boat on the far shore, Noah and I put on our snowshoes and set off through the wet snow, making our own trail as we attempted to find Elijah's. It didn't take long to give up on that idea, though. The heavy snowfall over the time it took us to gear up and get across the lake had been enough to erase any trace of him. There was no sign of the boat he'd taken over, which was undoubtedly stolen. He must have hidden it in the bush.

As we started up the slope toward the memorial, the snow finally stopped falling. Once the morning sun peeked through the clouds, the temperature hovered just above zero, and melting snow slid off tree branches in large clumps. Drops from the canopy above dripped down on us as if it were raining. I pulled up the hood on my jacket. As we sidestepped up the steep slope in our snowshoes, the snow mushed under foot, the consistency of butter. We stuck to the clearings as much as possible, wary of the grizzly that haunted these woods, avoiding the base of trees, the potential tree wells, as we headed up to the spot where I had stumbled across the Christmas tree and the memorial, where I had first spoken to Elijah.

When I finally saw the Christmas decorations catching light and glinting through the trees on the slope above us, I motioned to Noah to slow down, to stop, to use caution. I put my finger to my lips. We listened, scanning the clearing up ahead that surrounded the Christmas tree and cairn, and then the spruce and fir forest above it.

"Do you think he's here?" Noah whispered.

"Only one way to find out. Wait here." I started snowshoeing toward Elijah's memorial.

"But you said he doesn't want you there."

"I'm counting on it." If I hung out at his memorial, if I made a nuisance of myself, Elijah would be forced to talk to me. In any case, it seemed he *did* want to talk with me, alone. He had already attempted to do so.

I shuffled uphill in my snowshoes, ducking the branches of several smaller trees before entering the clearing. Up ahead, the decorations on the Christmas tree were wet, and a few had fallen to the ground and were half-buried in snow. Elijah's memorial to his wife was completely free of snow, though, and there was a small potted poinsettia, brilliant red against the grey of the rock and snow, at the base of the cross. He must have just stolen the plant from one of our neighbours on his expedition to break into our house. If he wasn't here now, then he had only just left. I thought I could feel his eyes on me, though I might have been imagining it.

"Elijah!" I called. "Elijah, are you here? I need to talk to you." I waited, listening. "It's Piper," I added. "*The wife.*" Snow continued to fall from trees in the forest, each time making a resounding *whump*. "Elijah!"

I called and called. After a time, Noah stomped up the hill to reach me.

"I told you to stay back," I said.

"What if he doesn't show?"

"Then we'll keep trying." I gestured at the memorial just up the slope from us, at Andrea's teddy bear and necklace hanging there. "He'll come back here for her." He would always come back, I thought, just as I would never stop searching for Ben. "My guess is he's close by now, watching us." Somewhere on the forested hill above, perhaps, hiding in the snow-heavy trees. "He'll show himself, soon enough." I glanced at my stepson. "Seriously, Noah. Elijah was armed when I was here last. You need to get back, take cover in those trees."

Noah shook his head. "Dad told me to take care of you," he said. "Especially when we were out here."

I shuffled around awkwardly in my snowshoes to face him. As he was on the downslope from me, we were nearly at eye level. "He told *me* to take care of *you*," I said, smiling.

He rolled his shoulders back. In his parka, he looked like a man, not a seventeen-year-old. He *would* be a man, in a year. "Then I guess we'll just have to take care of each other," he said, and grinned.

I nodded. "Okay. But try to stay out of sight. Elijah wanted to talk with me alone."

He shifted back, staying low within a patch of bush.

I cupped my hands to my face to call out into the forest. "Elijah!"

We listened. An eagle circling over the lake cried out. I called again, and again. As the minutes ticked away, I stamped my feet, clapped my mitted hands to keep warm. The sun slid up the sky, but snow clouds loomed overhead.

"We should try the drones before it starts snowing again," Noah said, coming out of hiding.

"Let's grab a coffee first, warm up a little."

I pulled out the Thermos, poured us both cups. Steam rose around our faces as we drank. Then my radio crackled, and Libby's voice rang out over the clearing. "Piper, you there?"

I tossed the last of my coffee to the snow as I pulled my radio from my pocket. "What is it, Libby?"

"Piper? Can you hear me? Piper?"

"I'm here," I told her.

"Piper? You said you'd stay in contact."

Noah grinned. "She doesn't know how to use the radio," he said.

I tucked my cup into my backpack. "Libby, listen. You've got to let go of the push-to-talk button after you talk, or you won't hear me."

"Piper?"

I waited, radio in hand, for her to give up trying so I could call her back. "Libby, you there? You have to let go of the button to hear me. Over."

"Finally! Thank god. You said you'd call." She paused. "Over."

"We're okay. Just a little busy climbing this mountain."

"I was so worried about you I had a panic attack," Libby said. "I thought I was having a heart attack. You hear me? A heart attack!"

"Libby. Libby, calm down." But she went on like that, her thumb firmly on the push-to-talk button, about how I had caused her anxiety, and a long list of past sins too. (I had failed to return her calls and texts. I hadn't invited her, *my own mother*, to my backyard wedding. I hadn't phoned her when Ben went missing. She repeated that last one. "I had to find out on the news," she said, as she had on her arrival. "The news!") Now that she had control of the radio, she wasn't going to let me get a word in.

Noah rinsed out his cup with a fistful of snow, one of Ben's habits, and I once again felt that stab of pain, of *fear*, in my ribs that I'd come to understand was grief. He nodded at my radio, my mother's voice blaring and crackling. "The Green Man isn't going to come out of hiding with this shit going on."

"You're right." I tried talking on the radio. "Libby, listen. I have to go now. I'm turning off the radio for a while. Libby—" But she kept her thumb firmly on the talk button. Not getting through to her, I finally turned off the radio. "I'll call her back in a bit. I can never talk to her when she gets like this."

"Has she been drinking?"

"I don't know. I hope not." As far as I knew, she had stayed sober for years.

Noah stooped to tuck his cup in his pack. "I don't like it when you drink," he said. "I mean, like you have this week. I've never seen you drink like that before."

I looked at my stepson and away. "I'm sorry, Noah." I rubbed my chilled face with both hands. "With your dad gone, and my mother here, I guess I fell into old habits." Family habits.

"The way you acted when you drank last night . . ." He stood to face me. "It was like—"

"I wasn't myself."

"Yeah."

I pressed my snowshoes into the snow, creating a step on the hillside. "I used to think that about my dad. When he was sober, he was the man I thought I knew, my father." Fierce and funny, always armed with a pun, a dad joke, affectionate and quick to hug, but also quick to judge. "And then he'd have a bad shift, and he'd drink to calm down, and he was somebody else entirely." An angry, wounded, rampaging bear of a man, roaring and breaking dishes, hurling his pain at me and my mother until, exhausted from the effort of violence, he collapsed in his recliner within his man cave to sleep while my mother and I retreated into our respective rooms to tend our bruises, alone.

Noah hugged himself. "Do you need, I don't know, *help*?"

"To stop drinking?" The question caught me off guard. I didn't think of myself as a drunk, not the way my mother had been, or my father. But I also knew when worry or anxiety surfaced, so did the craving. Could I stop self-medicating? Not alone. "Maybe," I said.

"Will you get it?" Noah held my gaze for a long, uncomfortable moment.

"Yes," I said. "I will." Then I clapped my hands together, to end this excruciating conversation. "Let's try the drones," I said.

"They may scare off the bushman."

"Or we might get lucky and catch a glimpse of him."

We pulled the machines out of our packs and launched them into the air. Their noisy whine set birds flying from the trees. I flew Ben's drone awkwardly at first, but the thing was programmed to keep its distance from trees and other obstacles, and I quickly got the hang of it again. I tipped my head back to watch it scale the trees until it was hovering over us, and then watched the screen images of Noah and me as I spun the drone, circling around the clearing. Noah set his drone on a grid search, and it paced methodically back and forth over our heads.

"See anything?" I asked Noah.

"Just a lot of trees and snow."

"Keep in mind, Elijah's hiding."

"So how would we see him under this heavy cover?"

"I don't know." The morning was passing quickly, and I was starting to wonder if we *would* find Elijah. Why did I think I could track the bushman down when Ben, the RCMP, Jackson and others hadn't been able to?

Because he had come to me. He had led me to him with the drone. He had broken into my house to talk to me, I felt certain. And he had taken Ben's things to make my husband comfortable. Maybe that was also his way of letting me know Ben was still alive.

A shower of snow fell from a tree nearby. And then I *felt* it. The hair rose on the back of my neck. I was no longer imagining it. "He's here," I said. "Watching us."

"You sure?"

I had felt him watching in this forest so many times before. "Elijah, I know you're here." I scanned the snow-laden trees, the branches sparkling with drops of melting snow, the patches of white in the open sections, the dark shadows of the brush beneath the canopy.

Above us the drones whined and whined, but we saw no sign of Elijah in the bush. The battery icon flashed on, signalling the drone's power was low. "We should stop," I said. "I think you're right. The drones will just scare him off."

"Just give me a minute," Noah said. "I think I saw something."

I hit the home button to bring Ben's drone back down, but Noah continued to search the area just below us. He was so much more adept at flying a drone than I was.

"Anything?" I asked, standing near him to look down at the screen of his controller.

"I thought I saw someone down there, coming up the slope behind us, but it must have been a shadow. I'll do one more pass."

But right then, the crack of a rifle echoed through the forest from below us, and Noah's drone exploded in the air above as the bullet hit.

# 33

Noah's drone spiralled to the ground in pieces, disappearing into the heavy bush on the slope below us.

"Oh, man!" Noah's voice held more disappointment than fear, and he started down the hill in the direction of the fallen drone, but I grabbed his arm and forced him to his knees with me. Noah, only now registering we could be shot at too, took a heartbeat longer to crouch down.

"Elijah!" I cried out. "Elijah, don't shoot!" I stood gingerly, hands above my head.

"What are you *doing?*" Noah asked from the snow at my feet.

"We've obviously got his attention," I said. Then, louder, "Elijah, I need to talk to you. About Ben." When I got no response, I told Noah, "Stay here, and stay low. Whatever you do, don't join me. I mean it."

I sidestepped uphill in my snowshoes to Elijah's memorial to his wife, the stone cross, her necklace hanging there, wet and sparkling in the winter sun. I hesitated, then lifted the necklace from the cairn. *That* would get his attention.

"Leave that alone!" Elijah's voice rang out from somewhere in the trees above me, rather than below, as I had expected. So who had fired down Noah's drone from below?

"Elijah? Please don't shoot. I just want to talk to you."

"Put it back!"

"Piper," Noah said from the snow downslope from me. "This isn't a good idea."

I hung the necklace back around the cross and held up both hands as I stepped away from the Christmas tree, the memorial. "I know you don't want us here," I said to Elijah, looking uphill into the trees. "I know this is your special place, your wife's place. But I'm not leaving until you talk to me."

He was quiet for a time, as if considering that. A breeze picked up, swaying the younger trees around us, releasing more snow to the ground.

"Elijah, do you hear me?" I listened. "Do you have Ben?" There was a rustle in the bush from below. Had the bushman somehow moved downhill? He had a snowboard. I swung around, but still couldn't see him. "You broke into our house and took Ben's sweater, his mug, his book." I paused. "Our wedding photo. You took those for Ben, didn't you? To make him comfortable."

There was a long pause, and then his voice rang out again, from the trees on the hill directly above me. "He brought those things for me, when I was in the hospital," he said. "Ben took care of me. When there was nobody else."

I scanned the trees above me, trying to see him. "And now you're taking care of Ben, aren't you? Is he badly injured?"

"Bears, so many bears," Elijah said.

"What's he talking about?" Noah said, his voice low.

"Dangers, you mean," I said to Elijah. "You're protecting him." I paused. "From what?" Or who?

Catching a flicker of movement, I suddenly saw him on the slope above us, where he must have been standing all along. His green form in the shadow under a fir.

"There is someone else below us," I said to Noah. "Someone else shot your drone."

"Who?"

"I don't know. Stay down."

But I took several steps up the hill toward Elijah. I had to find my husband. "Where are you hiding Ben?"

I waited for him to respond, but his attention was elsewhere, on the slope below us. His form was rigid, like a deer on alert. "He's here," Elijah said, and his voice seemed choked with, what? Fear, anger?

"Who is it?" I asked Elijah. Who had shot down Noah's drone?

"You need to leave."

Right then, I heard the crack of a gunshot fired from below, and Elijah ducked as a bullet whizzed over his head. I threw myself to the ground. "Noah!" I cried, shimmying downhill on my belly toward him.

There was another blast, and Elijah answered with a shot of his own, protecting himself and, it appeared, us as well. Nevertheless, Noah and I were caught in the open, in this clearing, between the two riflemen, the bushman on the hill above, and someone else below. I peered down at the heavily treed slope. The second shooter could be anywhere. When another shot rang out from below, I wrapped an arm over Noah. He clutched both hands over his head, his cheek to the snow.

"Could that be Owen?" I asked myself more than Noah. "But how would he know we're here?"

"Shit."

"What?"

"I texted Tucker, told him what you said about Elijah, that Dad could be alive, and we were coming over here to find him. I didn't think he would, but he might have told his dad." Noah scanned the slope. "But Owen wouldn't shoot at us, would he?"

"Not unless . . ." Not unless he had something to hide and he figured I was getting too close to the truth. And why fire on Elijah unless the bushman knew something about what had happened to Ben?

Still lying in the snow, I pulled out the radio and switched it on. "Libby, Libby, are you there? Over." I listened to the static. "Libby, please respond. Over." She had likely wandered away from the radio, giving up on it after I turned mine off. Or perhaps something was blocking reception. "Libby, if you can hear me, we need help. Call Jackson. Ask him to come over to the far shore."

Unless he was already here. Was Jackson the shooter?

The rifleman fired right over our heads, nicking a branch from the Christmas tree on the slope above us. I tried calling my mother on the radio again, but as soon as I did, another bullet plowed into the tree directly over our heads. The second rifleman clearly didn't want me calling for help.

"Shit." I pocketed the radio. I had to fix this, protect Noah at all costs. I stood, awkwardly, my snowshoes still strapped to my feet. Then I ducked as another shot rang over my head from below.

"What are you doing?" Noah hissed.

"Keep your head down," I told him. Then, facing the forest downslope, I cried out, "Hey! Owen, is that you? For god's sake, stop firing on us."

I stepped away from Noah with my hands up, but kept my distance from the Christmas tree, Elijah's memorial. I couldn't risk angering him again. He was still close by, just up the slope, watching us, with a loaded rifle.

I called out, facing downhill. "Owen, I don't know what you think you're doing, but this needs to end now." I listened. A crow's wings whistled as it flew over our heads. "Owen? Please. Put down that rifle and talk to me. Whatever you did to Ben, we can work it out. It doesn't have to end in any more bloodshed." I paused. "Owen, you hear me?"

A branch on a younger tree below us shook off its load of snow and bounced back in place as a figure shifted behind its trunk. But it wasn't Owen hiding there in the shadows, rifle in hand.

It was Tucker.

# 34

"Tucker?" I squinted at him, trying to make sense of things. The kid had no snowshoes and, dressed in his blue monosuit, he was up to his calves in mushy snow. He sank a little farther as I said his name again. "*Tucker?*"

Noah staggered up. "What the hell, man?"

"*Noah*," I warned, gesturing for him to stay down.

"Dad didn't do nothing," Tucker called out. "I told you, he didn't hurt Ben."

I took several steps down the slope in my snowshoes. I had to get that rifle out of the kid's hands before Elijah shot him, by accident or on purpose. "Tucker, why did you fire on us?"

"I didn't want to hurt you," he said. "I shot over your heads." He hesitated. "I thought you were the Green Man."

"Bullshit," Noah shouted. "You shot down my drone!" Despite my warning, Noah sidestepped the slope toward us. "You *knew* it was my drone." No one else in town owned a drone. "You didn't want us to see you."

I scowled at my stepson, to get him to be quiet, and waved him back, then slogged several more steps downhill until I stood in front of the tree Tucker was hiding behind, aware that Elijah was on the slope above, watching us, and likely had his rifle trained on the boy.

"Tucker," I said quietly, "you need to give me that rifle before Elijah—the Green Man—fires on you again." I looked up the hill, where I could see his green form against the trees. "He thinks he's protecting Noah and me—from you."

I held out a hand, expecting him to offer me the gun. But instead, he aimed it at me, and shouted up the slope into the forest, to Elijah. "You fire on me again, you crazy asshole, I'll shoot Piper."

Noah swore at Tucker. "What the fuck, man?"

I echoed him. "What the hell are you *doing*?"

Tucker's gaze slid to the right, to the left of me, over the play of light and dark shadows on the snow. I was close enough now that I could clearly see his bruised face, his piercing hazel eyes, so like his father's. In the overcast light, they were greenish yellow, like a cougar's. There was something about the long line of his body in the monosuit that reminded me of a wild cat too, his muscles coiled as if about to spring.

"Why were you shooting at us?" I asked again. "Why were you shooting at *Elijah*?" And then things started to click into place. "Elijah stole Ben's controller from *you*, didn't he?" I asked. Not Owen. "*You* found the controller. Or did you take it off Ben?" Off Ben's body.

"Ben—he dropped it." Tucker's voice broke. "He dropped it as he fell. But I never spied on you through it, I swear."

"But you did try to steal the drone from our house, from my room." And then jumped out Ben's office window when I surprised him.

"I needed the SD card in case the drone camera had caught me up on that ridge. It would be proof that I . . ." He paused, his eyes darting to my feet. "And I wanted my own drone."

Noah shook his head, disgusted. "You were supposed to be my friend. And you tried to steal Dad's drone?"

"I was never going to get one of my own," Tucker said, as if that justified his actions. "Dad said he wouldn't give me the money for a useless piece of shit like that. I tried to tell him we could use it for logging, to find the best trees, keep an eye out for Ben or anyone who might—"

I finished the sentence. "Catch you poaching trees."

"But he just didn't get it. I mean, Jesus, he's not even on Facebook. He barely knows how to work the fucking TV remote."

"You said Ben fell?" I asked. "Where did he fall?"

"I didn't mean to kill him. You've got to believe me."

So it *was* guilt I saw in Tucker when he was sick on the mountain. But I had thought he was covering for his father, not himself.

And then the impact of what he had said fully hit me, like the heat of an explosion following a sound wave. "You *killed* him?" I said.

"I'm so sorry." Tucker fell to the snow on his knees, in tears. But he still held the gun.

"Tucker, what did you *do*?"

Tucker squinted into the overcast sky as if it might give us answers.

"You were out here with Owen, weren't you?" I asked Tucker. "When Ben died. You were out here cutting up that old tree."

"No! Dad and Nelson had started to cut it and haul it out during my school week, but then one of the ATVs got stuck in the snow up on that ridge on Friday, so they rode the other four-wheeler out. They planned on bringing back chains to pull it out on Saturday. Good thing they left when they did, too, or they would have run into Jackson. He was snooping around the Boulders Friday afternoon."

So Owen *had* spray-painted *I'm watching you* on the door of my truck on his way back from that trip, as he drove the logging road over Hunter's Creek and back down the mountain.

Tucker gripped the rifle in both hands. "And then, outside the diner, I heard you guys talking like Ben was boating over to check things out. So Dad sent me out here alone early Saturday morning to pick up things, to get the four-wheeler out before Ben found our stuff. He said if Ben caught me, I was less likely to be fined, charged."

"Because you're only seventeen." I shook my head. Owen was willing to slap the consequences of his crimes on his own kid. "But what did you do to Ben?"

Tucker swung his head from side to side but didn't answer.

"Dad stumbled on you in the forest, didn't he?" Noah said. "You were the one we saw in the drone images."

"I was trying to get the four-wheeler out of the mud up on that ridge when I saw Ben's drone flying right at me. I tried to take it down." He lifted his rifle, the muzzle pointing to the clouds. "But it was up too high, and I couldn't hit it. So I hid with the second ATV under tree cover."

"But Ben had already seen you," I said.

"I guess he must have, 'cause after the drone stopped flying, he climbed up to the ridge as I was trying to get the four-wheeler unstuck. When I saw him up there, I figured Ben knew for sure Dad and Nelson had taken down that old-growth tree. I mean, he must have found the lunch box Dad forgot by the Hourglass, because Dad and me and Nelson never did find it."

"That's what you guys were looking for the first night of the search," Noah said.

Tucker nodded. "I guess it must have got dumped when Ben's boat capsized in the lake."

"But what happened to Ben?" I asked.

Tucker's face crumpled. "You've got to understand." He wiped his nose with his sleeve. "I mean, even if I wasn't charged, Dad and Nelson would've been fined, maybe put in jail, and it would have been *my* fault. Dad would've killed me. I mean, literally. He would have fucking *killed* me."

"So you shot Ben?"

Tucker turned away as he spoke. "I just—I don't know. I fired on him before I thought about it. I had to get rid of him, or I knew my dad—"

"So you *killed* him?"

"No, I missed. But he spun around—the shot scared him—and he lost his footing and fell down into the ravine. When I went to look . . ." Tucker set the butt of his rifle into the snow to push himself up, and then bent over as if he was about to be sick. He spit. "Ben was so busted up. There was blood on his head, and his legs were all weird."

In that instant, I saw my father on the floor of our kitchen, his legs bent and arms out as if he were a grotesque origami, blood oozing from his head. Blood on the corner of the granite countertop.

And then I became keenly aware of Elijah on the hill above us, listening to all this. "Is it possible Ben could still be alive?" I asked. "Elijah stole things from our house to take to him. Ben's sweater, his mug and book, our wedding photo."

Tucker looked up the steep slope above me, at Elijah, lowering his voice. "That bushman's got a screw loose. Maybe he's got Ben's corpse hidden away somewhere for company."

"You're the one with the fucking screw loose!" Noah shouted, and Tucker's face fell, and then grew hard.

I shot Noah a look, to get him to be quiet. Then I turned back to Tucker. "*Could* he be alive?" I asked him.

Tucker shook his head slowly. "He was messed up, man. Like, there was no way he'd survive that fall. Even if I'd called for help, he would have been dead long before anyone got there."

"But his body wasn't where you saw him last, was it?" I asked. "When Noah flew the drone into the gully, you thought he should have been there, by that egg-shaped boulder."

"I figure that grizzly hauled his body off and buried it. They do that, you know. Bury what they don't eat."

"What the fuck, Tucker?" Noah launched forward in the snow toward the kid. "You left my dad's body for a bear? You left him to be *eaten*?"

Tucker aimed the rifle at him, and I pulled Noah back again.

"So, then what?" I asked. "You let his boat loose in the lake to cover your tracks?"

"No, I didn't think—I didn't even think of it. I was way up on that ridge, and I had brought the second four-wheeler. I just—I finally pulled the ATV out of the snow, like Dad told me to. Then I towed it up the trail toward Hunter's Creek, where I'd parked the truck. I wish I *had* thought of it, or been smart about it, picked up Ben's drone so I didn't have to try to break into your place for it later."

"But we found Ben's boat on the water," I said.

He shrugged. "The storm hit, and I guess it just floated out, overturned in the waves. When we came across Ben's boat on the lake, I thought—"

"You thought you'd gotten away with it."

Noah pointed at him. "You hung out with me right after you killed Dad, played games with me."

"I had to get the images off the drone, right? I had to find out just how much you guys knew."

Or suspected.

"So you just hung out with me to save your own ass."

"It wasn't like that. I came over because I wanted to." Tucker tried for a grin. "You're my buddy, right?"

Noah snorted.

"Tucker," I said. "People don't aim guns at their friends. People don't shoot at their friends."

Tucker dropped the muzzle of the gun a little, then brought it back up again.

"Does Owen know?" I asked him. "Did you tell him? Is that how you got that shiner?"

Tucker shook his head. "He hit me because I didn't find his lunch box." He touched the bruising on his face, now turning yellow as it healed. "And then because I talked back." He looked up at me. "But he doesn't know what I did. He *can't* know."

"What exactly do you think is going to happen now?" I asked. "Now that we know, now that you've told us."

"You can't tell anyone. You can't tell Dad."

"Tucker, I'll be telling the police."

He swung the rifle back and forth between us. "No, no, you can't do that. Dad would kill me. I'm serious. He would fucking *kill* me!"

"You can't just pretend this never happened."

Just then I heard my mother's voice through the radio in my pocket. "Piper? You there? Over?"

Tucker held out a gloved hand as he kept his rifle trained on me. "Give me the radio."

I put a hand to my pocket as my mother called again.

"Give it to me!" His shout echoed through the forest. Then, more quietly, he said, "Toss it here."

I tossed it to him. He fumbled to catch it, and it dropped in the snow at his feet. I reached for my bear spray, to use on him, but he kept his eye on me as he bent to retrieve the radio and turned it off, with the gun still trained on us. Then he ran his tongue over his bottom lip as he apparently tried to think what to do. "Nobody can know."

"Okay," I said. "We can keep this between ourselves."

"You're lying. I know you'll just tell." He gripped his gun over and over again, his fists clasping and unclasping the metal. "I've got to figure this out."

I held one hand out as I slipped the other to my bear spray holster. "Tucker, just give me the gun."

"No!" He lifted the rifle. "Step back. Step back! I've got to stop you from telling Dad, from going to the cops. It's the only way."

"You're going to kill us?" Noah asked, astonished.

"You'll tell. Sooner or later, you'll tell. Then I'll be charged. And then Dad—"

"You're seventeen," Noah said. "They won't charge you as an adult. Right, Piper?" His look said, *Help me out here.*

"Tucker, I don't know what will happen to you," I said. "But I do know that if you come clean, if you confess, if you're honest and tell the cops what happened, things will go so much easier for you. The charges, the consequences, will be much less."

"But Dad—"

"I'm sure, if anything, he'll be proud of you for taking responsibility."

"Bullshit. He won't."

No, he wouldn't. He would beat the crap out of Tucker the first chance he got. Was he capable of murdering his own son, as Tucker seemed to think? Maybe, though I was sure that wasn't what Tucker really feared. If he came clean with all this, Owen and Nelson would undoubtedly face a variety of charges, or at least fines. Tucker was terrified of disappointing his critical father again.

"I'm so sorry," Tucker said, glancing at Noah and then me. "This isn't how I wanted things to end up. I didn't want any of this to happen." But he cocked the gun. "Please, just turn around."

So he didn't have to see our faces when he shot us.

"Fuck you," Noah said.

Tucker's lips pruned. "Turn around!"

But then the crack of a rifle shot rang out and Tucker dropped to the ground. A bullet, shot not from the hill above but from below, had narrowly missed him, plowing into the tree trunk beside him. There was a third man with a rifle in these woods.

"Who is that?" Tucker cried.

"I don't know."

"That wasn't the Green Man," Noah said, looking up the hill behind us.

"Who did you bring with you?" Tucker asked, scrutinizing the bush below.

As he was briefly turned away, I quickly uncapped the bear spray and aimed it at him, spraying as soon as he turned back in our direction.

"Shit!" Coughing, his eyes watering and stinging, he dropped the rifle and grabbed handfuls of snow in a desperate attempt to wash the bear spray away.

"Run!" I told Noah, tossing the used canister into the snow. "Run!"

# 35

Running in snow, in snowshoes, wasn't easy. We shuffled, ungainly, sideways down the slope, away from Tucker but also, hopefully, away from whoever had shot at him from below, staying clear of the trail we had followed to reach the memorial. I glanced back to see if Tucker was following, but he was still trying to wash away the bear spray with snow, coughing as he did so. The bear spray hit humans just as hard as bears, but unlike a bear, Tucker could wash it off. Given the distance I'd been from Tucker when I used it, I figured the swelling and stinging in his eyes, nose and throat would last fifteen minutes or so. But if he cleared it out of his eyes and nose, he might be after us in much less time.

"Who *was* that shooting at Tucker from below?" Noah asked as we fled. "Obviously, it wasn't Elijah."

No. He had been on the hill above us. But at the sound of the last rifle crack, he had thrown down his snowboard and taken off sideways, skidding, swerving, disappearing and reappearing as his camouflaged shape moved between trees and in and out of shadow, his rifle in his holster slung over his back. He was going downhill but taking a different route than the one we'd taken on our way up as he also attempted to avoid the third rifleman who had fired at Tucker from below.

"Hurry," I said, taking Noah by the arm and leading him to Elijah's trail.

"What are you doing? Elijah went that way."

"He knows this forest better than anyone, where to hide." I glanced back at Tucker. He was now slogging his way through the snow toward us, trying to keep the trees between himself and whoever had shot at him from below. "In any case, Elijah was firing on Tucker, protecting us."

"And you still believe that he knows where Dad is," he said. "That he has Dad."

I pressed my lips together, nodded.

As we wound down the slope, we moved from the fir and spruce forest into the giant cedar and hemlock trees, keeping to the patches of deep canopy, the bush, avoiding clearings, as Elijah had. But we kept looking back, aware that Tucker was likely following us. Still, he had no snowshoes and he'd have to fight his way through the snow in boots. Hopefully we could outrun him.

We followed Elijah's trail all the way down to the Boulders. At the base of the giant Hourglass, his trail abruptly ended at the bush surrounding it, where it seemed he'd dismounted his snowboard.

Noah turned a circle. "Where did he go?"

"Could Elijah have climbed this thing?" I put a hand to the Hourglass. The huge monolith towered above us, both ends tapering to a waist in the middle. The sheer rock face of the boulder went straight up. *Could* Elijah have climbed that? He and his wife had come here on their honeymoon, in part, for bouldering. They were both experienced cavers and free climbers, so he likely could. But why would he climb it now?

I pointed at the ground at the back of the boulder where Elijah's trail ended. "Noah, this is where I saw Ben standing. Right here."

I searched the area. "It almost looks too smooth right here, like Elijah swept it clean." I inspected the bush around the base of the Hourglass. Could he be hiding in there? It was a thick growth of young trees, boxwood and rhododendron that bloomed white blossoms in the spring. I pushed back some of the bush to get at the base of the boulder. "Huh. A few of these branches are broken, like someone's been here."

Noah leaned into the space between the bush and the base of the boulder with me. "There are skid marks in the snow there," he said. "Like that rock has been moved forward."

"Jesus, you're right." I tried pushing the rock back, but it was too heavy for me.

Noah nudged me out of the way. "Here, let me try." He slid the rock back to reveal a gaping black hole high and wide enough for even a large person to wiggle through.

"A cave!" I dug in my pack for a flashlight and, squatting, aimed it into the dark. The entrance opened right up. "There's a tunnel," I said. "I think we found Elijah's hideout."

Noah and I exchanged a giddy glance, and I stepped back as Noah got down on his belly in front of the opening to the cave. I turned to see if there was any sign of Tucker, and then, for a moment at least, common sense kicked in. "Noah, wait. I don't think we should—"

If we went into that cave and something happened, we'd never be found. But when I turned back, Noah had already shimmied headfirst down into the opening until only his feet stuck out. Then they too disappeared. A light emanated from the hole below as he tapped on the flashlight app on his phone. "Oh, man! Piper, you've got to see this."

On the other hand, I thought, Tucker and that second shooter were still out there. If we ran out to shore, or jumped in the boat, either one of them would have a clear shot. We were likely safer in this cave right now.

Noah's voice echoed up from the void. "Piper, seriously. You've got to come in here."

I got down on my belly and, holding the flashlight ahead of me, slid down into the cave headfirst. Below, the passageway enlarged to the point where we could stand upright.

Noah held out his hand to help me up, grinning. "Wow, huh?" he said.

The entrance to the cave was almost like a foyer, and from it, a winding tunnel, like a hallway, led into the blackness under the slope of the mountain.

Noah shone his light up to the low ceiling. Water, trickling down the face of the rock, had formed ice on the walls of the passageway. I could hear water dripping from somewhere, in the blackness. "I didn't know this cave was here," he said.

"No one did. There were stories about Valentine's cave—"

Noah nodded excitedly. "Yeah, yeah, some guy named Valentine stumbled on a cave out here, and wrote about it, but he wouldn't tell anyone exactly where it was, because he wanted to make money off it and he had to buy the land first. But then he died, and no one ever found it again. I remember our teacher showing us an old newspaper story about it."

I had read the newspaper stories too, in my research on the history of Moston. "But everyone thought it was a fabrication, a tall tale," I said.

"You really think this is where the Green Man lives?"

"Elijah," I corrected him. "It would certainly explain why no one could find him. If he is here, and I'm right—"Then Ben could be here too.

I brandished my flashlight against the dark. "Let's find out."

We crept into the netherworld, ducking when the ceiling lowered, one hand on the icy rock wall to stop from slipping on the wet floor. It was a talus cave system, I realized, openings between rock that were either deposited by glaciers or had fallen from a cliff face above over time.

I had done a little amateur caving in the past. The smell of wet earth here was hard to describe. Not that after-a-rain smell. Something deeper. More primal. More terrifying because it came with the knowledge we were buried beneath the earth. And the dark here was like nothing I'd experienced in the surface world. If we switched off our lights, we'd see nothing, absolutely nothing, at least until a half-hour later, when our night vision would kick in and we would see the hazy black-and-white world of ghosts. But in the time in between, I knew, our brains would attempt to make sense of this alien world, a quiet and dark that deprived the senses. It was common for cavers to hallucinate. Even now, I stopped to listen as I thought I heard the hush of whispers.

"What?" Noah asked.

"Shush."

But the whispers became the sound of many drops of water tapping on rock from somewhere in the cave system, likely snow melting within the crevices of the rock, I imagined. I stepped cautiously forward.

As the passageway twisted and turned, I could only see the rocky walls a few feet ahead. I started to lose my nerve. Elijah could be around any corner, and he had a gun. What were we doing here?

Spooked by the dark, Noah seemed to be thinking the same thing. "Maybe we should go back," he said. "Try to get to the boat."

"Tucker is out there. If we go to the beach, he could fire on us from the slope above."

Noah tugged my jacket nervously like a much younger child. "Maybe we can catch bars if we go outside. If Dad really is here, we need to get Jackson, his team. They have the equipment, the know-how, to get him out."

"Let's keep going. We've already come this far."

But then I stopped short as I saw something glinting in the dark just ahead: the muzzle of a rifle, aimed at us.

# 36

I jumped back as the rifle emerged from the darkness. And then, as I focused the light on him, I saw Elijah's bare green hands, his camouflage pants and shirt, his green face, his beard and hair festooned in twigs and leaves. I waved to get Noah to step back, behind me.

"This is my place, my space, my chase." Elijah said. "I don't want you here."

"You found Valentine's cave," I said, trying to sound cheerful. "You and your wife. Ben said you had been searching for it. That must have been exciting."

He scratched his head madly with one hand as he kept the gun trained on us. "No, Andrea and me never found it, not when she was alive. The bear, the bear—" And then his nervous tics stopped all at once and he stood motionless, his eyes on the middle distance, the dark behind us. He was gone, I thought, *there*, in the terrible moment when he lost his wife to that grizzly.

"Elijah?" I took a step forward, thinking I'd take the gun from his hands, but he startled, as if awakened, and snatched it away.

"After, after she—I had to find it. I had to find it!"

"The cave, you mean." I used a soothing tone. "So, after your hospital stay, you came back here, to this forest, to find Valentine's cave."

"Andrea led me here."

"After she died, you mean?"

"Do you see her?" Noah asked. "Her ghost?"

Elijah's eyes shone strangely in the light from my flashlight. "Of course I do," he said, as if that should be perfectly obvious. "That's why I stay. I stay and pray. Stay all day. To be with her."

I had seen or heard Ben's ghost several times over the days since his disappearance, even at the entrance to this cave. Was that how Elijah's grief had begun to take him over? Was I on my way to that madness now? I couldn't take Noah down with me. And yet here I was, leading him into this cave.

Still, I knew now that I was right. I *knew* it. "Ben is inside this cave, isn't he?" I asked Elijah. But was he alive?

Elijah shifted the rifle into one hand and pulled out his flashlight, flicking it on and aiming it toward me so I couldn't see his face. But he seemed to be considering mine. Beyond him, the winding passage with a low, rocky ceiling stretched into darkness.

He turned abruptly. "Watch your head," he said brightly. "Bed head. Bled head. Dread, dread."

I glanced back at Noah. Elijah hadn't said Ben was in here, but he hadn't said he wasn't. Following, we ducked our heads as the passageway grew narrow and cramped. Water droplets glittered above us in the light from our flashlights.

Elijah disappeared from view around a corner, and the light of my flashlight bounced off the rock wall in front of us. I slipped on the icy floor, nearly falling, and felt panic well up. "Elijah?"

His voice echoed as if from a great distance. "This way." And then his voice grew singsong. "This way, all the way. Into grey. Decay."

I rounded the corner and inhaled a shocked, awed breath as the narrow passage opened into a cavern—no, a cathedral—within the rocky hillside. More, the cavern floor was covered in bulbous icicles growing *up* from the floor. Shining my light to the ceiling,

I saw why: thousands of water droplets had condensed in the relatively warmer air above, clinging to the ceiling before dropping to the cold below, where they froze to create reverse icicles that I imagined would only grow larger over the course of the winter. The icicles were everywhere, like miniature crystal palaces, creating a fanciful, otherworldly environment. Even the walls glittered with ice formations. In a newspaper story, Valentine had called this cave "glorious," and it was.

"Oh my god," I said, my voice reverberating around the chamber.

Noah's voice was filled with wonder as he turned to me. "You know what this means?"

I nodded. A destination, a tourist attraction that would undoubtedly bring cavers and ecotourists from all over to rebuild the economy of the town. Both a blessing and a curse. Provided we got out of this alive, we would get our park now, I was sure of it, and the forest would be protected, but this wilderness would then be under pressure from the humans wanting to vacation here.

"Something, huh?" Elijah said. "Something, something, something."

Here and there along the walls there were gaping holes, large and small, the entrances to passages, leading off between the rocks. From one of them, far off, I heard the rushing of a waterfall, melt from above.

"This is incredible," I said.

"My home," said Elijah. He lifted his lantern to light a ledge and overhang just a step up, where the water didn't drip and where, I imagined, the air was a little warmer than it was on the floor. There was a folding table there, a camp chair, a cooler, a cot, blankets and pillows, stacks of books, a camp stove, all likely stolen from the cabins around the lake. I recognized a folding chair that had gone missing from our beach.

Elijah put a finger to his lips. *Shush*. "Can't tell anyone," he said, almost singing. "No, no, no!"

Noah laughed. "Are you kidding? We've got to tell everyone! This cave will put Moston on the map. People will *pay* to see this place."

"*Noah*," I said, warning him not to say anything more on the topic.

Elijah grew agitated, shaking his head over and over, his hand fluttering like a bathing bird. "Oh, no, no, you can't tell anyone. Can't tell anyone."

He took a swift step forward, angry now, and, reacting from instinct, I put an arm out in front of Noah to protect him.

"You're not going to tell anyone!" Elijah patted his chest. "This is our place, mine and Andrea's. I won't let you tell anybody else. I only brought you here to show you, to show you . . ." He waved a hand behind him, at the ledge.

From that dark corner, I heard a low groan that, amplified by the cavern, sounded at first like a grizzly's growl. I startled, fearing we'd walked into a bear's den. But then I shone my light in the direction of the noise, the light bouncing off the dark walls, and there, in the corner of the ledge, lying on a makeshift litter and covered in blankets, was Ben.

# 37

"Ben? Ben!" I rushed to him, stepping up to the ledge and kneeling beside him to take his hand.

"Piper?" He squinted up at me, blinded by the light of my flashlight. "Piper!"

His beard was a bit fuller, his face thinner. The smell of him rose up, sweat, urine, *human*. A milk jug, which he'd apparently used to pee in, sat to one side. His hands were bound together with zip ties, and when I tossed back the blankets to inspect his injuries, I found that his pants had been cut away, and both legs, apparently broken in his fall, were held straight in front of him in splints, cross-country ski poles fixed in place with duct tape. At least it appeared his legs had suffered closed fractures, the skin not punctured by broken bone, which lowered the chance of infection; otherwise, he likely wouldn't have survived this long in these conditions. Pillows were piled behind his head, and cedar boughs were heaped under the litter to keep the cold from seeping into him. That ugly green sweater I had knitted him was wrapped around his shoulders. His favourite mug sat beside him on top of the thriller he'd kept on his nightstand. And beside Ben's head, where he only had to turn to see it, was our wedding photo.

I tucked the blankets back around him. "Ben," I said again. "I'm here." I looked back down at Noah. "Noah and I are both here."

"Dad?"

Ben flinched, holding his bruised ribs, as he tried to look down at his son. "Noah, how are you doing, buddy?"

"How are *you* doing?"

Ben tried for a grin. "I've been better."

"He was hurt, he was hurt, that bear, that bear got him." Elijah pointed at the litter under Ben, fashioned out of branches, duct tape and rope. "I dragged him here." He stood a little straighter. "I took care of him."

"It seems Elijah brought me here to protect me," Ben said. He looked over at the young man. "He seems, I don't know, like he's reliving what he went through with his wife."

"Only this time he's saving you, in a way he couldn't save his wife."

"Yes."

Elijah pointed at Ben. "It's my job to save you," he said. "It's my job." As a paramedic.

My husband turned back to me. "I told him to tell you where I was, but he kept saying you were working or plotting with 'the bear,' whoever that is. He seemed to think you were involved in some kind of conspiracy to kill me."

Perhaps, I thought, Elijah's traumatized mind was working through his own guilt at not saving his wife.

"Well, it appears he changed his mind," I said. "He led us to you."

Ben nodded, then held his head. When I shone the flashlight into his face to look at his injuries, he held up his bound hands to block the light. "That's too bright."

But I kept the light on him a moment longer, because the pupil in one eye—the eye I'd seen as dead in my vision of him—was larger than the other, and a spot of blood floated in the corner. There was a deep gash on the side of his head. As I checked his head wounds, he winced.

"He's been having headaches?" I asked Elijah as I inspected the injury. "He's clearly sensitive to light." But of course, that could be from days spent in the dark.

Still, Elijah confirmed my fears. "He has a TBI," he said, pointing at the wound on Ben's head. "TBI." Then he repeated it like a chant.

"TBI?" Noah asked me.

"Traumatic brain injury," I explained. "He means your dad has a concussion. From what Tucker said, it sounded like he must have been out cold at the bottom of that ravine."

"Shit. How bad?"

"I don't know." I turned back to my husband. "Ben, do you have any idea what day it is? Do you know where you are?"

"The far shore. Valentine's Cave. I'm not sure what day it is. It's so dark in here it's hard to tell. Thursday?"

"Friday." At least his speech wasn't slurred. "Get these off me?" Ben lifted his cupped hands, and I saw the raw red marks where the plastic had cut into his wrists.

"Sorry, yes, of course."

I pulled my jackknife from my backpack, slit the plastic. Ben rubbed his wrists and let out a sigh of relief as he rolled his head back into the pillow.

"Was that really necessary?" I asked Elijah. "Tying him up?"

"He wouldn't let me take care of him. He tried to escape."

Noah snorted. "I wonder why."

"He—he dragged himself down, into the ice." There were broken icicles beneath the ledge as evidence. Elijah pointed a finger at Ben and, briefly, a more lucid Elijah, the man who had once been a paramedic, rose to the surface. "You could have hurt yourself further, Ben."

My husband put his hand to my face lovingly, then squinted

down at his son. "I'm so glad to see you both," he said. "You have no idea." And then he cried. My husband was not one to cry.

"He cries a lot," Elijah said. "Cries and dies. Pies and fries."

And then Ben put a hand to his mouth. "I feel like I'm going to be sick."

"He throws up," Elijah said. "He throws up a lot."

I grabbed an empty plastic shopping bag and handed it to Ben. He hacked, spit up into it. "Crying and vomiting are both symptoms of a concussion," I told Noah. "We've got to get back to the surface, radio Jackson for help to get him out of here."

"Tucker has our radio," Noah said.

And he was somewhere outside with a rifle. I couldn't leave Noah here with Ben, not with Elijah carrying that gun. I couldn't send him outside either, not with Tucker and god knew who else lurking out there.

Ben cried out as he lay back on the pillow. "Everything hurts," he said.

Elijah rummaged for a pill bottle, handed Ben a tablet.

"Whoa, wait," I said. "Let me see that bottle. What kind of pain meds have you got him on? Ibuprofen, acetaminophen with codeine?"

"Morphine," he said.

I looked down at the label. "*Morphine?*"

Ben cupped the pill. "He had to keep adjusting the dose," he said. "I was seeing things, thought I was someplace else." My husband gripped my hand. "I thought I was at home, with you."

Elijah repeated the word as he shook the bottle of morphine tablets. "Home, home, home."

I exchanged a glance with Noah. "We both saw your ghost," I said to Ben. "Or your doppelgänger. At home and out here, standing in front of the cave entrance. You told us to find you."

He laughed but didn't seem surprised. "Like I said, half the time I thought I was at home." He swallowed the pill. "Did you think I was dead when you saw my ghost?"

I didn't want to admit that there were moments when I had given up, so I didn't answer the question. "What do you remember?" I asked Ben. "From before you got here."

"I was hiking along the ridge above Silver Creek—"

"That grizzly was following you," Noah said.

"She was?" He squinted up at his son. "I don't remember."

"You may not have seen the bear," I said. "She was some distance behind you."

"A four-wheeler—I saw a quad on the screen."

"And you hiked up to the ridge to check it out," I said.

"But when I got up there . . ." Ben pointed a finger into the darkness. "Tucker . . ." He stopped there, as if the effort of coming up with the words was too much.

I squeezed his hand. "He shot at you. We know. You fell into the ravine. You got banged up pretty good."

Ben touched the eye with the enlarged pupil, the red spot. "Tucker left me for dead. I don't understand."

"He's an asshole," said Noah. "I can't believe I hung out with him."

"He's wounded," I said. "Mentally ill. He needs help. Tucker got it in his head that you would throw him and his father in jail over the tree poaching, that they would face huge fines." I paused, remembering my argument with Owen at the diner on Friday. *I had put the idea in his head.*

"So he shoots at me?"

"He was afraid of his father," I said. "Afraid of letting him down. Of what Owen might do to him now that you had evidence of their tree poaching."

"Evidence. You mean the photos the drone took of the ATV?"

"I understand Owen also left his lunch box on site, with his name on it. Tucker couldn't find it."

Elijah pointed at his encampment, and I trained my flashlight on it, revealing Owen's lunch box on the floor under the folding card table.

"Elijah and I shared his sandwiches," Ben said grinning. "Peanut butter and jam. And a bag of chips. Salt and vinegar." He laughed a little and then held his ribs. "I guess I owe Owen lunch."

"You don't owe him anything," I said.

"We searched for you, but then we found your boat in the water," Noah said.

"Along with your life jacket, coat and radio," I added. "How *did* your radio and coat get in the water?"

Ben pointed at Elijah. "He took them off me."

I turned to the bushman. "You threw Ben's coat and radio in the water, didn't you? So we'd finally call off the search."

Elijah rolled his shoulders as if the tag on his shirt was causing him discomfort. "All those people," he said. "All over. All over. They wouldn't go away."

"So you made everyone believe Dad drowned?" Noah asked.

"I had to take care of him, protect him from the bear," Elijah said. "And I couldn't let them find me. No, no."

I climbed down from the ledge. "I've got to get help," I said. "Get you both out of here."

"No. No." Elijah said again, gripping the gun with both hands. "The bear's out there. If he goes out, the bear will get him."

"Elijah, I have to get Jackson and his crew back here, to take Ben to a hospital. Just like they got you to the hospital. Do you understand?"

"They'll know about the cave, then. I would have to leave. I would have to leave Andrea." Elijah's eyes hardened on me. "I'm not leaving Andrea." He shook his head. "I can't let you tell. I won't let you tell."

He climbed to his little encampment and grabbed a couple of zip ties.

"Elijah, what are you doing?" I asked. "You can't keep us here."

"There's no other way," he said. "You'll have to stay too. I'll have to figure this out." Then he hit the side of his head with his thumb. "I need time to figure this out! Out! Out!"

Just then there was the echo of footfalls in the tunnel, and the light of a flashlight danced across the wall of the passageway.

And there was Tucker, holding his rifle.

# 38

"Holy shit," said Tucker, aiming his flashlight at the ceiling above, at the many icicles on the floor. "This is wild." Though his eyes were still red and watery, his voice hoarse from the bear spray, his face was lit up in excitement at finding this cave, as any teen's would be. But this teen was carrying a gun.

Elijah stormed toward him. "I don't want you here. You don't belong here! This is my home. My home!"

But Tucker lazily turned his rifle on Elijah, forcing him to step back, as he continued to look around.

"What are you doing here?" I asked. "How did you find us?"

He shrugged. "I followed your tracks."

"The rock," Elijah said, pointing at me as if he were instructing a child. "You need to put the rock back over the hole when you come inside. Otherwise, people will find you."

"Is this like a grizzly den or something?" Tucker shone the light in Elijah's face. "Is this where that bear that killed your wife lived? And now you live here. That's just sick, man."

"Think about it, idiot," Noah said. "Could a bear get in through that opening you climbed through?"

*Maybe*, I thought.

But Tucker didn't react to Noah's anger. "This place is huge. There's got to be another entrance someplace." He dropped the muzzle of his gun as he aimed the flashlight at a far wall, at one of the gaps in the rock leading to another passageway. "There could be a bear over there right now."

"There's a bear here. A bear here!" Elijah cried, and his voice echoed off the walls in the chamber. But he was pointing at Tucker.

"What the hell is he talking about?" Tucker asked.

"He means you're a danger," I said. "It seems in his mind dangers are bears."

"So I'm a bear now." Tucker kicked one of the icicles, breaking it. "I like that." It seemed he was becoming more and more like his father.

"Tucker, how about you put that gun down," I said, then glanced pointedly at Elijah's rifle. "We don't want anyone else hurt here today."

Tucker rubbed his swollen eyes. "Like you didn't hurt me already," he said. "What the fuck, man?" He shone the beam of his flashlight on me, and then on Ben, and stepped back, visibly shaken. "*Shit*."

"Hello, Tucker," Ben said.

"You're—you're not dead."

Ben laughed a little and then winced as he held his ribs. "Reports of my death have been greatly exaggerated."

"But I saw you in the ravine. You *were* dead."

"He was unconscious," I said.

"I saved him," Elijah said, and his eyes flicked to me. "I owed him."

"You owed him?" Tucker said. "Man, you are one first-class fuck-up. You save him by kidnapping him and keeping him cooped up in here?"

"I saved him from *you*." Elijah aimed his rifle at Tucker. "I hid him from you. So you couldn't hurt him anymore."

"Whoa." Tucker trained his gun on Elijah in return.

I stepped between them with my hands up. "That's enough," I said.

Elijah lowered his gun, but when Tucker turned both his flashlight and his rifle on Ben, he raised it again.

"This is so fucked," Tucker said. "You're supposed to be *dead*. Everyone thinks you're dead." He looked up at me. "They still think that, right? Who else knows you're here? Your mother. She knows, right?" He stuffed his flashlight in his pocket and gripped his rifle with both hands. "You couldn't have told Jackson, or he'd be here."

I backed up, easing my body between Tucker and my husband. "What are you saying, exactly?" I asked. "You plan to kill all of us, and Libby too?"

"*That's* fucked," Noah said.

But Tucker kept his rifle trained on me. "I don't want to kill any of you, but I've got to. I don't have a choice."

"Tucker!" Ben boomed. But he was stuck on the litter, his legs broken and in splints. It was up to me to get this situation under control.

"What are you talking about, Tucker?" I said gently. "Of course you have a choice."

"It's either you or me. Dad finds out and I'm dead." He stepped to the side, gripped the rifle with sweaty hands and took aim at my husband.

He wasn't going to kill Ben or Noah. He *wasn't*.

I threw my body at Tucker and knocked him off his feet. He fell on several icicles, breaking them, sending ice tinkling across the cavern floor. Yet he hung on to the gun. I tried wrestling it from him, but he was stronger than me. As we both gripped the rifle, he lifted his elbow hard under my chin. I fell back, reeling from the blow, breaking more of the icicles.

"Piper!" Ben cried.

And then Noah was there, trying to take the gun out of Tucker's hand, pushing him back to the floor.

Both Ben and I called out at the same time. "No!"

I could hear Ben struggling to get up, his grunts of pain, as I pulled Noah away. As I did so, Elijah stood over Tucker with his rifle aimed at the boy's head. "Drop it," Elijah said. And Tucker let go of the rifle. It rattled to the rock floor before Elijah picked it up.

Then Elijah brandished the gun at Noah and me. "Just—just sit," he said.

Noah and I climbed back up to the ledge and sat next to Ben. The cold of the rock floor seeped into my seat.

Elijah pointed the gun back at Tucker. "You stay there. I've got to think. Think, think, think." He retreated to his folding card table, placing Tucker's gun on the floor, and pointed his own at Tucker. But he could just as easily aim that thing at us.

I leaned into Noah to whisper. "We've got to get that radio from Tucker and get outside to call for help."

"How the hell are we going to do that?"

"No talking!" Elijah said, his voice ringing in the chamber. He hit his head again. "I'm *thinking*."

After a few moments, he got up, started to pace on the ledge. In the interval when he had his back to me, I mouthed to Tucker, *Give me the radio.*

He frowned at me, not understanding at first.

"You expect him to *help* us?" Noah whispered. "After all this shit?"

"No talking!" Elijah boomed. He stared at us, then went back to pacing, mumbling to himself.

I tried Tucker again. *The radio.*

He reached in his pocket and held it up. *You want this?*

I nodded.

277

He put it back in his pocket. The little shit.

"We were *friends*," I said out loud to him.

Tucker shook his head. "You didn't want me around. No one wants me around."

"That's not true. I asked you if you wanted to live with us until you graduate."

Ben craned his neck toward me. "You did?"

"To get you away from your father," I told Tucker. "You would have had a home with us."

"Why would you care?"

"Because I've been there, Tucker. My dad was a cop. He saw, experienced, a lot of shit that hurt him. So he drank, and when he drank, he hit me and my mother." I turned to Elijah. "My father was a bear," I said, and it was only then that I realized the grizzly that had killed Elijah's wife likely wasn't the only "bear" the bushman had faced in his life, or his wife's death wouldn't have broken him the way it had. He had told Ben and me that his brother had died in an accident caused by his drunk father. So he must have faced similar abuse to what I'd experienced as a child. That trauma had likely led him to choose a career as a paramedic, so he could save himself as he saved others. Tucker, Elijah and I were all haunted by our own raging, wounded bears.

And then, as if talking about my father had conjured him, the shadow of a bear slid across the cave wall.

"Owen," I said, as he stepped into the cavern carrying a gun. So he was the third rifleman. It was bad enough to face a scared kid with a rifle. Did Owen, an experienced hunter, intend to use that thing on us?

Tucker leapt to his feet. "Dad?"

"You get out of here!" Elijah cried as he jumped up. "Git!" he said, as if Owen was a stray dog.

But Owen's eyes were on my husband. "Ben," he said, and he was almost giddy with relief. "Oh, thank god, Ben. I thought Tucker had—" Owen took several steps forward into the cavern, picking his way through the ice formations, his shadow diminishing as he approached, and as he did so, Elijah withdrew into the shadows. But the bushman still held his gun.

"You followed me down the mountain?" Tucker asked. "*You* shot at me?" Tucker's brows puckered at this betrayal.

"Oh, for god's sake, I wouldn't have killed you," Owen said. "But I had to stop you from killing them." He nodded sideways at Noah and me. "What the hell, son?"

"So you really didn't know about all this?" I asked.

"About Ben? Hell no. I thought he drowned in the lake, same as everyone else. But then you came over with your crazy-ass theory about the Green Man stealing Ben's controller from our house. Thing is, I had seen it in Tucker's room. I didn't think anything of it at the time. Just another gadget. But after you came over, I looked, and it wasn't there no more." He turned to his son. "And that got me thinking about how nutty you've been acting since Ben went missing. And I finally pieced things together. You went and tried to kill Ben, didn't you?"

"I'm sorry," Tucker said to his father. "I'm so sorry."

Owen backhanded him, the smack of skin on skin echoing around the chamber. "You'll be sorry, all right."

Elijah jumped up, holding the gun.

"Owen, stop it!" I cried.

"If he isn't punished, he's never going to learn."

"How do you think he learned to behave this way in the first place?" I asked.

"You putting the blame on me again?"

"You beat him, Owen, any time he did anything you didn't like."

"Mostly only when he was drunk," Tucker said.

"Shut it," Owen told him.

"He would do anything to avoid disappointing you," I said. "Anything."

"I was trying to protect you," Tucker said to his father.

"By nearly killing a man? Threatening to kill his wife and son?"

Tucker's gaze slid toward Ben. "He knew it was us who took down that tree, and the others. He was going to throw us in jail, fine us a *million dollars*."

Ben tried to sit up. "Who told you that?" he said.

Tucker glanced at me.

"I may have said something to that effect at the diner," I said.

Ben settled back. "Well, the reality is, penalties are rarely that high."

Tucker spat like his father so often did. "Doesn't matter. Now I'm going to end up in jail for shooting at you."

"Tucker," Ben said, his voice whispery from exhaustion. "I'm not pressing charges."

Noah waved a hand at Tucker. "But he shot at you, Dad. Left you for dead."

"Tucker needs help, not jail time." Ben wagged a finger at Owen to get him to come closer so he didn't have to project his voice. "But he gets the care he needs, understood?"

"Psychiatric care," I added.

"And the tree poaching has got to end, Owen. You understand me? Obviously, I've got enough now to build a case against you. You *will* be facing a fine." Ben struggled to sit up again, grunting with the effort. "And, Owen, you *will* stop hurting your son and get counselling for this shit, or so help me god, I will make sure you are charged with assault."

Owen ran a finger under his nose. "That's the deal?"

"That's the deal."

Owen nodded. "Okay," he said, resigned.

Ben slumped back into his pillow, exhausted from the effort. "We need to call for help," I said. "Get Jackson out here."

"Either of you got a radio?" Owen asked.

"Tucker took it."

Owen held out his hand to his son. "Give it to me." When Tucker hesitated, he raised his voice to a roar that filled the cave. "Give it!"

The boy handed it over and Owen pocketed the radio. "I'll go out and call for help." He took his son by the upper arm. "Come on," he said, and led him back up the passageway to the outside world.

"Maybe you should go with them," I told Noah. "Keep an eye on Tucker. I doubt Owen will lay a finger on him now with you there." Not after Ben had stated his terms.

"Yeah, sure."

As Noah followed Owen and Tucker out, I returned my focus to my husband. "You comfortable?" I asked. "How's the pain?"

"I'll survive." He looked toward the little table, to the dark figure hovering in the corner. "But what about Elijah?" He lowered his voice. "You've got to get through to him, Piper."

I pulled the blanket up to Ben's chin, then picked my way over the uneven floor of the ledge to reach Elijah. He cowered a little as I approached, even though he was the one holding the gun. I tried laying a hand on his arm, to reassure him, but he jerked away as if I had burnt him.

"Elijah, listen to me." I squatted next to him. "Maybe it's time to leave this cave?"

"No. Andrea is still here. I can't leave her."

"I'm so sorry, Elijah. Even if I wanted to keep this cave a secret, the search and rescue team will have to come and take Ben out of

281

here. You know they will." I paused. "And they'll be here in less than an hour."

Elijah jumped up. "I have to go. I have to—" He started gathering his things, manically, stuffing them into plastic grocery bags, a ragged backpack, muttering to himself as he did so. In a city, he would be the guy pushing a grocery cart, his home on wheels.

I followed him as he went to and fro. "Elijah, we can help you get back on your feet. We can get you medical help, a place to live and, eventually, a job."

He shook his head over and over. "No, no. Andrea's here. I can't leave Andrea. She's all alone. I can't leave her alone. I left her alone. I left her. I ran from the bear. I left her." He bundled his things together and skuttled into the dark tunnel that led out of the cave.

"Piper, don't let him go," Ben cried.

"Elijah, wait."

I followed him, but the tunnel was slippery, the going slow. "Elijah," I called. "Please let us help you."

I reached the entrance to the tunnel just as he pulled himself headfirst out onto the snow after his belongings. By the time I climbed out from behind the bush at the base of the Hourglass, he had disappeared into the forest.

"Elijah," I called out, knowing he was somewhere out there, listening. "When you're ready to leave, we'll be here to help you."

# 39

After checking in with Noah and Owen to make sure help was on the way, I returned to the cave, to Ben. He lay in the dark with his eyes half closed. I kissed his cheek. "You okay?"

He smiled a little. He had been shot at, left for dead, kidnapped by a bushman and hidden in a cave for a week, and here I was asking him if he was okay. "No," he said, "but I'm a whole lot better now that you're here." He looked around. "What happened to Elijah?"

"He's gone."

"Shit." Ben grunted, holding his bruised ribs as he lay back in his makeshift bed. "I'll try to track him down. We've got to help him."

"Shush," I said. "Stay still. Jackson and his team will be here shortly." We would find Elijah only if he wanted to be found, and even then, he would have to navigate his own way out of his grief. In any case, it would be weeks, months, a year or more before Ben would be up to hiking these mountains.

I held my husband's hand, stroked his hair, careful to avoid his head wound, and cried at the miracle of finding him alive. Within the hour, I heard voices in the passageway leading to the cavern, then saw lights reflecting off the reverse icicles, and then Jackson appeared in full SAR gear, hardhat and headlamp, his crew similarly geared up behind him, carrying a litter. Noah and then Owen and Tucker followed to see if they could lend a hand. I stepped back as the SAR team lifted Ben carefully onto the litter, putting my hand over my mouth and hugging Noah close when my husband cried out in pain. Once Ben was strapped in place, Jackson and his crew carried him up the passageway and, with some difficulty, managed to get him through the cave opening and down to the beach. Even before the crew had loaded Ben into the SAR inflatable, Owen and Tucker were already in their boat and heading across the lake.

I held Ben's hand all the way across the water. I couldn't take my eyes off him. He was *alive*. My husband was alive. Noah sat on the other side of him in the boat. At one point, my stepson offered me an infectious smile. "We did it," he said.

I grinned back. We hadn't given up. We had found Ben.

The ambulance was waiting when we reached the shore. As Libby watched from the deck, and as Noah and I followed, Jackson and his crew rushed Ben's litter up the snowy beach and helped the paramedics transfer him onto the stretcher and load him into the ambulance.

"We'll follow you to the hospital," I called out to Ben. It was a drive of more than an hour away. "We'll be right behind you."

As soon as the ambulance left our driveway, and before the SAR crew started to disperse, I thanked them all, telling them we'd have a barbecue once Ben was back home, to show our appreciation. But as the team headed to their trucks, Jackson pulled me to the side. "Piper, a word."

I held up a hand to Noah and Libby, asking them to give me a minute, and they went inside to get ready to leave for the hospital.

Jackson ran his fingers over his moustache, taming it. "I guess I should apologize for not believing you," he said.

I sank my hands into the pockets of my ski pants. "I gave you no real reason to."

"I can't tell you how delighted I am that you found Ben, that it all worked out. But going over there to face the bushman was reckless. Why didn't you me call as soon as Elijah broke into your bedroom?"

"You'd made it clear you weren't going to restart the search. I thought you'd stop me. And . . ." I scratched my cheek. Okay, out with it. "When I was over at your place, I saw all those photos you took of me."

Jackson nodded once. "Ah."

"You were watching me."

"You figured I was *stalking* you?" Jackson laughed a little. "Seriously?"

"The thought had crossed my mind."

"So that's why you acted so strangely, why you didn't stay for dinner."

I felt my face flush.

Jackson put his hands on his hips and contemplated the ground for a moment. Then he looked back up at me. "Remember the day I went over to the Boulders to catch up with you and Ben? It was, what, the beginning of September? We met on the far shore to discuss where to locate the trail system."

I sank my head into my hands, to hide. *Shit.* In the craziness of this past week, I had forgotten.

"Before I reached you, I grabbed a few shots of you and Ben together, and then of each of you separately. Candid shots. I figured I'd grab one or two of Noah too, and then frame a collage of the photos for a Christmas gift."

"Oh, Jackson. I was such an idiot."

"No, you were a scared woman who was trying to find out what had happened to her husband."

"Can you forgive me?" I asked.

"Done."

"But you're never going to let me live this down, are you?"

He grinned. "Nope."

And that, of all things, made me cry. Jackson opened his arms to me. "Come here." He hugged me, patting my back. "It's been a hell of a week," he said.

I sniffled into his chest. "You can say that again."

• • •

Late that evening, I sat next to my mother in the orange plastic chairs fixed to the floor of the Clifton emergency waiting room as the ER doctor put casts on both of Ben's legs and tended to his many smaller wounds. Noah had come with us to the hospital, but we had been waiting so long that he'd searched out the cafeteria and was now eating there for the second time. Libby had stepped outside for a couple of smokes and now, as she chewed the nail on her thumb, she seemed due for a third.

"I'm sorry this is taking so long," I said. "I do appreciate you coming with me, and for making the journey to Moston."

"I'm your mother," she said. "That's what I'm here for. I *want* to be a part of your life." She paused for effect. "If you would just let me."

I nodded slowly. "I should have phoned you as soon as Ben went missing."

"Exactly."

"And I'm sorry I didn't invite you to our wedding."

"That one hurt," my mother said.

"I know. I just—"

"You were embarrassed of me."

"That's not it."

"I know I behaved badly in the past, when I was still drinking. But that was years ago."

"Really, it wasn't that." Or not only that. I paused, looking around at the unhappy gathering in the waiting room to make sure we didn't have an audience. "When I was around you . . . it was a reminder of what I did, of what we did, to Dad. I didn't want to bring that into my wedding day."

My mother sat back to look at me, as if that surprised her. "What happened to your father was all on me," she said. "It was my decision. I told you to wait." When a pregnant woman in a nearby wheelchair looked up from her magazine to watch us, Libby lowered her voice to a near whisper. "You were only a child. I was your mother. You did what I told you to do."

"I was old enough to know better."

We sat for some time in an uncomfortable silence, reliving that other day we had spent together in an emergency waiting room, as my father hovered between life and death.

After a time, my mother said, "At the very least you could have invited me to visit you, to meet your new husband. I haven't even met Ben yet."

"You're right. I should have." I had come to Moston to start over, to leave my past behind, but it seemed it had only followed me here. "Since you're here now, maybe you can stay in Moston for a bit. Get to know Ben."

"And my grandson."

"Yes, and Noah."

Libby raised an eyebrow as she regarded me. "And you would think a daughter would want to spend a little time with her mother."

"Yes, Mom. That too."

Libby grinned.

"What?" I asked.

"You called me *Mom*."

"I guess I did." Likely for the first time in fifteen years.

287

The pregnant woman in the wheelchair smiled into her magazine.

"All right," my mother said. "I'll stay for a bit, help you out around the house while Ben recovers." She must have registered the alarm on my face because she added, "But maybe I'll rent a cabin while I'm here."

"That's probably a good idea."

"Jackson was telling me I could sell my house in Vancouver, buy a cottage here on the lake and live out my days on the difference." She raised an eyebrow. "What do you think of *that* idea?"

I hesitated. "We'll talk," I said. The truth was, the idea warmed me, to have her close.

But not too close.

I stood as the doctor came into the waiting room and nodded at me. "You can see Ben now," she said.

"Finally," Libby said.

I quickly texted Noah to tell him where we'd be. Then I looped my arm through Libby's and patted her hand. "Come on, Mom," I said. "Let me introduce you to my husband."

# SPRING

# 40

In the spring, I was back in the entrance to the underworld, Valentine's cave, standing with our neighbours, all of us in hard-hats, as Jackson announced that the government had finally agreed to establish the Boulders as a provincial park. All our work to protect this small island of old-growth forest had finally paid off, it seemed, but the deciding factor was the discovery of this cave system that threaded through the mountain like veins, a darkly glittering world that we'd only begun to map, bringing with it the potential for real tourism, the kind of international attention that would pump life back into our ailing town.

Jackson wanted the community to hear it first before the news was released to the media, and so we'd made an event of it, encouraging everyone to jump in their boats and join us in the cave. In the weeks before, Noah and Libby had helped us clean out the mess Elijah had left after he disappeared, and we'd set up lights all around to spotlight the rock features. The generator that powered them hummed outside. Noah now stood not far from me, at the back of the crowd with a couple of friends, all of them excitedly pointing around at the cave. The magical icicle formations were gone now, of course, but would form again in winter.

As Jackson gave his speech, one I had written, Ben stood at his side, surrounded by others on the park committee, Hen and Archie at the forefront, as they had initiated the fight to protect this forest so many years before.

Ben caught my eye and smiled in that way that made my heart skip a beat. There he was: my love. Dressed casually in jeans, a Cowichan sweater and hiking boots, his hair freshly cut, his beard trimmed, he was literally back on his feet, though he used two canes for support and his legs still hurt if he walked for too long. His boss in the office had assured him that his job was waiting for him when he was ready. He would be back patrolling not only the park but the vast wilderness that surrounded it. But for now, he was still in recovery and regaining his strength. With treatment, the symptoms of his concussion had all but disappeared, except that he was still a bit more prone to tears and easily fatigued. Loud environments, like the diner, bothered him, but he seemed to be holding his own today.

In any case, all that was a small price to pay. Ben was *alive* in this forest that could have absorbed him into itself as easily as it had Elijah, the Green Man, and had almost swallowed me. My husband was right here, with me. I was, as Ben called me, *the wife*, and not *the widow*, though I very well could have been. I had come so close. I was the almost widow.

I blew my husband a kiss. Still smiling, Ben glanced at Owen and raised an eyebrow as if to say, *What's he doing here?*

I turned to Owen. Arriving late, he had chosen to stand next to me within this crowd, his meaty arms crossed over his wide chest like he was a bouncer guarding an entrance. I expected him to heckle, to throw his complaints at Jackson during his speech celebrating the park formation, but he didn't. His eyes scanned the crowd as if he was gauging the shifting winds, the changing attitudes of his neighbours, whose faces were flush with excitement and awe over this strange cathedral we stood within, and the future of the park. I felt a little sorry for Owen then. As local opinions about logging and the environment swung toward protection, his status within the community was sinking, and through his son's actions toward Ben, it had already taken a hit. The few times I'd seen Owen at Maggie's diner over the winter, he'd seemed subdued. He kept to himself, eating alone in his booth at the back. Nelson had taken to dining with chattier locals at other tables.

Jackson clapped his hands together as he wound up his speech, pulling my attention back to him. "Okay, everyone!" he said. "Let's eat!" Outside, down at the beach, Maggie had set up a picnic for us all, to celebrate. Libby was helping her out there. Since my mother's move to Moston, into a tiny lakefront cottage that was walking distance to the village, Libby and Maggie had become fast friends. Maggie had offered Libby a few shifts a week at the diner, to get my mother out of the house, she said, but also, I think, to keep Libby from getting underfoot at our place. Bless her. My mother visited us almost every day she wasn't working.

As Jackson led the group back out the mouth of the cave, which we had cleared of bush and widened, and then down the trail through the Boulders, I found myself once again near Owen, walking with him, as if he had planned it.

I nodded at him. "Owen," I said.

"Piper."

"I was surprised to see you here," I said.

He scratched his nose. "Yeah, well, it seems the whole town is over here today. I never miss a party. Or free food."

"The cave is quite something, isn't it?"

He tipped his head sideways, a half nod. "Don't see how that hole in the ground's going to make the town any money, though."

And there he was, the old Owen. But then we turned a corner, stepping out from under the tree canopy and into sunlight. The spring warmth felt so good on my skin after a long, cold winter. I stopped, soaked it in. And then Owen shrugged. "But I'll check out some of the cave passages. Maybe I'll find myself some silver." That was as close as we would get to his approval for the park.

When Ben had confronted him about the tree poaching, he had done the smart thing and owned up, and he now faced a fine, but no jail time, as Ben had promised.

"Have you found work?" I asked him.

He moved on down the trail. "Not much work to be had." A bit of jab, a guilt trip, I thought, for making him give up his good living, the tree poaching.

"Well, that's changing," I said. "We could sure use your expertise, your equipment, in creating the trails and mapping out the cave system. Jackson said you were into caving at one time." When he was younger, thinner.

"Are you offering me a paying job?"

"That's exactly what I'm doing."

"Then I'll take it."

I nodded. "Okay. I'll let Jackson know." I looked back at the tree line, the cliff above, the monolithic tip of the Hourglass boulder towering over the trees. "When we get word out about this cave system, I have a feeling there will be more than enough work in this town for everyone." Jackson and I had already been compiling photos and stories to release as soon as the trail system was ready and we could get tourists out here without damaging the surrounding forest.

"I'll take any work you throw my way," Owen said. "Got to support Tucker through trade school this fall. That ain't cheap. He's talking about doing a cabinetry program."

"That's so good to hear," I said. I found myself talking to his broad back as we hit a narrow section of the path and he took the lead. "How is Tucker doing, anyway?"

Owen spoke over his shoulder. "He's out now." Out of the psychiatric ward. "He's living with my sister in Vancouver." Where I heard he'd enrolled in a new high school for students who were struggling. Owen paused. "Meds are helping." And the visits to the psychiatrist too, I'd heard from Noah. After several long months of anger and grief over what Tucker had done, Noah had finally shot a text Tucker's way. Then, when he didn't answer, a few more. He tried again on Discord when he saw Tucker was on, invited him to play a game. At that, finally, Tucker replied with a one-word message. *Hey.*

Over time, over games, their friendship reignited, or at least a new version of it did, to the point where Tucker was now confiding in Noah again, about his therapy, a girlfriend, the shitty kids in the new school, how rattled and disconnected he'd been from reality in those months leading up to Ben's disappearance, how he'd hidden it from us all. Noah had found it within himself to forgive Tucker, sort of. Kids were, indeed, resilient, far more resilient than me. I still harboured flashes of anger at Tucker for what he'd done to Ben, and at Owen for the harm he'd done to his own son, but perhaps my counsellor was right: my anger was more about me, targeted at the kid *I* had been, at what I had done, than about Tucker. And I was already well aware that my anger at Owen had been more about my father than about him. After I had addressed the circumstances of my father's death, my guilt, with my therapist, I told Ben about it, thinking he would most certainly pull away. But instead he hugged me and said he fully understood me now, particularly when it came to my reactions to Owen, which had often puzzled him.

Now, as we hit the pebbles of the beach, I expected Owen to stride away, but he hung back a little, allowing me to walk at his side, inviting conversation. Ben glanced back at me and Owen, and raised an eyebrow, surprised to see the two of us chatting amicably. Noah walked with him.

"Will Tucker be moving back here this summer?" I asked Owen. I wasn't entirely sure I wanted Noah hanging out with him anymore, whether he was better or not, though I realized that was uncharitable. Noah would be going to university in the fall, in any case.

Owen kept his eyes on the trail ahead of us. "I don't think he'll ever come back."

"I'm so sorry, Owen."

"Yeah, well, that one is on me, isn't it?" Was he asking for forgiveness?

"I think that one is on all of us," I said.

We walked on until we were almost at Maggie's picnic site on the beach, the folding tables and spread of sandwiches, chips and squares. Maggie and Libby continued to unpack boxes, adding more plates of food as what was there quickly disappeared. A long lineup had formed as people loaded up their paper plates. But Owen didn't join them. He stuck with me, standing off to the side, like he had something on his mind.

"I stopped drinking," he said finally.

"Oh?"

"Been clean a few months now."

"I'm glad to hear that."

"AA," he said. "Meetings in Clifton." He ran that nicotine-yellowed finger under his nose. I hadn't seen him light up a cigarette since he'd landed on this side of the lake. Had he quit smoking too? "I'd like to say sorry to you," he said, "for all the harm I done. I'll do what I can to make things right."

So that's why he had hung back with me, to make amends as part of his recovery program.

"The things I said, the way I threatened you when I was drunk."

Pushing me around in the diner, the graffiti on the door of my pickup, the ugly message keyed into the paint on the tailgate: *Go home bitch*.

His hazel eyes searched mine. "My counsellor says I felt threatened by you. I laughed when he said that. Me, afraid of that little thing?" When Owen laughed again, I eyed him, and his smile fell. "But then I got it," he said. "I'd lost my job, and it was easy to blame you for everything. A city asshat in my face about taking down those trees. Throwing all that stuff about the park up on the net, trying to bring more city asshats into Moston."

"This is an *apology*?" I said, grinning a little.

"I'm trying to say, *I* was the asshat, not you. And yes, I am sorry for that." His feet kicked the rounded stones. "I'm sorry about a lot of things."

"I think it's safe to say we both acted like assholes with each other."

He looked back at me. "Your dad drank, didn't he?" Owen asked.

I didn't answer. Had Ben said something to him?

"I could tell, the way you acted around me, like you were fighting a ghost. My dad drank too. Hit me. I know it isn't an excuse for how I treated Tucker, or my wife, or you, but it was all I knew, right? I didn't know nothing different. Or more like, it was what I went to when I wasn't thinking, when I was on autopilot, when I drank, when I got mad."

In that moment I saw not Owen but my father standing there in front of me, explaining himself, apologizing to me. Could I ever forgive him for what he had done to my mother and me? Could I forgive myself for what we had done to him?

I had to if I was ever going to get past it.

My mind went to the grizzly, the cinnamon sow, which Ben

and Jackson had finally trapped that winter. They had released it in an even more remote area, where it wouldn't be able to hunt another human. At least they hadn't had to euthanize the animal. *Euthanize*: a kinder word for *kill*.

"I'm glad you got real help," I told Owen. "I wish to god my father had."

And there it was, a few faltering steps toward recovery, for us both.

As the lineup to the food dwindled, we joined it, grabbing our paper plates. Owen piled on the squares, and I noticed his paunch had grown thicker even though he'd given up beer. So he *had* quit smoking.

After lunch, as Owen and the others left in their flotilla of boats, Ben, Jackson, Noah, Libby and I helped Maggie fold tables and pack things up. As I placed boxes of leftover food in our boat, I saw a lone figure emerge from the bush.

I tugged on my husband's sleeve. "Ben, look."

It was Elijah. But he was no longer the Green Man. He wore no green face paint or camouflage. He was dressed like any one of us, in jeans and a T-shirt, a hoodie. He had shaved and given himself a haircut, albeit a choppy one.

Ben raised his hand, and after a pause, Elijah waved back. The surprise on Ben's face mirrored my own.

And then, as Noah, Libby, Jackson and Maggie watched from beside our boats, Ben and I walked slowly toward Elijah, just as he tentatively edged toward us.

Once we reached him, Ben tucked his second cane under his arm and held out his hand. "It's good to see you," he said.

Elijah looked down at Ben's hand for a long moment, then finally shook it. He glanced up at my husband, smiling, his eyes watering. "It's good to see you too."

It had been several months since we had seen him last, in November, in that cave of icicles. When he had run off into the forest, I had told him that when he was ready to leave this wilderness, we would be there to help him.

Now, as he held my gaze, he nodded, his chin trembling. "I'm ready," he said.

# THANKS

My deepest thanks, once again, to my editor Iris Tupholme and my agent, Jackie Kaiser, for giving me the opportunity to write this thriller. The experience has rejuvenated my writing life. I also offer my gratitude to my editor Janice Zawerbny for helping me develop and refine the story into the novel you have in your hands.

The town of Moston, its people and its surrounding landscape are fabricated, constructed to serve this story. I found inspiration for this community from all over British Columbia and the Pacific Northwest of the US, plucking ideas from many articles online, including the April 20, 2015, *Times Colonist* piece titled "B.C.'s Tiniest Towns Set Sights on Growth by Reinventing Themselves," and, of course, by visiting many rural and wilderness areas in BC.

The area I called the Boulders in the novel was inspired by the amazing boulders at English Creek, southeast of Three Valley Gap, near Revelstoke, BC, as well as other bouldering areas throughout the province. The idea for the cave Elijah hides within came from the story of a real-life bushman, John Bjornstrom, who hid from authorities within a cave on Shuswap Lake. (The character Elijah is wholly imagined, however, and not based on Bjornstrom, who passed away some time ago. My father was a mountain man, and I grew up hearing story after story about bushmen, going back to the 1930s, from my parents, and I had written about bushmen in my first novel, before John Bjornstrom's infamous activities in the

Shuswap.) Details of my fictional cave were inspired by those found in the story of a legendary cave said to exist somewhere in the Shuswap, recounted in the March 4, 2020, *Salmon Arm Observer* story "History Mystery: Mammoth-Sized Cave Discovered at Shuswap Lake," which offers a link to the original *Summerland Review* story about the cave from October 4, 1923. I learned about the unique reverse icicles of Cody Caves from *The Nature of Things* video on the CBC Docs page titled "In B.C.'s Cody Caves, Beautiful 'Reverse Icicles' Grow from the Ground Up," posted January 12, 2021, and included that magical detail into my fictional cave.

The epigraph that opens the novel is from page one of C.S. Lewis's *A Grief Observed* (New York: HarperCollins, 1994).

I owe a debt to my husband, Mitch Krupp, who is a GIS expert and drone pilot and worked in forestry for many years, for his brainstorming sessions on logging, drones and the BC wilderness.

Any errors in the novel on any topic, are, of course, my own.

Lastly, I offer my thanks to those involved in the fight to protect our old-growth forests, to the men and women serving as Natural Resource and Conservation Officers and, of course, to the search and rescue volunteers who find those lost in our wilderness areas. Writing this novel made me realize what a difficult and enormous task you all have. Please forgive the many liberties I took with reality in order to create this suspenseful story.